Doc Voodoo:
Aces & Eights

A novel by
DALE LUCAS

To Marc —
Enjoy!

Published 2011 by Beating Windward Press LLC

For contact information, please visit:
www.BeatingWindward.com

First Edition
ISBN: 978-0-9838252-0-3

For Mom and Dad. *Finally.*

Haitian vodou, like organized crime, is a hierarchy: a complex system of patrons and clients; bosses, captains, and soldiers. Everything works on a basic quid pro quo principle as old as time: this for that; a favor for a favor; you scratch my back, I scratch yours. Collectively, the gods of vodou are known as the lwa.

At the top of the lwa pyramid are the Orishas: the movers and shakers; the matriarchs and patriarchs of a number of elemental clans whose powers bind all those beneath them: the cool, fluid Rada; the fierce and fiery Petro; and the Ghede, the house made up of the ancestors, the dead, and their chthonic keepers.

Doing the work of the Orishas and running their own stables of servants and soldiers are the caporegime of the vodou realms: the Barons.

And at the bottom of the heap—the minor spirits, dead souls, and lingering ancestors who do the grunt work of the Orishas and the Barons, along with everyday Joes like you and me: people of flesh and blood who give the Barons and Orishas offerings in exchange for blessings and curses; and who sometimes give their bodies over to possession as shuttles and mouthpieces for the lwa.

Small wonder that when we're saddled by the lwa, doing their dirty work, they call us horses...

The question inevitably arises: Will the
Negroes of Harlem be able to hold it?

—James Weldon Johnson, 1930

1

Wooley's hands shook, so Johnson offered him a tug on the reefer and Wooley took it. The sweet-grass filled his throat and nostrils, then his lungs, and he held it. Moments later, his brain felt like a wad of soggy cotton and every moment seemed to live in a perfect little bubble, separate from the last, like pearls on a string. His hands didn't shake anymore, and Johnson grinned beside him in the dark, teeth bright white in his mahogany face.

"Dig this! Wooley's grinnin' ear to ear!"

Tibbs rode shotgun. He huffed and jacked the breech on his pump twelve to make sure a shell was ready and waiting. "That mean you niggers are ready to roll?"

Johnson's reply, "Who you callin' nigger, nigger?" came with a smile, but there was venom in it. Wooley took another tug on the reefer and handed it back to Johnson. He blew on it, and the cherry glowed in the darkness of their idling Model T.

"Cocked and locked?" Bedoux asked from behind the wheel. Wooley answered with a snort, as did the others, and Bedoux eased the accelerator. The car crawled up the street toward their targets.

Wooley saw them up ahead through the windscreen: Lester Bernice, with the little tin lunch pail he used to shuttle the bolito slips from his route; his policy-boss, Chester, next to another one of the Harlem Knight block-bosses, Frupp; and a kid that Wooley didn't know, probably not even seventeen yet.

Not much younger than Wooley himself.

XX

"So pay attention," Lester said, and Beau did his best to listen, though it was getting late and he knew Fralene would want him home soon. If he wasn't careful, he'd have to explain to Lester, Chester, and Frupp why his sister was out wandering up and down Lenox Avenue after midnight, calling Beau by his unwieldy Christian name, Buchanan.

Lester plunged into his umpteenth explanation. "The pail's full of dough and slips. You bring it back to your block-boss, and they collect and give you blank slips for the following day. Never hand over the slips or the dough unless there's at least one witness, if not more. You don't want to do it out in front of God and everybody, but for fuck sakes, don't be dumb enough to hand over a pail fulla cash to anybody—anybody!—when there ain't somebody else there to vouch for you makin' your drop."

"Sound advice," Chester said, eyes still on the checkerboard before him. He and Frupp were melted into their chairs in front of Frupp's Barbershop, which had been closed for hours, but which Frupp never seemed to leave. The old barber and the bolito boss sat smoking thin little Mexican cigars, munching boiled peanuts, mulling over whether to jump or crown next.

"You gonna move?" Frupp asked. "Slow as molasses in goddamn January..." Frupp was boss for this block, but Beau was apprenticed with Lester, who made his slip and dough deliveries to Chester. Chester had promised that the game would soon be over and they'd all cross 128th and 129th Streets back to his block to see the slips and dough safely deposited at the night bank. But presently, the game didn't seem close to ending, and Beau was more than a little nervous, standing out on the street in the middle of the night next to a middle-aged Negro numbers runner carrying a tin lunch-pail filled with hundreds of dollars in coin and small bills, not to mention the receipts for the first flush of the following day's policy slips. Still, best to keep his mouth shut and go with it. They were the experts, he the newbie.

Chester made a double jump. Frupp countered with a triple, leading to a king. "Son of a bitch!" Chester huffed. Frupp burst out with a round of wizened laughter that sounded like a dull handsaw on a termite-ridden log.

"Shit on a stick, Ches," Lester moaned. "I saw that comin'. You didn't see that comin'? You blind, old man?"

Beau heard a click behind them and turned in time to see a heavy woman in a loose housedress come stomping out of the brownstone next to Frupp's Barbershop. She looked pissed, and something about the flip-flop of her slippers on the stoop stones and the sway of her ample bosom under the housedress filled Beau with maternal terror.

"Y'all wanna shut your filthy old mouths?" the woman hissed. "I got my little ones sleeping right inside—" she indicated the ground-floor window just a coin-flip from where Beau stood, "and I don't need you wakin' 'em up with all your carryin' on. Ain't you got gin joints to patronize?"

"Well, ma'am," Chester began, with a mock courtesy that Beau had seen him employ a hundred times in the name of good-natured sarcasm, "first and foremost, I'm insulted that you'd even suggest gentlemen such as we would patronize any establishment that'd serve liquor. This is a dry nation, after all."

"Here here," Frupp chimed in. "Goin' on five—naw—six years dry! That's Prohibition, miss! The law of the land, case you didn't know!"

Chester waggled a finger at her. "You'd do well to keep your own sorry after-dark activities to yourself, miss!"

Beau laughed in spite of himself and the fat woman in the housedress came pounding down the stoop steps toward them, thick lips pursed, eyes bulging angrily.

That's when the black Model T rolled into view and the gun chatter started.

XX

This was Wooley's first spitfire for the West Indies, but he hoped it wouldn't be his last. Running numbers was fine and good; likewise dealing at Papa House's card tables or crouping at the dice games; but real money and respect came by the gun. Kings didn't trust wetworks to just any flunky, and if your king offered you the opportunity—as Papa House had offered Wooley—then you took it and you made damn sure you didn't screw the pooch and spank her.

Part of Wooley felt bad when he saw the fat lady in the house dress appear on the stoop and knew she'd be walking right into the line of fire. But that small, remorseful bit of him was forgotten when his weed-addled brain moved on to its next bubble-moment and he was back on Papa House's dime: a lean, mean killin' machine.

So Wooley did just what Johnson told him, leaning right out the side window of the Sedan and squeezing the trigger of the Tommy gun with the muzzle low. It kicked and the gunfire made his ears ring and his teeth chattered and flossy tongues of flame spat from the muzzle in strobe-quick bursts. Above and behind him, he heard Johnson doing his part with a pair of Smith & Wesson six shooters, while next to Wooley, Tibbs made boom-chakka-boom music with his pump shotgun.

He sprayed the stoop and the brownstone and the barbershop with his Tommy; and Johnson took pot-shots at the numbers-runners, ventilating each in turn; and Tibbs provided the insurance, following Wooley's lead spray and Johnson's target practice with a carpet of buckshot.

The funny thing was that once he opened up, Wooley had no clue what was happening. The noise from the guns blew his hearing and the world was all bells; the muzzle flashes and gun smoke dropped an iridescent haze in front of him that he could barely see through; and the dust, mortar, and shattering glass from the brownstone and the barbershop clouded their targets. The only thing he saw clearly was a lunch pail that went flying upward, splaying its coins, bills, and numbers slips into the cold night air, so much expensive confetti.

Then the car lurched under him, their targets shrank behind, the cold wind kissed his face, and Wooley knew that Bedoux had his foot on the accelerator and their work was done. Away they went. Faintly, behind the alarm-clock ring in his ears, Wooley heard the fat lady screaming, voice echoing up and down the block.

So that was that. Wooley ducked back into the car.

XX

Beau thought he might be bleeding, but he'd just pissed himself. Strangely, he wasn't embarrassed, just glad to be alive. He even welcomed the fat lady's screams in his ringing ears—further proof that he was still breathing; still in the game.

Frupp lay folded backward through his shattered barbershop window, stitched up and down with the raspberry-jam pockmarks of bullet wounds. Chester had taken a belly-full of the Tommy slugs and a face-full of buckshot. A piece of his brain and skull stuck to the brick lintel above the barbershop door. Lester lay in a heap of coins, small bills, and pink bolito slips. He had a small pistol in his hand—a little .32 that Beau knew he always carried at the small of his back. The little revolver gleamed in the gun-smoked, lamp-lit haze.

When Beau saw the Model T speeding away down the block, heard its brakes squealing as it rounded the nearest corner and cut due south, he knew what he had to do. Those sons-of-bitches in that car made him piss himself! They weren't gonna roll off without a little bit of lead lip from Beau Farnes!

So he snatched up Lester's gun and took off running, cutting south through the nearest alleyway, hoping that he might get to 127th Street in time to catch them on their double-back. As he pounded down the dark alley, he heard the fat lady screaming, louder now, surprise and shock giving way to stark horror.

"My baby! My baby boy! Those bastards shot my baby boy!"

XX

They cut from 128th down to 127th and turned hard right again, Wooley sliding over against the rear door, thinking he might go spilling out into the night.

"Shoulda cut down farther," Tibbs growled.

"I'm drivin'," Bedoux snapped. "You shut your trap and—what the fuck?"

Wooley leaned forward, peering over Bedoux's and Tibbs's shoulders through the windscreen. It was the kid. He broke out of an alley, ran right into the street, raised a little .32 popgun and started squeezing off rounds. The first went wild. The second put a hole in the windscreen and Wooley heard it buzz by his left ear before punching out the back.

The kid didn't have a mark on him. Impossible! He was standing right there with the others, and Wooley knew they'd all taken heat!

Bedoux hit the gas and the car lurched forward. Tibbs shoved three more rounds into his shotgun and jacked the first into the chamber.

Another round from the kid's .32 punched through the windscreen, veering too close for comfort to Bedoux in the driver's seat. Bedoux bent, and the car swerved.

Then something big and heavy bounced off the roof. The windshield shattered with the impact. With the wind in their faces, they were flying blind.

"Did you hit him?" Johnson brayed. "You hit that little bastard?"

Bedoux hit the brakes, the car careened sideways, and the whole rumbling mess screeched to a halt broadside in the middle of 127th Street. Wooley wondered what the hell Bedoux was doing, but before he could ask, Tibbs was out the passenger door, shotgun in hand, rounding the car.

"Wooley," the elder gun barked, "get your skinny little ass out here and—Jesus Christ!"

Wooley did as he was told. He threw open the back door and leapt out with his Tommy gun, ready to follow Tibbs and finish the kid.

Wooley saw the kid. He was still alive, tumbled over in the gutter, neither broken nor bleeding.

They hadn't hit him.

Tibbs wasn't looking at the kid, though. He was looking at something standing right out in the middle of the street, and there was fear in his eyes.

Tibbs is afraid, Wooley thought. *Tibbs ain't afraid of no man.*

So he followed Tibbs's gaze and saw what had him so spooked.

Death stood in the middle of 127th Street. He had a gun in each hand.

The apparition conjured a whole slew of bedtime stories from the dusty bins of Wooley's weed-addled brain. He was draped in a long overcoat and a coiled, serpentine scarf, both undulating and billowing in the night on a wind that wasn't there. The coat was coal black and the scarf was the angry red of hot iron or an open wound.

Buried amid the coils of the scarf and the upturned collar of the coat was a broad face painted white in the semblance of a skull, framed by hoary, ropy dreadlocks and crowned with a black top hat. From the shadows under the hat brim, black eyes burned out at them, smoldering like banked coals.

Fuck me! Wooley thought. *That's Baron Samedi! The gravelord! The Cemetery Man!*

Who called the Baron?

And who's he come to collect?

Tibbs, who was born in Jamaica and should have known the Baron on sight and been terrified of him, didn't seem fazed. He just hipped his scattergun and barked at the nasty apparition.

"You best be skinnin' out, mister! Three seconds, and you're goat meat!"

The Baron heard—Wooley saw the glint in his eyes that seemed to welcome the challenge, and the way his black-and-white painted lips seemed to sneer.

Tibbs opened fire.

The shotgun roared, ka-chacked, roared again. On Wooley's right, Johnson popped off round after round from his six shooters, laughing as he did so. Wooley raised his Tommy to throw a burst, but in the breath it took to do so, he saw the Baron's coat and scarf fan up before him. The slugs didn't draw blood. It was like the coat and scarf threw up a screen of black-hot heat before him, and all the lead that came barreling his way hit that screen and veered aside and left him untouched. Wooley even saw the shots going wild, kicking up scraps of cement, sparking off lamp-posts, shattering windows and popping the tires of parked cars.

But not a single shot touched the Baron.

Wooley's Tommy gun was heavy in his hands.

Tibbs kept firing, pumping, firing. When the scattergun was

dry, he threw it down and went for the Webley he kept stashed in the shoulder holster under his coat.

That's when the Baron raised his .45's and opened up on them.

Wooley dove. The twin autos sounded like cannons and he heard the bullets whiz by above him; heard their hot lead punching ragged, wet holes through Johnson and Tibbs; felt their blood on his bent back and shoulders; smelled gun smoke and gore as the two of them hit the pavement on either side of him. Wooley raised his head. The Baron stalked nearer, smoking guns still high.

Before Wooley could cry surrender, he heard the driver's door open and knew Bedoux was stepping out. The driver's own .45 coughed, throwing round after round at the Baron in the center of the street.

But the Baron marched on, putting two slugs in Bedoux without breaking stride. Then he was looming over Wooley, holstering one pistol beneath his living coat, reaching down with his black-gloved hand to take Wooley by the collar and haul him up onto his feet. Wooley heard his own voice, high and reedy, pleading with the lord of all the dead and the keeper of their houses; felt the sting of tears in his eyes, and the ring of ruined hearing in his ears from all the gunfire, and smelled the blood of his companions and the smoky cigar stink that wafted off the Baron, and looked into his black, smoldering eyes and knew that if he stared into those eyes too long or too hard, they'd swallow his soul and make mince of it.

He realized his feet were off the ground. The Baron held him aloft with one fist, sneering behind his painted skull-face, and spoke with a voice that sounded like a wind moaning through a cane break.

"Listen," the Baron said, and Wooley tried to listen, but his ears were ringing and he couldn't hear a goddamn thing but his own heart thudding in his chest and the blood thumping in his temples.

"Can't hear nothin', baron, sir," Wooley stammered, snot choking him, tears salty on his tongue, "shit, sir, I can't hear nothin'..."

"Listen!" the Baron commanded, and suddenly Wooley heard it—the fat lady, a block or more away, screaming into the night, lamenting a lost child. The chill on her soul was clear as a song in his ears, ringing like a cold razor on a communion bell.

"We didn't mean it!" Wooley spat. "Didn't mean nothin'! We was just after the runners! Papa said they were too close to our turf! Said we had to put the fear'a God in 'em!"

The Baron pulled him close and Wooley smelled sour rum and cigar smoke on his breath. "Well, now I'm puttin' the fear'a God into you, Gordon Woolsey. You feel that?"

He knew his name! The Baron knew Wooley's name! "Christ, sir, please," he cried, "I'm beggin' you... pleadin'... please, my mama..."

"Your mama's ashamed you were ever born," the Baron snarled, then threw Wooley down hard. Through the ringing in his ears, he heard the click of the Baron's pistol and felt the still-warm muzzle as it pressed against his forehead. Wooley closed his eyes and waited for the big bang and the bigger black that would follow.

"You're a West Indy? One of Papa House's boys?" the Baron asked.

Wooley nodded, but his voice was gone for good.

"If you can deliver a message, Wooley, you can walk away from this. Can you do that?"

Wooley nodded again.

"Tell Papa House that Harlem ain't his battleground. Tell him if he wants to wage war on the Knights or the Mount Morris Boys or the Sugar Hill Gang or who the hell ever, he does it without a single drop of innocent blood being shed. He's got one dead child on his hands now, and that's enough to bring me down on him. If he lays off, mayhap we can keep the peace and this won't have to get ugly... or personal. You remember all that, Wooley?"

Wooley nodded. "Yessir," he managed to say. "Yessir, yessir, yessir, yes I can."

He heard the mute click of the hammer being eased down on the shiny black Colt. "And one more thing," the Baron added.

Wooley waited, but he wouldn't raise his eyes.

"You don't work for Papa House or any of the bankers

anymore, you hear me? You're turnin' over a new leaf, Wooley, and you're gonna make your mama proud."

"What am I gonna do now?" Wooley managed to ask.

"Just do the right thing," the Baron said, and suddenly the muzzle of the gun was gone and the Baron took a long step back, and Wooley felt warmer now that the shadow was off him.

"Beat feet, Wooley, before you forget what we talked about."

Wooley rose and went lurching down the street, leaving the Baron far behind, never stopping, never looking back.

XX

Beau saw the whole thing. He saw the Baron leap off a ledge four stories above, bounce off the roof of the speeding car and land square and upright in the middle of the street; saw the stand-off and gunfight; saw the Baron offer cryptic counsel to the skinny young gunman and then send him running off down the street. Beau knew he should cut and run, lucky not to have taken a bullet or been run down, but it was all too strange, too wondrous, to just flee from.

But he regretted the decision to stay the moment the Baron turned and laid his brimstone gaze on Beau and marched toward him. Finally, Beau found his legs, turned tail, and ran back down the alley he'd used to cut down to 127th Street.

Just as he made the shadows, a huge, immovable wall of darkness melted out of the alleyway before him, and there was the Baron, blocking his path.

Beau tried to skid to a halt, but he ran right into the gravelord and felt the demon's black grip on him. The Baron drew Beau into the shadows and lifted him off the ground.

"I didn't do nothin'!" Beau managed. "Those sons-a-bitches sprayed the fuckin' block! Killed Chester and Lester and Frupp and that fat lady's kid! Lemme go, man! Lemme go!"

"You're in over your head, Beau," the Baron said, shaking him a little. "I know you think you're on the road to bein' a swell, maybe runnin' a gin joint or bein' a bolito boss for the Queen Bee one of these days, but I'm here to say it ain't all wine and roses, and you'd do well to beat another path through those tangled woods right now."

Beau stared, the gravelord's eyes like open tombs. Still, he saw something like the ghost of concern in them.

"Looks like you took some of Frupp's window in the spray. Deep cuts on your face and neck."

"Who are you?" Beau dared.

"I'm the one who's always watching," the Baron said. "Remember that."

He tossed Beau aside, and Beau landed hard amid a trio of trash bins.

"See a doctor about those cuts!" the Baron called, voice echoing through the alleyway. When Beau finally made his feet again and searched the alleyway, the Baron was gone.

XX

Wooley gave Papa House the message, just like the Baron told him. Though he knew that Papa wouldn't be keen to hear it, he didn't expect to get dangled upside down by his skinny legs above the muddy pit in the waterfront warehouse where Papa kept his pet alligator, Napoleon.

Still, there he was, Papa's goons each holding a leg like a wishbone, all the blood rushing to his head. Below him, fat, green Napoleon grinning his reptilian grin, roaring his bull gator roar and snapping at intervals as his head dipped too close to his gaping jaws.

Papa stood on the wooden catwalk beside his goons, snarling in his Trinidadi clip, demanding answers that Wooley didn't have. "Who the fuck was he, Wooley?" Papa growled.

"He didn't say, Papa, I swear! I told you, his face was painted like a skull! Looked just like the Baron, Papa! Baron Samedi! From the island stories!"

"You expect me to believe that, you skinny little bastard? The Baron deigned to manifest on 127th Street just to smoke my boys and let your skinny ass go?"

"I was scared and he took pity, Papa! I was cryin'! I nearly pissed myself!"

He couldn't see Papa, but he heard a smile in his voice. "Looks like you done it now, Wooley. Too bad. I thought you were braver than that."

"Papa, please! I's just givin' the message the Baron gave me! Please, don't drop me, please!"

"You say you think he took pity 'cause you were a cryin', blubberin' mess, Wooley? That's your opinion?"

"I don't know," Wooley said, choking on the snot that was creeping down the back of his inverted throat. "I don't know, Papa, I's just scared, that's all. I ain't never seen a man like that! Never looked into a pair of eyes like that!"

"Well, Wooley-boy," Papa said, voice softening to a velvet purr. "Ain't nothin' to be scared of. Not anymore."

Wooley looked up and caught a brief glimpse of Papa's broad face; a face sometimes capable of the most radiant, assuring warmth, and alternately of the most terrible, unblinking cruelty. The cruelty of a dictator or a god, mad on his own power and might.

And presently, the face he looked into was the latter.

"Papa," was all Wooley managed to say, then he felt the grip of Papa's goons loose, and he fell, and he hit the mud and it was soft and damp and cool.

Then Napoleon closed his jaws on Wooley's head, and Wooley couldn't see anything at all.

2

The place had been empty for over fifteen years, but Madame Maybelle Merriwether—known to her crew and the people of Harlem as Madame Marie, the Queen Bee, or simply the Queen—got a good vibe off it. Gideon Mann— her lieutenant and chief enforcer—had reservations, as did her bookkeeper and her attorney. But the Queen Bee knew her own mind, and therein, Aces & Eights was a unique solution to many of her problems, as well as those facing all Harlem.

Workmen arranged tables and chairs under the watchful eye of Atticus, the maître d'. Cheedle and Sylvia, the decorators, orchestrated a small army of hands and eyes on stage, while beyond the proscenium, electricians worked on the lighting system and stagehands tested the ropes, pulleys and counterweights of the flies. From where she stood, the Queen Bee even imagined she heard clink and chatter from the kitchens where the chefs and their help planned and organized the menus. Only ten days remained until their Grand Opening, but the Queen Bee had made it clear she wanted things in order sooner for a soft welcome. True to form, her worker bees and drones all buzzed and did as they were told... all to keep the Queen Bee happy.

She thought it over as she inspected her work-in-progress, her crowning achievement. Ever since the welcome-but-abortive interest sparked a few years earlier with all things African—what literary sorts prone to naming things had taken to calling 'The Harlem Renaissance'—pale-faced mid-towners had been tooling further and further uptown in search of new haunts, new music, new dance, and new thrills. Sure, they were after what they were always after from the quaint little darkies in their Negro capitol city—booze, sex, gambling, narcotics—but for once, the black market stuff hadn't been the end of white interest in Harlem.

Madame Marie had heard it bemoaned a thousand times, from Gideon himself on down to that Ohio poet she patronized, Hughes: it had gotten harder and harder to find a gin joint north of 125th Street that didn't have more white faces than black. As if to prove the point, the downtown racketeers had even come uptown and legitimized the white man's interest in all things black when Harry Flood opened the Jungle Room, a swank supper club with hot black jazz, fine black dancers, great food and service courtesy of an all-black staff—but with a strict NO JIGS ALLOWED door policy. So, once and for all, timid souls with pale faces could cruise uptown to fan their Jungle Fever, but have no fear regarding the color of the company they kept.

But the Queen Bee had her own ideas, and she'd been searching for the perfect empty space to cram those ideas into. Here, at Aces & Eights, she'd found it: a space where she could give the Jungle Room a run for its money; and more importantly, let whoever she wanted through the door—colored, kike, cracker, dago, Mick, kraut, beaner or otherwise. The money would be good, so long as she played the right society connections. And all that money, once it had passed through the sieves of her organization, would flow right back out the doors and onto the streets of Harlem. She planned to beat that Hell's Kitchen son of a bitch Flood at his own game without firing a single shot. She'd simply pay better, build a better stable of performers, serve better food and better booze (meaning she'd have to pay off cops of greater rank and influence than Flood paid off), and open the doors to anybody with the swag to afford a seat at one of the tables.

Thus, she could feel proud of herself. She wasn't just an old gangster maid with a head for numbers and a nose for which angles to play. She'd be doing something for Harlem—dragging her whole community a few steps up the ladder toward self-sufficiency, economic prosperity, and personal pride. So what if the same people that she hoped to pay well for their service would also be feeding that money right back into her pockets playing the numbers? She wasn't twisting their arms.

Green, green, green—a big wheel, going round and round and round. And every time it turned, more money fell into her purse.

Gideon lit one of his brandy-dipped French cigars and took a long, puzzled drag. "You know, I got a hospitable streak, too," he said, shaking his head, "but this night club business..."

The Queen Bee looked at her number one soldier and confidante. "You don't approve?"

"There are better rackets to make more money with less risk. Not to mention that those other rackets are straight legit, or straight black market, with no strings in between. But running an operation like this—you're half above-board, half under-the-table, tryin' to make sure that everything balances out and that what you're doing down below doesn't topple what's on top..." he shook his head, taking another long drag.

"It's risky," she conceded. "But what, worth doing, isn't risky? Tell me that?"

"You know your own mind," he said. "I'm not tryin' to change it. I'm behind you all the way, Queen Bee... I just want you to know I have reservations, and that's how I'm gonna proceed—with caution. With a skeptic's eye."

Marie felt a moment's warmth and pride as she studied her young lieutenant. He'd worked his way up from the gutter, but he wore the trappings of success and respectability well. She patted his smooth, dark cheek with one silk-gloved hand. "And that's what I pay you for, chéri. If things don't work out, I give you permission to tell me I-told-you-so."

He raised his eyebrows. "I ain't got the sand for that, Queen Bee, whether I'm right or not."

She shook her head. "I don't believe that for a moment."

She heard trouble's approach before she saw it: heavy footfalls crossed the carpeted floor from the main entryway, quick steps following. She turned and saw a short, thick policeman and his partner marching toward her. Lamont, the doorman, tried to keep pace behind them. Madame Marie managed a soft smile: she'd known this was coming—she just didn't know when.

The cop, one Officer Heaney, doffed his hat. Madame Marie knew that had to kill him—paying tribute, even as a matter of course, to a colored woman and her right-hand man—but his Irish brogue and the patently false smile on his broad, pink face told her that he was here on business, and he was doing his best to leave his pride and preferences at the door.

"Top o' the mornin' to ye, Miss Merriwether. Here I've been passin' by for months now, and didn't know, until this very day, that you were engaged in preparing to open a fine new supper club right here in the midst of my beat." He studied the work-in-progress that was Aces & Eights.

Lamont took the opportunity to break in. "I told him we weren't open, Miss Marie, but he wouldn't take no for an answer."

"That'll do, Lamont," Marie said, and her harried doorman bustled away, still looking perturbed at the Irishman's presence.

Heaney whistled and nodded approvingly. "Looks like a lovely room for music and dance." He turned to his partner, a young Mickey Finn with early gin buds on his knob nose and ruddy cheeks. "Take note, Leary. Some night when you're lookin' to impress one of the many young ladies you're inclined to dabble about with, you may want to bring them uptown, to this very place... providin' she goes in for soul food and race music."

Madame Marie held onto her composure. The man was an artist when it came to making compliments and insults indistinguishable. Young Patrolman Leary, for his part, just nodded soberly and studied the room, perhaps actually considering it as a date destination. There was a long, puzzling silence, then Heaney nodded, and Marie knew he was about to get down to business.

"Well, far be it from me to level false accusations," he said, clasping his fat hands behind his back, "but I'd be remiss if I didn't ask: there wouldn't happen to be any liquor on the premises would there?"

"Not a drop," Gideon broke in. "But I'm parched at the moment, Officer Heaney. How's about a snort off that flask you got warming in your left rear pocket?"

Heaney didn't even blink. His grin just broadened. "Holy

water, I assure you, Mr. Mann," he responded smoothly. "Never know when some heathen jig might need the pope's own blessings to save his benighted African soul."

Marie laid a hand on Gideon's arm, eager to diffuse their pissing contest before it got out of hand. "Gideon, dearest, why don't you give Officers Heaney and Leary the two-bit tour? Assure them that there's not a drop of liquor on the premises."

"Oh, that's very kind of you," Officer Heaney purred.

Gideon looked at her sideways, clearly displeased with his assignment but loath to balk outright. Marie persisted. "Some vouchers for free supper of an evening couldn't hurt either, neh?" She tried to make her orders clear in her level stare: *grease them and get them out the door.*

"Suppose not," Gideon said, and she read his reply: *As you wish, Queen Bee—but I don't have to like it.* He turned to the cops. "Gentlemen?"

As he walked on and Heaney and Leary fell in step behind him, Marie heard Heaney's departing compliment. "Might I say, Mr. Mann, that's a fine suit! You wear it well and proper!"

For a nigger, that is.

Marie took a deep breath. No doubt, Heaney and his friends on the police force were, somewhere along the way, connected to Harry Flood and his Hell's Kitchen Irishmen—thus, in turn, to at least one of the Italian gangs for whom the Irishmen worked, and further up the line, Tammany Hall. Marie's plan had been to warm up to Clayton Carr at Tammany Hall one-on-one and skip the middle men... but Officer Heaney's initiative had blown that plan out of the water. Her bribes would now have to work their way up a longer ladder, and therefore, start larger than she preferred, to assure that the right amount reached the right hands intact.

There was no way to avoid greasing the authorities when one's primary concern was getting people drunk. Period.

She did her best to dispel her bitterness and moved on. She caught Cheedle and Sylvia arguing over the placement of a pair of pulpits for the band leader while stage hands stood by with the bulky adornments, eager to put them down. The lights in the flies blinked off and on, off and on, in a whole rainbow of colors. The spectacle struck her as the sign of something being born, and it pleased her.

She moved toward the raised dais that bordered the room, intending to get a feel for the evolving lay-out, the views, and the problems that might be presented by the windows on the west wall. It was on this meandering path through the garden of not-quite-placed tables that the Queen Bee found herself once more interrupted.

He appeared on stage: Papa Solomon House, street warlord turned gangster philanthropist; leader of the West Indies; the only serious competition that the Queen Bee knew for total control of Harlem.

Papa Solomon House: the only man that Madame Marie, the Queen Bee herself, actually felt a little twinge of fear for.

There he stood, flanked by his bodyguards, Wash and Timmons. On her stage. In her club.

She'd gotten the word first thing this morning about the hit on her 127th Street bolito drop last night. It was buckshot to swat a fly—Chester and Lester were barely worth the nasty excess of lead that House used to down them.

But sense wasn't the point, was it? House was making a statement: *I'm moving north, and your runners are in my way. If I can't scare them away, I'll tear them out at the roots like weeds.*

It was an act of excessive force designed to induce fear and create fewer problems in the future—his standard M.O.

The bitch of it was, more often than not, it worked.

She decided to stay right where she was and make him come to her. She wished Gideon were on hand, but he was no doubt still haggling with that fat Irishman Heaney in the back about what booze Heaney would take with him and how much green would be in the brown paper sack that would carry it. She checked the main entrance, saw that Dorey and Croaker were close at hand, but felt no relief. They were hired help. She could probably count on them in a pinch, but they had no judgment to exercise and no ambition beyond living to see next week.

Damn. The dining room was full of drones. The Queen Bee was on her own.

House marched out onto the long, thrusting stage, studying the space as he went. He was tall and broad, but there seemed to be no fat on him. Unlike a lot of street thugs turned bosses, he hadn't gone to sod. He was still strong as an ox and tight as a steamer's guy-line. He wore a dark blue, double-breasted suit with light pinstripes, a starched collar, wing-tip shoes, and a dark blue homburg hat. A blue-gray camel hair coat was draped over his broad shoulders like a cloak. Wash and Timmons smoldered on either side of him, eager pit bulls on their master's chain.

Marie waited. House made it to the end of the thrusting stage, caught her eye, and smiled a bright, Caribbean smile out of his night-dark face. Marie managed a lopsided smirk. The bastard looked surprised to see her—as if this weren't *her* place, but his.

"Madame Marie! Good morning!" House offered, voice smooth as coconut milk. "This is good space you got here. Good light. Good air. I'd say you're gonna blow the Jungle Room out the water."

"Compliment accepted," Marie answered, chilly and non-committal. "I thought I was clear the last time you dropped in for a palaver that I didn't want to see your face without ample warning and approval first?"

His smile never faltered. "Unkind, Queen Bee, unkind. Can't two business associates have a friendly chat? Perhaps a drink?"

"Awful early in the morning for a drink, Mr. House," Marie answered, but she was already moving away from the brass rail that ran the breadth of the dais, getting Dorey and Croaker's combined attentions and waving them near.

House was off the stage now, rounding toward the stairs onto the dais. "Never too early for such as we, milady."

Croaker arrived first and he got the order: two Bloody Marys for the Queen Bee and her guest—top shelf stuff in hers; basement-brewed turpentine for House. Croaker hurried into the back. Dorey, at the silent behest of Marie, moved up onto the dais and stood close at hand. She waited for House to fold himself into a chair that seemed too small for his big frame, then she sat across from him, her dainty, gloved hands folded in her lap.

"So that answers my first question," House said, removing his hat and laying it on the table.

"Being?"

"Is there booze?" House answered. "My next question follows: what about the other rackets? You gonna run a game room backstage? Upstairs or down, maybe? Perhaps billiards?" The latter designation—*billiards*—was a common euphemism among the bosses for a cathouse.

"I'm in the business of hospitality, Mr. House," Marie answered. "Whatever my patrons want, they can have, so long as they're willing to pay for it."

The Bloody Marys arrived and Marie let House take the first sip. He complimented her bartender with a smile and wink. She countered with a stiff drought of her own.

"You need someone to run the game tables or the billiards?" House offered casually.

"You can't possibly think that I'm not equipped to run my own dice, cards, and whores, Papa. Even you're not that stupid."

"But you know I'm better at it," House countered, smile brightening. "You know I can make more money for you, if you'll let me."

"I make out," Marie said. "I don't need you. Especially after last night."

"Last night?" The smile remained. He wanted to hear her say it.

"You think I don't know it was you? That mess on 127th Street? All you did was seed a lot of ill will, Papa. Maybe the next time you have your goons throw down, you should have them do it where some poor, innocent child in his bed isn't going to take a stray bullet."

His smile faltered now. "Christ, you're a stubborn woman."

"What's your angle, Papa? You got balls the size of watermelons to show your face in here this morning, of all mornings."

He leaned forward, pointing one long, thick finger at her. "A woman talked to me like that once back in Trinidad," he snarled. "I sowed up her flapping lips, then cut off her teats and curried them. If you want to test me—"

"Oh, I think it's clear I'm testing you," Marie said, "and you're always found wanting. You've got a nose for angles and a talent for graft, but you're just a monkey-chasin' thug off a banana boat whose only real talent is getting anybody weaker and dumber than you to knuckle under—all because you're willing to pull insensible shit like that dust-up last night. Well, I'm not weaker *or* dumber than you, House, and I knuckle under to no man. If you really thought you could waltz in here and charm your way into a piece of this place, you're even dumber than I thought."

He looked at his Bloody Mary, clearly wanting another drink, but wondering if doing so was a sign of weakness somehow. She was insulting him, after all. Shouldn't he toss her drink back in her face?

If he had the sand to do it, Marie thought, *I might actually give him the honor of a death at Gideon's hands. But as it is, he won't. He's just gonna fume and play the part of the angry child.*

"Who is he? The Baron?"

Marie had no idea what he was talking about. "Baron who?"

"One of my boys told me everything—how some freak in white-face and a top hat took out three of the four associates who I sent up 127th Street to stake my claim. Who was he, Queen Bee?"

Marie felt a twinge of curiosity. She hadn't heard this part of it. She knew Chester, Lester, and Frupp took lead in the drive-by. She'd also heard that by pure, rotten luck, some poor kid sleeping in a front bedroom next door to the barbershop bought it as well. The new kid, Beau, was laying low. Three of Papa's boys—the gunmen—were found with new lead jackets a block from the hit, splayed out in the street like road kill, their bullet-riddled, flat-tired Ford nearby.

Truth be told, Marie had no inkling of who'd taken out the shooters. She figured that would come out in the long run—more of her soldiers who happened to be nearby? Pissed-off tenants from the building that took strays? Maybe even the kid Beau—though she seriously doubted the latter.

But what was this bullshit from House? A Baron? In white face and a top hat?

"You're talking about Baron Samedi? The Cemetery Man?"

"I'm talkin' about your gunman," House countered. "Whoever the fuck he is and wherever the fuck he's from. I hit your boys and you hit back. That's three and three, so we oughta be even now."

"You don't negotiate with the stray dog that keeps killin' your chickens," Madame Marie said, feeling her confidence returning because she could clearly see how this talk of the Baron shook House to his wing-tipped shoes. "You set traps and you exterminate him, plain and simple."

"I'm warning you," House said, "this time it's fair and square. But if your hoodoo man comes down my way, I'm gonna see him laid low, plain and simple."

"You haven't even considered that he doesn't work for me?" Marie did her best now to stay aloof and non-committal. Let him wonder; let him puzzle over it.

House chuckled, smiled, and took another sip of his drink. "I may be dumb, Queen Bee, but I ain't that dumb."

She was about to say something snide—something piquant that she'd savor for the rest of her days—but a new arrival interrupted the palaver, and the day went from bad to worse.

First, there was his smell: the smell of boiled cabbage, beer-yeast, and sen-sen peppermints. Then, as Marie was still turning to see who had arrived—who could possibly smell like that—he spoke.

"Nice joint, jigs and all," he said, his accent a shitty mix of Lower East side roil and Old World sibilance. Marie studied the new arrival, and though she didn't know him by sight, she put two and two together fast and deduced who he was based on his nefarious reputation.

And his smell. She'd heard about that repugnant, beer hall smell with the hint of peppermint to sweeten it from more than one friend and enemy. His mother had named him Adolph von Sturmundranger. Nowadays, he went by Dolph Storms.

He was a big, pasty kike with bad hair plastered down by a combination of too much tonic and too little washing, a complexion somewhere south of Bratwurst, and watery, red-rimmed eyes that reminded Marie of a couple white stones left to molder in a shallow pond. His suit was off-the-rack, rumpled, and sporting mustard on the lapels and small, dark freckles at the sleeves—dried blood, no doubt.

Two more sheenies flanked him—bruisers with better skin and better suits. Nonetheless, his place in the forefront made it clear that he was the alpha dog in this pack; the star attraction, no matter how unkempt and repugnant he might be. Marie remembered the word on him: a Yorkville thug who had, little by little, worked his way up as a brew baron under the watchful aegis of Teddy Michansky, the brains behind the east side Jew gang sometimes called the Dandies, because they all dressed so well.

All except Storms, anyway.

And here he stood, in her club, studying she and Papa House like they were close as cousins.

They all look alike, he was probably thinking.

Storms studied the two of them, then looked at Marie. "I hear you're the jungle bunny in charge. That right?"

Marie took a deep breath. It wasn't even noon, but it was shaping up to be a long, trying day. "So rumor has it," she said coolly. "What can I do for you, sir?"

He smiled. There were crumbs in his crooked yellow teeth. "Yeah, you're all right. You high yella dames can almost pass for whites, 'cept for that shovel nose of yours."

Dorey and Croaker were well behind her, out of her line of sight, but Marie felt them both tense, as if their sudden rage threw sparks into the air. She raised one hand slowly, to tell them both to keep silent and keep cool, then met Dolph Storms's watery, lecherous gaze. "You got a name, Abe?" she asked, knowing it full well.

"Dolph Storms. Here as an emissary of a popular and well-to-do brew concern that'd like to open contract negotiations."

"What sort of contract?" Marie asked.

"Whaddya think, Queen Brownie? We brew suds for the whole East Side. Seein' as you're in the neighborhood—"

"Your neighborhood's back in Yorkville," Marie countered, "south of 110th street. Shit, I'm surprised those nice, well-heeled heebs and huns down that way'd let a pasty-faced white gorilla like you walk their immaculate streets. No, Dolphus—you look like you're Lower East Side all the way to me. So my question is, what a cheap Five Points hood like you doin' all the way Uptown?"

He stared, clearly not amused by her patter, or her insults. She took advantage of his momentary silence.

"Shit, boy... something nasty could happen to you all the way up here, so far from home."

Storms summoned a crooked grin and snorted derisively, managing to follow it all with a sickly laugh. "You're a smart piece of coon-tail, ain't you? Well, you listen to me, powder burn—"

She cut him off. "No, you listen to me, you mocky fishmonger: you call me jig, coon, brownie, or powder burn one more time and you'll see just how smart I can be." She heard Dorey and Croaker's hands tickle their pistols under their coats and knew they would back her up. She gave the word, they'd throw down, no questions.

Storms stuck his tongue in his cheek and rolled it around. "Fine," he said, leaning close, as though talking to a child. His sauerkraut and sen-sen breath blew in Marie's face. "Let me spell it out for you, Madame... you wanna open the doors on this fine establishment, you gotta have suds and bugjuice. We brew suds. You give us green, we give you suds. You and your darkie friends can play your jungle music and shake your asses while getting sauced as can be on our product, and we leave you be. Elsewise, if you wanna crack smart and try to contract elsewhere for your contraband liquor and deny us the revenue that is rightfully ours, we'll see this place burned to the fuckin' ground, and all your little monkey ashes mixed in with the smokin' coals. And just for good measure, Madame, I might even stumble down here after a night off on a toot and piss on your poor, black ashes myself." Again, the crooked grin. "Clear?"

"Clear," Marie answered. "Let me honor you with equal clarity, Mr. Storms: we will not buy your brew. We do not want or need the cheap soap-piss you try to foist off as good beer. You will not have a dime of my money. And if you do not put your hat back on your filthy head and turn tail and leave my club in the span of twenty seconds, I *will* see you dead, silent, and finally respectful. Am I clear?"

Storms stared at her, shot glances at Dorey and Croaker, even looked to Papa House and his back-up. He was a big, bad bruiser, and he traveled with two dogs close at hand, but he was outnumbered, and in the wrong neighborhood. Marie wasn't dumb enough to think that she wouldn't have to deal with Storms or his employer again... but for the time being, her point had been made.

Storms put his homburg back on his head, jammed his hands in his pockets, and spat a neat wad of phlegm onto the floor at Marie's feet. "You got a mouth on you, Queen Bee. Come a day soon, maybe I'll get those flappin' lips of yours around my schvatz."

And with that, he was gone, and Marie was left alone again with Papa House and his bulldogs. House was smiling. Marie wanted to bust her Bloody Mary glass against his face and watch him bleed.

"Well-handled," he said.

"Are you still here?" she asked.

House's smile fled. He leveled a finger at her. "You've been warned," he said, then made a big show of rising from his chair and putting his hat back on his head again. He towered over her, but Marie didn't move. She decided that to stay where she was, seated, in his shadow, but totally unafraid, was the best of all possible approaches.

Then she heard Gideon's voice off to her right, approaching at last from the kitchens.

"There a problem, Queen Bee?" he asked as he neared.

Madame Marie looked up at Solomon House and smiled. She saw the fury and confusion on his face; saw that, for the moment, she had the upper hand and had done a fine job mind-fucking him. "No, Gideon, dear. Papa was just leaving."

House did as he was told, and Marie finished her Bloody Mary.

3

The name on his birth certificate was Booker Dubois Butler Corveaux, but the shingle that hung in front of his ground-floor office at 220 West 136th Street, just west of 7th Avenue, said simply:

B. D. CORVEAUX, M.D.

Though he owned the building and had keys to every door, inside and out—a fact unknown to almost everyone except for the dentist and attorney who were ground-floor office space tenants—he nonetheless always arrived by the public entrance in front. His secretary and nurse, Cecile, used to think this strange, but she knew his habits well now, and thought so no longer.

Every morning, before the sun was up, the young doctor took a long walk—meditation and exercise in one, he would tell her—then stop for a leisurely breakfast at some cozy little kitchenette, and finally arrive back where he started at around eight in the morning. Sometimes he would have an early morning walk-in, but most of the time his appointments didn't begin until nine and carried through until one in the afternoon. Then, he went out again for a one hour lunch, and upon returning, saw patients straight through until five or six in the evening. Usually, Dr. Corveaux remained in the office, finishing paperwork, making notes, and considering the health of his patients long after Cecile was already tipping out the door for the evening.

Thus, he was a creature of habit, and Cecile found that part of his personality comforting.

But there was another side to him as well. He could be puzzling and contradictory, moody and mysterious. Cecile made a point of never asking too many questions—he was her employer, after all, and it just wasn't proper—but she was curious nonetheless, and had extracted some information both directly and indirectly in the six months she had been in his employ.

Observation told her that he was a handsome young man of dark chocolate complexion, with serious eyes and a mouth that could alternately support terrible, ponderous frowns or bright, blinding grins. She didn't know if he sang, or even if he went to church on Sundays, but his silky basso profundo voice suggested that he could belt a spiritual with the best of them, or possibly even dabble in opera, if he so desired.

He was born in Louisiana, raised by a northern-born Negro father and southern-born Creole mother. At least part of his childhood was spent on a sugar cane plantation in Haiti, and his maternal family name, Corveaux, was well known around the world as a high quality brand of rum. He was also a decorated serviceman of the Great War, having served with Harlem's own favored sons, the 369th Infantry Division. That part of his past was no real mystery, for the young doctor kept a large photograph on the wall of the 369th's triumphant return march down Lenox Avenue, and would proudly point to a certain little black dot in the crowd of soldiers on parade in the photo and say, whenever asked, "There I am, right there, in full dress. Bet the white man never saw so many Negroes with rifles in one spot, eh?"

That last bit always got a laugh from whomever had asked about the picture—patient, creditor, vendor, or deliveryman.

Then there were the other little snatches of info that Cecile had derived from her employer, less solidified: he'd gone to school at Harvard stateside and earned his medical doctorate overseas, at the University of Munich. He copped to intimate knowledge of white women, particularly in France, but Cecile tried not to hold that against him—what a young man did when he was away at war was his business, and he could hardly be blamed for it. Most mysteriously, he seemed to speak of broad travels in Europe, Asia, Africa, and the Caribbean, but Cecile was loath to press for more details, and he never seemed to offer them. Thus, her knowledge of her young employer's broad meanderings remained incomplete, but tantalizing in its haziness.

Still, these were all speculations. For the most part, Cecile kept her knowledge of her employer's comings and goings, his leisure activities, and the company he kept, beyond her own reach. She was nosy by nature and would have loved to know more about him—given her employer's easy nature, no doubt he would have answered any question she asked—but nonetheless, she never allowed herself to ask, because somehow, she knew it was none of her business.

Still, it puzzled her a little when he arrived one late October morning, fresh from his breakfast, wearing no smile and looking more than a little tired and preoccupied. She almost hated to tell him that he had an unexpected, early morning appointment. He figured that out soon enough, however, upon sweeping into the office and finding a pretty young woman and her teenage brother in the waiting room. When he looked to Cecile, she was quick to assure him that these were walk-ins, not a forgotten appointment.

"Miss Fralene Farnes," Cecile said, suggesting the pretty thing in the fine coat and well-worn hat. And next to her, a young man with his sister's fine features, but none of her quiet assurance. "That's her younger brother, Buchanan."

"But everybody calls me Beau," Buchanan Farnes said.

Cecile puzzled over young Dr. Corveaux's aspect—the knit in his brow, the neutral set of that heavy mouth of his, usually smiling at this time of the morning. He studied the woman and her younger brother for only a moment, then a grin rose like the sun on his face, and his distraction seemed to burn off like an early-morning fog. Cecile even thought she caught a strange, ironic bend in the doctor's grin as he held out his hand to shake the hand of young Buchanan.

"Dr. Corveaux," he said, shaking Beau's hand first, then Fralene's. Cecile wasn't just imagining that she saw the light of sexual interest in the doctor's study of the young woman. And who could blame him? He was well-to-do and unattached—why not study a pretty young thing like her and make his interest known with a twinkle in his eyes?

But then his gaze was back on Beau Farnes, taking in the storm of fine slashes and lacerations on his face and neck. "Looks like you had a tumble in something sharp and fine," Dr. Corveaux said, by way of a welcome.

"He says he got rolled up near Sugar Hill last night. A fight over cards," Miss Farnes said indignantly. "But don't you believe it, doctor. Ask me, I think something untoward happened to my brother, and I'd like to know what."

Then Cecile saw the pleading dew in the young man's eyes, and Dr. Corveaux recognized it too. *Yeah, I lied to my sister,* that look said, *but it ain't her business, doc. Just patch me up and help me out.*

Cecile had seen that same pleading look given more than once in the waiting room, though it was usually a mother and son, or a husband and wife. Beau—who couldn't be more than seventeen if he was a day—must be the ward of his big sister, and her motherly instincts were clearly at odds with his young man's coltishness.

"Well, give me two shakes to shed my coat and hat," Dr. Corveaux said with a smile, "and I'll take a look at that mess on your face, Beau."

Beau rose and so did Fralene. The doctor looked to Fralene Farnes and suggested that she sit again. "I'll see your brother alone, Miss Farnes—no need of you to trouble yourself. I'm sure Cecile'd be happy to make you a cup of coffee if you like."

"Just percolated," Cecile said earnestly, trying to help her employer save young Beau Farnes's dignity.

"But he's my responsibility—" young Miss Farnes began.

The doctor was hanging his coat just inside the office nook where Cecile held sway and tossed his brown fedora onto a hook beside it. "Oh, it's just the size of the examination room, that's all," the doctor said easily. "No need to crowd us all in. Beau, come on back."

And with that, Beau was up out of his chair, disappearing with the young doctor into the examination room, and Cecile was left alone with a rather indignant-looking Miss Fralene Farnes, whose natural, milky-skinned beauty now looked flushed with insult and indignation.

Cecile stifled a giggle. The young doctor may have felt the first sting of Cupid's arrow at the sight of the lovely young colored woman, but he'd have a hard time getting dinner or a sundae out of her now that he'd ruffled her feathers.

XX

Beau Farnes winced as Dr. Corveaux dabbed iodine on the storm of cuts that stippled his face like splatters of paint. The doctor smiled a little. Though Corveaux knew otherwise, young Beau Farnes was sticking to his story, even separated from his sister.

"Those fellas up in Sugar Hill are rough," Farnes said, trying to talk away the sting of the iodine. "Grabbed me on the street, dragged me into an alley, rolled me in a trash heap. There musta been broken bottles or somethin' in there, maybe an old windowpane. I didn't even know I was cut up so bad 'til I got home and looked in a mirror."

"Well, you're lucky it wasn't worse," Corveaux said knowingly, and made a point to look the young man in the eye. "A lot worse."

Farnes nodded. The doctor's view of the young man was well in line with his estimation last night: untried, but not stupid... and certainly not lost for good.

Yet.

"I ain't goin' up that way anymore," Beau said, smiling. "Cross my heart."

"What was it drew you up that way?" the doctor asked. "Ladies, liquor, or games of chance?"

The young man's smile broadened. "Heck, sir... all three."

Corveaux smiled in spite of himself. He liked the kid. That's why he'd let him go the night before. He knew from the first that he wasn't a lost cause; that he hadn't pulled the trigger on anyone, stuck the knife in, or bloodied his hands. Sure, he was working an apprenticeship with the numbers-runners, but the way the doctor saw it, that was no crime in and of itself. There were worse sorts in the world.

The sorts employed by Papa House. The sorts he'd had to make short work of with his pistols...

But, back to the business at hand. The doctor held his smile, to make sure that Beau knew the advice to follow was offered out of friendly concern, not elderly reproach. "Ain't nothin' wrong with a toot or a roll of the dice. And believe me, Beau, I appreciate the company of ladies, myself... but use your head. Some of that stuff, if you wade in too deep, turns out to be a slippery slope with an undertow. You hear me?"

Beau was serious again. "Yessir, I hear you."

"And I take it your sister doesn't approve?"

Beau's eyes went wide, almost in fear. "No sir. You ain't gonna tell her any more—"

"Sounds like you told her what you wanted her to hear. You may not be a man, legal and all, but you're a big boy, and it seems you aren't a fool. So just use your head. What you tell your sister is between you and her."

He finished the last iodine swab. The boy had only needed a few stitches on a particularly nasty pair of cuts. The rest were largely superficial and would disappear soon enough. The stitched cuts would scar, but they'd be small—barely noticeable in time. The doctor began clean up of the implements of his trade. Beau slumped, perched on the examination table.

"She seems a might concerned about your pastimes," the doctor said.

"Fralene?" Beau said. "A might's a might short. She's like a mangy old hound keepin' this rooster in the chicken coop."

Dr. Corveaux turned to show Beau the smile that was on his face. "Forgive me for saying so, son, but of all the descriptions I could summon for your big sister, 'mangy old hound' isn't one of them."

Beau looked confused, as if the suggestion that his sister were anything but a nuisance was the strangest thing he'd ever heard. "Whatever you say, doc."

"She got somebody?" the doctor asked, hoping that he wasn't giving the young man too much grist on him, asking about his sister in such a way.

"Nobody'd want her," Beau said.

Now the doctor was confused. "Really? How's that?"

"Talk to her. You'll see."

He and Beau had barely cleared the examination room when Fralene Farnes shot to her feet. "Beau, go on to school, now. Don't be late. If you're late, I'll know."

Beau threw a glance back at the doctor—*see what I mean?*—and cleared out the door with only a muttered thanks, leaving the young doctor and his secretary alone with Miss Fralene Farnes.

She stepped up to meet Dr. Corveaux's advance. "He's going to be fine, Miss Farnes," he said assuringly. "I think he just had a rough night in a rough neighborhood."

"Well, doctor, that's my concern," Fralene Farnes said. "And I'd appreciate it if you wouldn't undermine my authority as my brother's keeper by closing me out of future examinations... assuming I bring him back here."

"Expecting more rolls in a trash-heap rife with broken glass?" the doctor asked.

"He gets into trouble more and more of late," Miss Farnes said. "I expect it might only get worse if I can't get him graduated and get him into school somewhere."

"That's his aim, then?" the doctor asked. "College?"

"That's my aim," Fralene answered. "And he's in *my* charge, so he'll do as *I* say."

The young doctor shot a glance at his secretary, saw Cecile resigned to stay out of the whole mess, then decided to try a different plan of attack. "Well, he sure is a lucky young man to have such a dedicated lady on his side."

Fralene Farnes eyed him suspiciously, as if she sensed the increased charm exuding from him and grew wary of it. She was smart, he gave her that; she had a subtle sensitivity to unspoken signals and motivation that most people only possessed on an unconscious level. Still, he got what he was after: the first little upturn at the corner of her slender, well-formed lips, suggesting an embryonic smile.

"Don't give me the high hat, doctor," she said smoothly. "You ran interference to save my brother's young pride—some brotherhood-of-men foolishness that somehow trumped what should have been your desire to please the person who was your patient's keeper—and, I might add, the one that'll pay his bills."

"Iodine and a few stitches," the young doctor replied, shrugging. "We'll call it fair and square. No charge this time."

"That won't do. We don't need charity and I pay fair for services rendered. What do I owe you?"

"Do you like curry?" the doctor asked.

"Excuse me?"

He shrugged. "Do you like curry? The sort you might get at a carib kitchen. Maybe some jerk chicken? Peas and rice?"

"Doctor, what are you talking about?"

"Call me Dub," he said, and knew Cecile was grinning now.

"What kind of a name is Dub for a doctor?"

"The sort I go by when I'm not called doctor. Dub's my name, yours is Fralene, and I, Dub, would like to take you, Fralene, out for curry and peas and rice and talk to you about any number of things that have nothing to do with your brother or my title. So how about it?"

She stared at him for a moment as though he were speaking a foreign language, then she, too smiled—albeit in a most puzzled and perplexed fashion—and he saw a blush in her cheeks and ears. "Well, that's forward."

"And to sweeten the deal," Dr. Dub Corveaux added, "the stitches and iodine are still free of charge, even if you say no."

"Well, how about I say that'd be fine, because I love peas and rice," Fralene answered, then dug a few dollars from her pocketbook and offered it, "but I'd still like to pay for the stitches and iodine—just to make sure that whatever services might be rendered, one way or the other, are fairly compensated and clearly distinguished."

Dub stared at the money, smiling in spite of himself. He'd gotten what he wanted. "Fair trade is never to be derided," he said. "Cecile, draw up a receipt for Miss Farnes."

Cecile went to work. Dub and Fralene stared at one another for a time, sharing something, puzzled and drawn by one another, eager and reticent all at once.

"Tonight?" he asked.

"Six o'clock," she said.

4

Wash parked the car in a narrow, untrod alleyway, as far back from the street as possible, and turned to address his boss over the seat. "You're sure about this, Papa?"

Solomon House studied Wash, then Timmons beside him, with cold, appraising eyes. "You scared of a few poor scrubs off the boat, boys?"

Wash and Timmons exchanged nervous glances. Papa almost laughed, because they looked ridiculous: big, strapping black bulldogs, heart-sick and troubled by the thought of a stroll among the dirty snowflakes on the Lower East Side.

Timmons shrugged. "We got your back, Papa," he said. "It's just... this ain't our turf. We don't belong here."

"What was your first clue?" House asked. His body-guards looked duly chastised. House drew out a cigarette, lit up, and took a long drag. "Just keep your eyes peeled and your nerves frosty."

Wash and Timmons exchanged worried glances again, then stepped out of the car. Timmons opened the door for House and he stepped out, buttoning up his camel hair coat as he did so. If he wasn't crazy, it was actually colder down here on the Lower East Side than up in Harlem. Maybe it was the closeness of all the old tenements; the narrow, sunless spaces in between. Truth be told, he felt bad hoodoo in the air, too, even as he smelled refuse and human waste in the open back-alley gutters and the sludgy banks of the East River a few blocks distant.

But he couldn't let the boys see fear. Whether there was something worth being afraid of hereabouts or not, showing fear to them was as good as asking one of them to bump him off and snatch his rackets. He was the king—he was Papa—he had to stay strong in their eyes.

So he led them out of the sunless alley onto the street. They were a few blocks shy of slum center. Up and down the avenue, House saw the remnants of industry: empty crates piled and left to molder; collapsed scaffolding leaning against ancient buildings; an old flatbed horse cart blocking the mouth of an alley, looking like it'd been abandoned since House himself was still a boy back in Trinidad. Above and around them, armies of spectral shirts and long johns flapped in the breeze on drying lines stretched between the block towers, choking the October sunlight and adding that special tang of human sweat and lye soap to the sour air.

"They's hoodoo ladies up in Harlem, boss," Wash offered. "Why we gotta come all the way down here?"

House was tired of explaining himself. He needed reliable security, not a couple of frightened, superstitious island monkeys in fine suits. "Ain't no telling which mambos uptown do business with the Queen Bee. 'Sides that, the Queen Bee's from the islands, too. So if we're gonna get someone to work some juju on our dime, we need juju that ain't in the Queen Bee's ken, get me? The kind of hoodoo that a mambo up in Harlem can't undo once we've done it. Now, both of you, keep your eyes open, grow some stones, and stay on me."

House marched off down the street. Wash and Timmons flanked him and followed.

He felt eyes on him immediately, and though not surprised — one big, dark skinned carib and his bigger bodyguards couldn't be too common down this way, especially when House and his boys wore finer suits than most of these poor saps had ever even seen in a store window—it still gave him the heebies. Street urchin kids with faces so dirty they were almost black; whiskered old rummies from any number of shitty, Eastern European dukedoms; East River longshoremen knocking off for the day and looking to get sauced or buy a poke before stumbling back to their nasty hole-in-the-wall homes, their dirty, lice-ridden wives and rheumatic children; strange old Jews with hoary beards, black coats, and hats, like the members of some ancient, religious *cosa nostra*—all of them studied House and his boys with the predatory gazes of vultures awaiting a kill.

House did his best to keep his gaze level and unswerving, his shoulders square, his gait steady. He knew, more or less, where he was going. Best to find the place and the old woman he'd heard tell of, buy the curse he'd come to buy, and get the hell out of there.

They rounded corners, took a few false trips down narrow side streets, and finally came to a tall, narrow brick building that looked so darkened and filthied by time that it could have been a thousand years old. The skeletal tenement squatted between two larger, newer buildings—themselves not terribly welcoming or pleasant to behold—and was set far back from the street. Sooty streamers fluttered in the yawning frames and sashes where no windowpanes remained. All in all, it gave the impression of being the wizened, invalid elder of a degenerating family, hidden in the shadows, its quick expiration and collapse prayed for by its devolving kin.

"This is the place," House said.

A half-dozen street urchins scurried out of the broken ground-floor and cellar-level windows, gathering before the dark doorway, studying House and his men with the beady, dark eyes of hyenas. The children were filthy, crawling with lice or breeding ticks on their pasty flesh. House smiled, trying to win them with charm before resorting to violence.

"Afternoon, boys," he said. He heard the fear in his own voice and cursed himself.

The kids said nothing.

"Beat it," Wash ordered.

One of them hawked phlegm and spat on Timmons's well-polished shoe. Timmons stared, too shocked to move.

House reached into his coat and pulled out the small wad of bills that he kept for just such emergencies. He peeled off a dollar and offered it to the pasty-faced leech who seemed to be the leader of the grub gang.

"This a toll road?" he asked, waving the bill.

The boy took the bill, shoved it in his pocket, but still didn't step aside or order the same from his gang. House waited for a long, uncomfortable moment, then offered another bill.

"Two dollars, boy. And that's all you get. Now, step aside or—"

They moved fast. The two urchins nearest the leader shot forward and stomped on Wash's and Timmon's toes. Wash and Timmons recoiled in pain and shock, and before House could tell them to get back on point, the leader of the gang had reached forward and snatched the roll of small bills from House's gloved hands. The street rats scattered every which way like a bunch of albino ants whose pile had been stepped in. Before House or his lieutenants could regroup, the urchins were gone, fled to the surrounding streets or dissolved once more into the yawning darkness of the tenement itself. The three of them were left alone before the open doorway, the air suddenly colder than it had been a moment before.

Wash and Timmons looked at House. House glared at both of them. "Fail me one more time like that," House growled, "and I'll leave one of you here for those little bastards to eat."

Wash and Timmons stared back. Clearly, they believed the little street urchins would eat them if given the opportunity. But House wasn't going to waste time scolding them. He hated this place as much as they did and wanted to go as well. So he pushed past them and stepped into the gloomy central hall of the old tenement. Wash and Timmons followed.

As his eyes adjusted to the darkness, House studied the interior of the old apartment house. Above, he saw open archways leading to deeper caves in the labyrinth. Filthy pale figures crouched and skulked in those doorways, watching with eager, or hungry, or wanting eyes. Drawing his camel hair coat closer about him, House mounted the stairway. He half-expected the steps to collapse beneath him; to plunge into the dank cellars of the old building, swarmed by pale, hungry termites. But the stairs only creaked beneath him, and he climbed into the darkness. Wash and Timmons followed.

Word had it that the hag lived on the sixth floor, and it took every ounce of House's will and determination to climb the stairs that far. On all the landings on every floor, they saw the remnants of men and beasts in the form of old bones, wrinkled scraps of flesh, tangled knots of dead hair and fur, and on occasion, a fresh puddle of piss or steaming pile of excrement. Strange sounds drifted out of the open doorways, as though whomever still lived there retreated as far from the street and its light and air as possible—fearful of them, reproaching them by withdrawing from them.

Then, at last, they had made the sixth floor. House could still see the purple-gray Lower East Side twilight beyond a glassless window hung with an old, bloodstained birth sheet. Within the tenement, however, there was almost no light at all; as though the bowels of the earth here festered above-ground, a cancerous tumor on the face of the world where human and animal pests of all sorts bred and thrived amid mold and darkness.

House marched down the long hallway, drawn by a stew of pungent smells from the far end. Nearing the corridor's terminus, the light fled. He sensed candlelight behind a filthy curtained doorway at the end of the hall on the left, saw the haze of cook-fire smoke, and smelled strange, stale tobacco mixed with other herbs that he couldn't identify. Before that door, he stopped and knocked on the crooked frame.

They waited in the darkness.

"Come," a knotty voice said beyond the curtain. House looked to Wash and Timmons, to make sure they were still with him, then ducked through the doorway.

The den of the old witch, whom hearsay named Magda, was the heart of the building. Geography placed it on a high floor, near the building's aft end, but nonetheless, House felt all the bad mojo in the house flowing into and out from that single chamber, and the darkness therein was tarry and permanent—the most terrible, close-cramped darkness he'd ever known. He instantly wanted to flee the place.

There was strange litter everywhere: flasks, sacks, and little totems; the skulls and bones of men, beasts, and things that House had never seen or imagined; potted herbs and weeds growing in every corner and on every surface; flayed skins, some tanned, some fresh, hanging from the low rafters above like cannibal streamers. But all of these things were not the source of the evil air that hung in the place, merely symptoms of it.

No, the hag was the source. And though she was slight and withered, bent in upon herself like a gnarled, wind-wracked, dog-legged tree, she was also the most hideous, unnatural, unsavory thing that House had ever laid eyes upon.

"Madame," House said.

"Papa," she answered, and far from flattering him, hearing his common title on her tongue made him sick to his stomach.

"I hear you're a lady who solves problems. I've got a problem needs solving."

The hag smiled in the fire-lit darkness. House felt his stomach turn like a cornered, coiling serpent. "What do you offer in trade?" she asked, and the bargaining began.

5

After being employed to pay off outstanding credit with a grocer, or cover a meal for a pair of families at some neighborhood diner, it went like this for a five dollar bill in Harlem: the grocer, diner owner or whomever, paid their protection money to the most-likely-Irish cop who walked the beat on their block. That five dollar bill joined more of its kind, part of a fat little roll that said officer of the law pocketed and bore back to his watch commander at the local precinct. Said watch commander kicked that wad of bills and others (less negligible courier fees for the flatfoots ferrying them, of course) up the line to the deputy police chief of the Harlem borough (William 'Burly Bill' Forsythe, who, not surprisingly, was Irish). Every Tuesday, the uptown bagman, Sean Farrell, picked up these community property funds from Burly Bill, usually arranged in neat bundles in an office accordion file (and perhaps a little lighter, as Burly Bill was entitled to a modest commission of his own). Farrell put the money-packed accordion file in his solicitor's briefcase and caught a ride with his driver, Tuck Mansfield, back downtown to Hell's Kitchen.

There, Mansfield would drop Farrell at the Auld Shillelagh Pub and take off to make another bagman ferry trip, probably to pick up Derry Hingle, over in Yorktown, or Tom Kelly, on the Lower East Side. Farrell, meanwhile, would sit himself down at the nearest empty table in the Auld Shillelagh and sip imported stout (on the house; perks to the bagman) while awaiting McCann's attentions.

And finally, whatever meeting McCann was in would disperse and he'd ask of Farrell, "You got those papers I asked for?" Farrell would rise, say, "Yes, I do, boss," open the briefcase, and hand over the accordion file. McCann would give it a cursory inspection, then slip Farrell his two hundred bucks and send him on his way. Every single time, Farrell hoped and prayed that McCann wouldn't notice the minor delivery fees he'd extracted from the bundle for his time and trouble.

It was an easy racket: pick-up and delivery; a free pint; and a two-hundred clover roll in his pocket. What could be easier?

But it was a little different for Terry McCann, because he wasn't some pimple-faced soldier or bored bagman like Sean Farrell. Terry McCann was a top earner and trusted captain in the Flood outfit, so he naturally had more responsibilities. Farrell's drop was one of many that he collected from his favorite back booth in the Auld Shillelagh. McCann's second, Matthew "Maddy the Paddy" Short, would take the deliveries, double-check the counts, and pack them into a small valise in the back room, under the eyes of Mickey Dewer, the owner of the pub, or sometimes Myra Dewer, Mickey's number-crunching wife and bookkeeper. Come four o' clock, court was closed, all deliveries should have been made, and McCann would get a final count before setting out in his brand new Cadillac—with Maddy the Paddy behind the wheel— to make his Tuesday afternoon delivery to Brendan Doll—who everyone called Danny—over at the waterfront warehouse where Doll held court in Chelsea.

So that five dollar bill rolled on, bundled with its fellows in a cardboard valise fat with cash graft payments a little after four on a Tuesday afternoon in late October. Said valise accompanied McCann and Maddy the Paddy to McCann's waiting Cadillac— parked under an awning in the alley to keep off the pigeon shit— then rolled west toward the river and the waterfront. In short order, the valise and its keepers would arrive at the cluster of old brick warehouses that formed the nerve center of Danny Doll's Chelsea crime dukedom.

As Farrell always found McCann in the same condition— meeting with someone, giving orders to someone—so McCann found Doll in familiar straits: usually poring over the books of his import-export operations, keen eyes checking and double-checking every penny and percentage, asking rapid-fire questions of his number-crunchers, demanding justification for the deliberately cryptic 'petty cash' or 'sundries' payments transcribed therein—which usually denoted pay-outs to Union bosses or harbormasters to make sure that the most important shipments made it onto the docks and into Doll's warehouses without trouble. McCann and Doll exchanged pleasantries; some good-natured, manly insults; shared shots of fine, imported Irish whiskey, and then got down to business.

Doll always counted the money first, then handed it off to his bean-counters, who verified the counts. Satisfied, he'd extract McCann's five percent, usually with a little extra based on timeliness and dependability, earning McCann a total of seven points on the whole take, and with handshakes and casual greetings to one another's respective families, they'd part company.

By this time on a Tuesday afternoon, Doll would have taken several deliveries himself, extracting the agreed-upon amounts for their deliverers (McCann was the only one who earned five points or more; the rest got closer to three or three-and-a-half, occasionally getting a tip to make it five if they'd done something shady at Doll's behest, or made him happy with the offering of more tribute than was demanded). Once the last delivery was made, usually getting on five or five-thirty in the afternoon, Danny Doll would unwind with final instructions to his warehouse staff, a quick, quiet moment of meditation, usually only as long as a single song on the RCA radio, and one more shot of Jameson. Then, knowing that the deliveries were counted and packed at the bottom of the cardboard office boxes he used for his deliveries to the next big fish up the food chain, Doll would slip into his enormous overcoat, squash his hat onto his big, red-shocked melon head, and order a roll-out.

He slid into the back of his touring car, the pair of medium-sized office boxes—now packed with file folders, to look like a simple delivery of paperwork or some such—waiting beside him on the rear seat, and he set out to make his weekly delivery, to Clayton Carr, boss of the New York Society of Democrats over at Tammany Hall.

Thus did the image of Old Abe Lincoln make progress through the soiled hands of Irish beggars.

Clayton Carr—a criminal in practice and instinct, but not by definition—didn't have the all-in-a-day's-work sense of normalcy or the self-control that any of his associates—notorious and nefarious sorts such as Terry McCann, Danny Doll, or the Flood brothers—possessed. To Doll or the Floods, weekly pay-offs were as natural as breathing; as unremarkable as the crop-payments of a medieval serf to his manor lord. But, for Clayton Carr—who loved money and the power it afforded, and felt a none-too-subtle thrill whenever he knew he was engaged in illegal moneymaking activities, which was quite often—the weekly deliveries were like a promised treat from a doting parent to a regularly spoiled child.

And so, Carr worked late on Tuesdays in anticipation of the deliveries he expected from his dependable waterfront Union rep, Danny Doll, of longshoreman rolls and timesheets—the sort regularly purchased by Tammany Hall to update their voter registration paperwork and reach out more effectively to the working-class community. Carr had similar deliveries all week long—from the Italians on Fridays, from the Chinese on Mondays, from the Bohemian and sundry immigrant gangs of the Lower East Side on Saturday mornings—but the Irish were his star earners. They had power and influence, mainly through the police force, and their kingdom spread far and wide over the face of Manhattan and the surrounding boroughs.

Carr's bosses—men of power, means, and strategic association—likewise demanded their fair share, so that the pay-offs could be redistributed among the higher echelons of the city's halls of power and Ivory Towers. It struck Carr sometimes as a strange sort of food chain: people at the bottom paying hard-earned cash to people above for the privelege of turning a blind eye or operating a racket; those middle-ground collectors kicking the cash further up the line to the bosses of the different neighborhoods and buroughs; those bosses kicking it up to Tammany Hall; and Tammany Hall passing it along finally to men so rich—so well-to-do by virtue of good birth and investment—that the payments meant nothing to them... at least, nothing in terms of the value of the cash itself.

But even the rich and powerful demanded their tribute. Carr had seen the men of that powerful inner circle—the high-toners who ran with Joseph Donnelly and J. P. Morgan—take their cash payments more than once and throw them straight away. Donnelly once even accepted his bundle of bills—several month's worth of wages for one of the poor immigrants of the city—and casually set the bundle on fire in order to light a cigar from it.

For the men whom Carr worked for, the issue wasn't money, or capital; it was respect. They wanted their fair piece of all the illegal tender that rolled around the pork barrel that was New York City. So long as they got their tribute, they let the gangsters, the bootleggers, the gamblers, and the whoremasters operate. If the payments flagged, they rattled their political sabers: the police were roused, like a hornet's nest; the prosecutors threatened indictments; the Feds loomed at the city's doorstep like midnight callers.

Bottom to top; top to bottom. It was a fascinating organism to be one small piece of, and Clayton Carr was simply thrilled that he was closer to the top than the bottom.

So he sipped imported Scotch, fed his parakeet and the fish in his grand aquarium, and soon enough, Danny Doll arrived. The two enjoyed small talk, shared grumblings about their respective families and social circles, then Doll departed and left Carr alone with his graft payments and boxes full of useless manila file folders loaded with old, redundant documents destined for the incinerator.

The greater portion of the money was cached in the two imbedded safes that made up Tammany Hall's private credit union, and a royal fifth was withheld and bundled into Carr's briefcase for delivery to the next big fish up the ladder. By the time the sun was down, Carr was finally locking up his office and marching out to his waiting car to be whisked toward a mid-town evening rendezvous with the Mayor, Paul Garrison.

Garrison was already finishing his dinner salad when Carr arrived to deliver the grease. The mayor—a big, thick fellow who was obviously of Italian ancestry but whose name, mysteriously, did not reflect it—didn't even look up when Carr sat down and ordered himself a ginger ale. Armstrong's, the steak house where they regularly met for such business, would happily serve elected officials and high society sorts any booze they asked for, but Carr had enjoyed two doubles back at the office and needed food before he drank anymore. Luckily, the menu was placed in his hands in short order, and it only took him moments to decide that he wanted a medium-rare Delmonico and pan-fried rosemary potatoes.

Garrison's salad plate was whisked away. The bearish mayor took a sip of water from his glass and folded his bruiser's hands before him. He looked tired. Carr even made note of it aloud.

"Long day," Garrison sighed. "The blacks want more police officers... *black* police officers. *Black* detectives. *Black* precinct commanders. The whole schmear."

"Panties in a twist?" Carr asked. His ginger ale arrived and he sipped.

"Some gang business last night. Shots were fired. Some poor tar baby, asleep in his bed, took stray buckshot. I had a visit from the Reverend Barnabus Farnes, the reverend's very vocal and strident niece, and our esteemed Harlem representative. I swear to Christ, Clay, I was kind as could be. Kinder than they deserved."

"You suggested that maybe the issue isn't one of needing more black cops, but fewer black criminals?"

Garrison gave Carr a mordant stare. "Advice of that sort will not get me re-elected, Clay. You know I need the jig vote. They love me up there."

Carr opened a poppy seed roll, slathered it with butter, and tore off little pieces, chewing around his words. "Most of them, anyway. Sounds like the good reverend and this niece of his gave you an earful."

Garrison shook his head, rubbing his temples. "Barnabus goddamn Farnes... and I thought that Garvey son of a bitch was a pain in my ass. And the niece... Christ, Clay, she's not an elected official—she doesn't even have a proper job, as far as I can tell! She just appointed herself a 'community representative' and tags along every time that bleeding heart uncle of hers comes to see me."

"The pitfalls of patronage," Carr said with a sly grin. "You're preaching to the choir, Paul. Believe me, I know."

"More black cops..." Garrison muttered again. "How do I tell my constituents that the good white folk of this city don't want to see more Negroes with guns? Even if they *are* in uniform?"

"You don't," Carr answered. His steak arrived and he situated himself, fork in one hand, knife in the other, and dug in. The meat was bloody red and well-peppered and it melted in his mouth. "You can't tell people like that the truth, because they don't want to hear it. You tell them what they want to hear and send them on their way. Nine times out of ten, the shiny paneling and fine leather in that office of yours puts the zap on their brains and they go their way figuring they really accomplished something, when all they got was the high hat."

"It may be—and I'm just thinking out loud, so don't think I'm getting ahead of myself here—but it may be, that in time, we'll have to deal with this issue a little more directly."

"You mean hire more black cops?"

Garrison screwed up his face: *don't be ridiculous*, that look said. "No, I mean force a little law and order by other means. Get Gino and his crew into Harlem. Maybe even Michansky or Flood or that Dicicco kid. I mean, fine—let the blacks have their uptown Mecca; but if they think the taxpayers of this city are going to put more Negroes in uniform just so those same blacks-in-blue can start sucking off the uptown rackets and act as enforcers for the West Indies or that brownie dame and her numbers runners... let me just assure you, that ain't gonna happen."

Carr decided it was time to see to business. He laid his briefcase on the table between them. Garrison, without a word, or even a bat of the eyes, opened the briefcase, drew out his cut, and stuffed the bundle of bills into his coat pocket. "I should hope it doesn't come to that," Carr added around a mouthful of beef. "The Negroes have to learn: they've got to render unto Caesar, just like everybody else in this city."

Garrison managed a little smile. "I'm glad you understand, Clay. Compromise keeps the wheels turning, not demands. And certainly not more spooks in blue."

Carr knew Garrison's plan before the mayor even voiced it; perhaps before the mayor himself had even finished formulating it. Garrison was a leader, but he wasn't a natural strategist. Therefore, nine times out of ten, Carr knew what the big man would be ruminating on before the big man did.

There'd be talk at the Lexington Club tonight with the high-toned sorts that Garrison kept company with. Resources would be earmarked and pooled. In a day or two, calls would go out and someone—Gino Soccorro, Teddy Michansky, Carman Dicicco, maybe even Danny Doll or one of the Flood brothers—would be given a mandate from City Hall to get Harlem under control.

By any means necessary.

XX

But opening Harlem to contractors from one of the other territories was still two or three days in the future. At the present moment—as Mayor Paul Garrison and Boss Clayton Carr of Tammany Hall enjoyed their steak and conversation at Armstrong's Midtown—Papa Solomon House was already making in-roads with his Mediterranean neighbors in the Upper East Side's Little Italy. Foot soldiers had been dispatched to scour woptown and find Gino Soccorro so that House could drop in unannounced for a personal meet-and-greet. He was taking a chance, waltzing into guinea territory without permission, but he figured Soccorro—or, more rightly, Soccorro's lieutenants—wouldn't listen to reason otherwise. So if he could just find the old greaseball and drop in, he should be able to talk sense.

The scouts paid off. Soccorro rolled into a little trattoria near Second Avenue and 96th Street every Tuesday night for veal and a late-night poker game in the cellar. When House arrived, he was still harried from his trip to the Lower East Side and bearing with him a bundle of bad juju devised by the witch lady. Still, he needed to be on-the-spot if he wanted to win Soccorro. So he centered himself as he stepped out of his Cadillac, marched into the trattoria, and found Soccorro just finishing his pasta course, swilling a glass of red that looked like thin blood, wiping tomato sauce from the pursed corners of his fattened, narrow little mouth.

There was a tense moment as House swept through the door. Guinea eyes all turned on him. Olive-skinned hands dove into overcoats, and suddenly Papa Solomon House was staring down a garden of gun barrels. He saw the old lady that must have owned the trattoria taking cover behind the counter in the back, urging her kitchen help to do the same.

Good thing House told his boys to play it cool when Soccorro's men skinned their smokers. Papa smiled, showed his empty hands, and gave the whole situation a few ticks to unwind. Soccorro's chief muscle, a tallish slab of ginzo named Franco Nasario, stood between House and Soccorro, blocking Papa's view of the big man.

"No pigs feet here, pops," Nasario said with a smirk. "Beat it."

"Already supped, Franco," House answered, and the gangster seemed a little disarmed that House already knew his name. But Papa prided himself on that front: he was big into details; into *knowing*; into putting names to faces. "I just thought I'd drop in, pay tribute to the big man, talk a little business."

"You got no business here," Nasario said.

Nasario moved to lay hands on Papa. Papa's men knew that that was the signal, and their pistols leapt out of their coats and into their hands. The two contingents squared off, guns pointed every which way, the prayers of the mistress of the house clearly audible behind the back counter.

House held his grin. "Five minutes, and I'll leave without trouble. You keep runnin' interference on me, Franco, and trouble there will be. I promise you."

"Boss?"

A muttered, raspy answer came, and Franco Nasario stepped aside. Papa House stood face to face, across a short span, with Angelino Soccorro, don of the East Side, uptown mob.

He gave the impression of a jowly, thick-lipped, Mediterranean Buddha: head and body round; small, dark eyes sunken into a soft, inscrutable face etched with deep folds and lines; hair slicked fast against his melon head with tonic and oil; a pencil-thin mustache above his blubbery mouth.

House approached and sat himself down in a chair opposite the big man. House knew his own height and broad shoulders often worked to his advantage in face-to-face meetings. He sensed the same sort of advantage in the old don, though in his case, it was his thickness, not his height that worked for him. House did his best to remain bright-faced and cool. The old don didn't blink; his mouth never even twitched.

The don snapped his fingers. Someone placed an empty wine glass before House, then filled it from the carafe on the table. House drank. "Grazzi," he said.

"Talk," the don countered.

"I've got a problem," House said. "I thought perhaps we could arrive at a mutually beneficial solution."

A long silence as the don mulled this. "Continue," he rasped.

"It's the Queen Bee," House said, and unfolded his dilemma.

6

Dr. Dub Corveaux arrived at Fralene Farnes's row house at six o'clock, and was more than a little embarrassed to realize that she was niece to the Reverend Barnabus Farnes of Harlem's Mother Zion African Methodist Church. Everybody knew the honorable Reverend Farnes. That Dub hadn't connected Fralene's surname to the cleric was just plain careless.

But he enjoyed short words and pleasantries with the reverend until Fralene showed herself, looking lovely and far less businesslike in a purple blouse and periwinkle skirt with a matching coat. She even smiled, seemingly eager to get their evening off to a start. So Dub gave the customary sincere but not-too-eager praises for the young lady's appearance, bid the reverend a warm farewell, and got them out the door.

They strolled to Lenox, and there moved south to Island Flavors, one of Dub's favorite evening supper spots. Helena, the pixie-ish West Indian proprietress, did a steady business, but had one of the best kept secrets in Harlem. Her Caribbean fare was to die for, but the little dining room was always mellow and warm, humming with easy conversation and the well-measured swing of jazz from Helena's radio on a pedestal behind the counter.

So Dub played the culinary tour guide. He ordered curried goat for himself and Helena's special fried chicken for Fralene. Both of them would have heaping sides of rice and peas. And if they had room after the meal proper, Dub would buy them each a slice of Helena's mango bread for the road.

"You look like you've got some creole in you," Dub offered, "what with your light skin and all."

"Not a drop that I'm aware of," Fralene said. "Then again,

who knows? Whose blood I've got in me isn't more than a matter of hearsay as far as I'm concerned."

Dub smiled and nodded. "True enough. I just know the folk that claimed my mother back in her parish swore I couldn't be her boy, 'cause I was too dark to be Creole."

"What about your father?" Fralene offered.

Dub nodded. "Mahogany. Antique."

"You favor him, I guess. He still around?"

Dub shook his head. He forced his smile to remain, as he answered, "No. Died some years ago."

Fralene caught his melancholy. Concern modulated the light in her big brown eyes. "Sorry to bring up bad memories."

He looked at her again. She was beautiful. Her eyes were sad now, but her mouth still turned upward at the corners a little, suggesting curiosity. Dub decided to take a chance on her. "It was bad business. We were living in Haiti at the time. Chaco rebels. Didn't like a North American Negro poking his educated nose into their business."

He could still hear his father's defiant curses and the laughter of the chacos; smell their greasy torches and the copper tang of his father's blood as their machetes rose and fell.

Then dinner arrived, a fragrant feast of rice and brown peas flavored with ginger and coconut milk, a stew for him of chopped goatmeat, roasted in a thick, yellow-brown curry gravy, and fried chicken for her, glossy with a bright red Caribbean hot sauce of Helena's own devising. The smell of the food and the light in Fralene's eyes drove the terrible memories of Dub's father's death from his memory and he smiled.

"Smell that," he said.

"Oh my," Fralene said.

They ate.

She took to the dinner, and the two of them cleaned their plates. Dub was determined to get Fralene a sample of the mango bread, so he ordered a single thick slice to go, and they were off again into the cool October night, the still-warm bread in a piece of wax paper. Dub had some ideas for where to go next, but wasn't sure if Fralene would be up for it.

"A trip to the islands needs a rum-and-coke," he said.

Fralene looked at him sideways. "Lead the way."

"Where to?"

Her smile was sly. "To whatever gin joint you've got in mind, Dr. Corveaux. Don't worry, I won't tell the police that our esteemed doctor drinks bootleg rum in Harlem cabarets."

"I've got a bottle of the family label back at my place," he offered.

She tightened her grip on his arm. "I'd sooner be seen in a speakeasy, doctor. After all, how would that look? Seeing your apartment on our very first evening together?"

He swallowed a chunk of mango bread. "It'd look pretty good to me."

She slapped his shoulder. Dub chuckled. "Fine. Gin joint it is."

So they strolled down Lenox to 130th Street, then turned eastward. They passed through Astor Row, past the strange, lovely houses that looked more like something from Dub's New Orleans days with their porches and little green yards out front, and finally made their destination, a little basement 'coffee house' called Edmond's. It was the sort of place where the liquor was imported in bottles from real distilleries—not the sort brewed in bathtubs or basement stills. Gingerbread Mae, the proprietress of the close little basement, welcomed Dub with a hard embrace and kisses on either cheek. Then she studied Fralene queerly and let her pass, seemingly in spite of her better judgment.

They sat at a small table in a corner, as far from the banjo and piano player in the rear corner of the space, who were picking and pounding out old-school ragtime while a pair of young, lanky boys from up Sugar Hill way (Dub had seen them before but couldn't remember their names) tapped and swayed for the smoking, well-into-their-cups patrons.

Fralene studied her surroundings. "Charming."

Dub couldn't tell if she was being straight or joshing him. "Ethel Waters used to sing here," he said, by way of justification. "Right here, going table to table."

Fralene let that pass with an accepting smile. They talked

some more about all sorts of things. He ordered a Cuba Libre—a rum and Coca Cola with a splash of lime—and Fralene ordered a coffee with a shot of brandy. Once their drinks had arrived, Fralene grew serious.

"What do you think of everything going on up here?"

"Everything being?" Dub asked.

She shrugged, eyes on her coffee. "The turf wars over the numbers rackets. Drugs. Booze. Seems like a night can't pass without hearing a gunshot or two. Sometimes worse."

"Like that mess last night?" Dub asked, knowing where she headed.

"Horrible," she said, shuddering a little. "As if dead men in the street weren't bad enough, that poor mama losing her baby like that."

Dub shrugged, trying to remain non-committal on the issue. Truly, though, he still rankled over the child's death. He should have been warned. He should have been able to stop it. "It's a tragedy," he said slowly, "but there are still worse places to be in the world."

"Like Haiti?" Fralene asked.

Dub's eyes met hers. The question was so random, and yet so strangely pointed, that he couldn't help but wonder precisely what she meant by it. "Pick your banana republic. Or, if you prefer, I'm sure you could talk to some folks in Germany who are still trying to get over the Great War."

"But aren't we supposed to be doing something better here?" Fralene asked, and he could tell that she was utterly sincere, and his heart broke for her because he knew she'd never be anything but disappointed in life.

"We as *Americans*?" Dub asked. "Or we as *black* Americans?"

"Both," she answered.

Dub shrugged, sipped his rum and coke. "We try."

"But it's getting worse," she countered.

"Sometimes it has to get worse before it gets better," Dub said, then forced a smile. "What are you on about, Miss Farnes. You a crusader? Like your reverend uncle, Mr. Barnabus?"

She smiled a little, but the sincere light remained in her

eyes. "A little, maybe. It just seems that for a while I saw things getting better... and now they're sliding downhill."

"Ebb and flow," Dub said. "Up and down. That's the way of the world."

"But it seems like the up part was so brief. So short."

"So what's your plan, Miss Anne?" Dub asked, knowing that the epithet would probably annoy the hell out of her.

He wasn't wrong. Her mouth set and her eyes grew serious. "Don't call me that. I've heard enough of that just because I haven't got an antique mahogany finish like you, Dr. Corveaux."

"But you didn't answer my question," he pressed. "What's your plan?"

"My uncle and I spoke with the mayor today. We've spoke with him a number of times. We're trying to get him to push through a mandate for more black police officers uptown... maybe even some black detectives."

"And what good will that do?"

"Don't play dumb, doctor," Fralene said. "I know you're not dumb. You know how the people up here see the cops."

He knew all too well. There were blacks in uniform, but most of the policemen who walked the beat in Harlem were Irish, bolstered by Italians and other sorts to round things out. The Irish cops in Harlem—hell, all over the city—still had ties to the Hell's Kitchen and Chelsea gangs, and through them, to Tammany Hall. They were almost all on the take. And on the take or not, their main purpose when on patrol was to keep the white downtowners who came up to Harlem for booze, jazz, and vice safe when they walked the streets. As for what darkies did to darkies when the cops weren't around: that wasn't their concern. Queen Bee Marie and Papa Solomon House could fill the gutters with rivers of Negro blood for all the Mickey Finns in blue cared.

So Fralene and her reverend uncle, no doubt bolstered by a few well-to-do and well-intentioned Harlemites, thought that badgering the mayor into putting more blacks in uniform would give Harlem a police force that actually policed.

It was a nice thought, but Dub wanted to tell Fralene that, even if she and her uncle got their way and the mayor hired more black cops, even promoted a few to detective, they'd most likely just end up on the payroll of the Queen Bee, or Solomon House, or one of the lesser black gangsters in Harlem. So they'd still have a police force tied up in the rackets; they'd just be tied up in black-owned, Harlem-based rackets instead of the concerns of the Italians or the Irish downtown.

But Dub didn't say that. All he did was shrug and say, "I know how the people up here see the cops. And I know how the cops up here see the people. But I don't see how the color of the cops is gonna change anything if it's the force itself—and the system it's part of—that's dirty."

"I didn't peg you for a pessimist, doctor," Fralene said, a little sadly.

He grinned, though he knew he wasn't fooling her. "Well, I *did* peg you for a crusader, Miss Farnes... but I'll try to forgive you for that."

She managed to smile, but he could tell she wanted to say more; to convince him of something; to change his mind. Her sort were always after that: changing hearts and minds. Dub Corveaux was past the point of thinking that hearts and minds could be changed.

At least, not without a little hellfire and bloody knuckles.

Someone broke out a cornet and started blowing a hot, staccato melody in concert with the jangly banjo and the tinkly little juke joint piano. The rear of the little cellar dive was coming to life, tables and chairs pushed out of the way, bodies sweating and swaying in the dim lamplight.

"Care to dance?" Dub asked.

Fralene didn't answer. She just offered her hand.

XX

The brandy loosened her and the coffee gave her a kick in the seat, and Miss Fralene Farnes proved that, when she wasn't trying to solve the world's many ills, she could cut quite a rug for herself. She spun and smiled and swayed, and more than once she pulled loose of Dub's arms and turned and sidled before him and he watched her hips curve back and forth and her well-formed buttocks move beneath her skirt, and though Dub Corveaux knew that Miss Fralene Farnes's heart was too pure and good and hopeful to be consort to a dark, divided heart like his own, still he found that he wanted her, and even loved her a little.

But, finally, it was close to midnight, so they left the little rhumba room and started their walk back to her home. Harlem's ills weren't brought up again. Fralene admitted that she'd actually known a little about Dub before meeting him: she'd read some of the poems and essays he'd published in *The Messenger* literary journal, and been taken with each and every one of them. She'd long intended to go seek him out at his office on 136th Street, but not until her brother showed himself at the breakfast table one morning with all his mysterious cuts and scrapes did she manage to do so.

"Now I feel taken," Dub said. "Mere prey for your keen hunter's eye."

"Predatory," Fralene said. "That's me. All the way."

They laughed easily, and suddenly, they were back at her stoop and the night was done. They stood looking at each other for a long time.

"It's been a fine evening, Miss Fralene Farnes," Dub said.

"Dr. Corveaux, you've been excellent company."

"I want to see you again."

She smiled, but made no move or indication that she wanted to be kissed. "You know where to find me," she said, then turned and climbed the stoop and disappeared into the house. Dub stood watching as she disappeared beyond the foyer and the porch light went out, then turned and marched for home, hands in his pockets.

He cut down toward 136th Street by way of a series of narrow alleys that snaked and intersected behind various buildings. Upon reaching the intersection of two such alleys just a block shy of home, Dub found a wizened old Negro in a slouch hat, smoking a corn-cob pipe and smelling of stale old tobacco.

The old man sat on a lidded trashcan, cross-legged, like a boney, ebony Buddha on a cheap pedestal. Dub had half-expected to find the old man here at the secret crossroads behind his building. That was why he took this particular route.

"She's a sweet girl," the old man, whose name was Legba, said. The old man smiled a little, black eyes catching the light of a single, bare light bulb shining above the back entrance of a nearby tenement.

"Why weren't you here last night?" Dub asked. "When I called you?"

"I don't come when called," the old man said. "I come when required."

"And you don't think you were required last night?" Dub persisted. "What good was that mess last night? A few more hoods off the street. A little fear in the air. Fine. But a child died. An *innocent* child."

"Innocents die," the old man said, puffing smoke from his pipe. "It can't be helped, and you know it well."

"But I thought it *could* be helped," Dub countered. "That's what I thought I was doing here."

"As you say," the old man agreed. "It *can* be helped. *Sometimes.* Not always. You're just one man. There's a difference to be made, but you ain't gonna change the world... or save everyone that needs saving."

Dub felt his anger rising. "Then what's the point?"

"You do what you can, when you can. But you can't do it all."

Dub snorted. "I never pegged the doorman at the crossroads for a pessimist."

"Well, I *did* peg you for a crusader, Dub Corveaux... but I'll try not to hold that against you."

Dub didn't like having his own words thrown back at him. Especially when they made him feel such a fool. "Do you have work for me tonight?"

"There's always work to be done."

Dub threw a glance up at the looming shadow of his brownstone above them. He thought of his attic sanctum... his other face... his guns.

XX

Owney'd had too much to drink, and he knew it. But he wasn't gonna let Deirdra guilt him; not this time. His number'd come up; he had swell new vines and a tight knot in his pocket to show for it; they'd burned up Jungle Alley, and now he was walking his Deedee back to her place, where he hoped to get some fair action in recompense for a fair—hell, a lavish—evening's expense.

The lights of the Lafayette Theater were behind them. In the dark, they were strolling nearer to the Good Luck chestnut tree on 131st Street. Owney threw himself at the big tree, arms around it in a shameless embrace. "That's my girl," he said happily. "Finally brought my numbers in!"

"You're drunk," Deirdre said.

"You ain't?" Owney asked.

Deirdre held her severe look for a good two or three breaths, then burst out laughing. He could see the clouds in her eyes now; the soft, easy manner of her smile. He'd done well; she was drunk as a skunk, just like him.

Tonight. Finally. Those silk stockings on her long, slender legs came off tonight.

They laughed together, then Deirdre had his hand and pulled him across Seventh Avenue, toward 130th Street. There was a lot of activity on the corner of 7th and 131st, as there always was—largely their fellow Harlemites out to stock 'the Corner' and watch the swell 'fays as they were dropped off at Connie's Inn. In moments, they were across the street, stumbling and laughing all the way, and Owney saw a big, yawning darkness ahead and drew up short, wary. Deirdre yanked on him.

"Come on," she said.

He pointed toward 130th Street. "That way," he said.

She pointed toward the alley in front of them. "This way. Shorter." Then she drew up, pressing herself against him and whispering in his ear. He smelled the cheap liquor on her breath and it got him hot. "Gotta get back to my place fast, Owney. You got my fuze burnin' and I don't wanna blow on the way."

He took her hand and drew her into the alley. It was his lucky night. He'd have to buy that good luck chestnut a park to go around it. He supposed that the six hundred bucks he hauled on bolito wouldn't exactly buy a park—but it was fine to dream, wasn't it?

"Lookit this," someone said, and Owney turned, trying to find the source of the voice in the dark, deep alleyway between the buildings that fronted 131st and 130th streets. Some distance behind him, he saw the lights of 7th Avenue, but already they seemed far away—as distant as the stars above bracketed by the dark, rising monoliths of tenements and store fronts on either side.

Then a trio of shadows came swaggering out of a darker side alleyway, surrounding he and Deirdre like sharks, circling, smiling, their teeth too bright and their faces too dark in the shadows. "Owney Potts," one of them said. "Fella who hit the numbers this afternoon."

Deirdre took a swing at the nearest one with her pocketbook.

"You dumb niggers best back off, 'fore my Owney gives you what for!" she snarled. Owney wanted to support the sentiment, but truth be told, he felt too scared—and too sober, all of the sudden—to give anybody much of anything.

One of them took a swipe at Deirdre, snatching the gold chain and locket that Owney had bought her just that afternoon and tearing it off her neck. It broke without resistance and she gave a little scream. "Nice!" the fellow hissed. "Sparkly, shiny!"

Owney felt rough hands on him, shaking him, diving into his coat pockets. "Where's it at?" the shadow with the ivory grin snarled. "Where's your knot, Owney?"

Owney started to lay hands on the fellow; started to put on a show of resisting, but secretly hoped that one of them would just knock him out, take what they wanted, and go, so he wouldn't have to try and be brave for too long. But then a new shadow melted down out of the high darkness in the alleyway, and he found himself more terrified than he'd ever been in his life.

The apparition came plummeting down from a high ledge above, landed with both feet on a jutting awning above the back door to some shop fronting on 130th Street, bounced, and landed light-as-a-cat on the pavement. Owney's three assailants all turned and stared. Deirdre gave a rough, strangled little scream and backed into the shadows, looking for a wall to huddle against.

The apparition tossed something; a pair of little round spheres about the size of grapefruit. The grapefruit hit the pavement at the feet of the two muggers on the wings of the trio. Owney heard the spheres break open, shattering like clay.

Flames engulfed the two outer hoods, but they were flames like Owney had never seen before. One firestorm was fire engine red and engulfed the hood foot-to-crown like a nest of roiling, slithering, fiery serpents. The flames on the other hood glowed blue and white, and seemed to wail and moan in mourning voices as they surrounded him. Both hoods collapsed, the flames licking at their bodies but seeming to do no damage.

At least none that Owney could see.

But they both screamed. Oh, how they screamed!

Owney's eyes shot back to the stranger himself. He didn't know the gent, but he felt a fear of hell itself as he stared at him: the white skull-face under the black top hat; the flowing tendrils of a bright red scarf and long black overcoat that seemed to sway and undulate by themselves, as if on a phantom wind; the faint, vengeful smile that seemed to paint the stranger's thick lips under his skull-face.

"Aw shit," the last hood muttered. Then he drew a switchblade, popped it in the dark, and closed on the newcomer. "Nice white-face, Mister Charlie, but I ain't afraid of all that southern-fried hoodoo bullshit!"

The skull-faced stranger straightened as the hood stepped up. His broad shoulders squared. "Drop the knife and beat it," the stranger said, and Owney thought that voice was the most terrible thing he'd ever heard; rusty iron scraping rusty iron; the old gates of a graveyard, yawning open to set the spirits of the dead free.

The two on the pavement still bucked and flopped like dying fish, screaming, begging mercy, all tied up in the red and blue flames from the clay grenades the hoodoo man had tossed.

The last hood came on. The knife flashed in a wide arc. The stranger caught the hood's knife-hand mid-swipe, drew something heavy from under his black coat, and slammed the hood hard right in the flank. The hood choked and bent double. The stranger's hand—he was holding a cold blue .45 automatic—brought the butt of the pistol-grip down on the hood's shoulder and the guy hit the pavement, knocked cold.

Deirdre screamed again. Owney looked to the skull-faced man with the drawn gun. The avenger stared back, gaze burning beneath the brim of his black top hat. "When your number comes up," he snarled, "stick to lighted streets."

Owney only nodded. The black coated apparition turned with a flourish and marched away, seeming to melt back into the shadows, then disappearing entirely into a side alley twenty yards distant. Then, suddenly, it seemed as if some dim light bled back into the world; as if the fellow's very presence had deepened the darkness. Owney heard Deirdre screaming, even as he fled toward the lights of 130th Street.

XX

Mookie and Trix were delighted. They knew they'd find good scratch in the southern-style houses on Astor Row, but they hadn't expected the haul they now drew out of a hidden drawer in a big, handmade armoire. Where the occupants of the house currently were—attending some church of Africa-for-the-Africans meeting, getting sauced in Jungle Alley, enjoying a jitterbug review at the Lafayette or the Lincoln—they didn't know and didn't care. All they knew was that something about this particular house had drawn them, and looky-looky here what they'd found in an upper bedroom: a little ivory-inlaid cedar box in this secret drawer, full of pearl strings, gold rings topped with fat stones, silver earrings and bangles, even some old gold and silver coins from around the world, fat and heavy enough to suggest value.

In the near-darkness, the only light coming from the nearby bedroom window, Mookie's eyes went wide. "Trix, lookit this!" he breathed, and held out the box.

Trix's thick fingers dove into the cache of precious metal, stone and coin. "Shee-yit! That's it! That's what we's after!"

Mookie started pocketing the stuff in his coat. He half-considered taking the whole box—certainly fine, lacquered cedar inlaid with ivory would get him something from the fence? But then he thought better of it. Too big and bulky. Close to impossible to conceal. The box stayed. Its contents would leave with he and Trix.

When both of them had filled their pockets, Trix moved for the window. "I'm thinkin' it's a good haul for one night," he said. They'd already hit two other houses on the row. The prize discovery they'd just made tripled their expected earnings for the night. "You wanna go hit Cyrus, then the Alley?"

Trix only ever had one thing on his mind: drinking, gambling, and whoring along Jungle Alley, on 133rd Street between Lenox and 7th Avenue. Mookie dug a good night out too, and if Cyrus could front them some cash, they'd have fat pockets and no reason not to hit the Alley. Hell, it was still early!

But Mookie also knew the fence business. Even if Cyrus was still puttering around his pawn shop fixing bicycles or music boxes—he probably wouldn't give them prime on the merchandise. It was a general pattern Mookie had noticed: hit a fence late at night, when your haul was still hot, and they'd be likely to filch you because they knew you were eager. Wait 'til first thing in the morning, catch them fresh after some eggs and coffee, and they'd be more likely to work with you and give you fair trade.

So Mookie turned toward the window to tell Trix that they should wait—they'd get more money that way—and he saw Trix, half-in and half-out of the window, one foot on the ledge, one hand braced on the underside of the double-hung pane, getting ready to duck through.

"It's too late," Mookie started to say, then a shadow fell across the window-pane, and strong hands grabbed Trix and yanked him through the little portal and tossed him out into the air and Trix was plunging down, end over end, his fall coming so fast, and so unexpectedly, that he didn't even cry out. He just gave a strangled, "Hey!" before gravity took him and he disappeared from Mookie's view.

Mookie rushed to the window. Trix lay on the floor of the alley below, crumpled like a rag doll, a spreading pool of blood below him glinting in the moonlight.

Then Mookie caught a whiff of stale cigar smoke and felt a heavy, cold shadow falling over him. He craned his head round to look upward.

The houses on Astor Row were fine and well-designed—the cornice- and brick-work was what made climbing to the second floor so easy—but Mookie didn't remember the buildings sporting gargoyles. Now he looked up into the face of one; a nasty creature seemingly cut from stone and shadow, wearing a long, black overcoat and top hat, crouching on the ledge above like something out of a preacher's vision of hell and damnation.

And was the gargoyle smoking a cigar? Did he see the little cherry of the cigar's fire glowing in the dark, reflected in the gargoyle's shadowed eyes? Clouds of smoke puffed out of the nasty, looming creature's pursed lips.

Then the gargoyle lunged down toward him, and Mookie almost knocked himself unconscious yanking his head back in the window. He stumbled back, well-clear of the window, vaguely aware that some of the jewels in his pockets fell loose and littered the floor. A moment later, the gargoyle dropped down onto the ledge outside the window, and he saw in the dim moonlight that the figure in black had a face painted white, like a grinning skull; and he thought of the stories his Trinidadi grandmother used to tell about the vodou barons and their grave-lord, Samedi.

The keeper of cemeteries. The lord of the dead.

Mookie Deuce was on his feet, pounding out of the strange bedroom, careening out through the empty corridors, thumping down the stairs, plunging headlong for the front door. It was locked, and he beat and scratched at its locks, cursing, hands shaking, but suddenly he had it open, and the cool night air greeted him, and he went stumbling out of the Astor Row house, through the little front yard, and into the street. At this point, he didn't care who saw him. He didn't care if the whole goddamn neighborhood were out on their front porches, enjoying the crisp October evening. He wanted out of the house; away from the gargoyle with Baron Samedi's skull face.

He was halfway down the street when he saw a dark form leap from the roof of a nearby row house, glide gracefully through the air, and arc down to land heavily in the street before him. The Baron had caught up; Mookie skidded to a halt, landing on his ass at the grave-lord's feet. The cigar-chomping avenger loomed over him, and in the moonlight Mookie saw the gravelord's serpentine red scarf move of its own accord. Its limp ends rose up on the Cemetery Man's shoulders like two lazy snakes, then reared and struck.

The serpentine ends of the angry red scarf coiled in an instant round Mookie's throat and hauled him to his feet. Choking, vision going snowy, Mookie stared into the Cemetery Man's burning black eyes.

XX

Wash was well aware that they were too big to hide easily, no matter how late it was, how dark it was, how deserted their destination was. But Papa gave orders, and Wash and Timmons obeyed. The big man didn't play, and though their trek to the darker corners of the Lower East Side and that terrifying, close-aired tenement where the witch lady holed up still put the zap on their brains, their exhaustion was nothing beside the fear and respect they bore their employer.

So they rolled up to West 139th Street, just east of Lenox, to make a late-night visit to the Queen Bee's new club, Aces & Eights. They bore with them a special bundle, about the size of a fat plowman's lunch, wrapped in dirty old oil cloth and smelling of old incense and ill will.

They watched the place for an hour, to make sure that no one lingered late, then finally left their touring car and searched the alleyways that skirted the club. They found a small cellar window that was open near the southwest corner of the building, and Timmons—the lankier of the two—shimmied through, then hurried back upstairs to let Wash inside.

The place was too spacious and too dark to welcome them. Though they'd seen it just that morning in Papa's company and been impressed by its class and good vibe, Wash now reflected that the same good vibe went south fast when everyone fled and the lights were out.

So they hurried downstairs into the cavernous basement and went searching through the roomy darkness with their flash lights for a suitable spot to stow the nasty package that Papa had entrusted to them. It was Timmons who located an old man-hole in a narrow back alcove, the shaft beneath the steel cover plugged with a round cement slab at a depth of about two feet.

"That'll do," Wash said, and laid out the bundle, drawing back the oilcloth to reveal its contents.

Therein lay Papa House's secret weapon, courtesy of the Lower East Side witch woman, Magda: a nasty-looking totem composed of two crossed human leg bones topped by a quartet of human skulls, each facing outward.

"Which way's west?" Wash asked, as Papa had told him to make sure the skulls faced the cardinal points.

Timmons considered, then pointed. "That way. Plant it."

Wash felt a tremor of revulsion as he picked up the hideous skull-and-bone sculpture, adorned above and beneath with crow-feathers, knucklebones and rat-skulls, painted with strange red-brown letters from alphabets older than any Wash or Timmons—both of whom could barely read English—had ever seen or imagined. Just touching the vile curse engine made Wash want to retch, and the moment he'd placed it at the bottom of the little cement well, he felt the residue of its latent evil on his hands and wanted to wash them in boiling water—to scrape the skin off if need be, before it was forever absorbed into his flesh.

They replaced the man-hole cover and stood. Wash suddenly noted that their breath plumed, as though the temperature in the basement had dropped to the frigidity of a meat locker. He and Timmons studied each other in the pale, narrow cones of light from their torches.

"You feel that?" Timmons asked.

Wash searched the darkness around them. It worked fast. The vast, echoing basement held the pall of a tomb, and he imagined that he already heard the whispering voices of the four skulls filling in the shadows around them, tittering in anticipation of mischief; clamoring for vengeance and ruin.

For the first time in his life, Wash actually felt sorry for one of Papa House's enemies. He had no idea what was in store for the Queen Bee and the people she employed here—but damned if he didn't feel more than a little nearer the fires of hell for doing them such a nasty turn as this.

"Fuck this," he said to Timmons. "Let's go."
They went, and their feet couldn't carry them fast enough.

XX

All through Harlem that night, the baser elements of that Negro Babylon met the gravelord, Baron Samedi, face to face. Muggers in dark alleys; sneak-thieves in fine, swank houses; racketeers planting firebombs in the stores and restaurants of honest businessmen who didn't want to pay for protection; loan sharks busy with roughing up their borrowers; drunken husbands beating their wives; philandering wives caught in the act of cheating on their husbands. The grave avenger seemed to be seen anywhere and everywhere from sundown to sunrise, and by the next morning, there was already talk on the streets of who or what the avenger might be—man or ghost or manifestation of the *lwa* or gangland enforcer or even a rough, ready guardian angel, particularly suited to duty in Harlem.

By breakfast, even the white cops that patrolled the neighborhood were trading stories of a crazy jig in white-face and a top hat who roughed up burglars, cracked mugger skulls, and laid low gun-toting hoods with a pair of cold, black .45 automatics. These cops—Micks, wops, krauts, and all sorts in between—alternately laughed at and shuddered over such stories. Some of *them* were on the take too, weren't they? How long before they were busy roughing up an informer in the night, or doing a little off-duty, in-uniform work for a patron, and this skull-faced kook came for *them*? Sure, they'd laugh amongst themselves—*Listen to the crazy, superstitious darkies! Listen to all their crazy hoodoo talk about spooks and devils! Get a load of those nutty Negroes!*

But the white men knew fear, too. Negro gunmen and pig-stickers were bad enough. Gangs like the Harlem Knights or the West Indies found strength and courage in numbers, and that was worse. But if there was some self-styled spook Lone Ranger in town—the sort who inspired more fear in the blacks than they, the white men in blue uniforms, inspired—and if said Spook Ranger started gunning for *them*, the boys in blue—

well, that was worse than a whole city full of nigger stick-up men.

This spook—the one the spades called The Dread Baron, and that the white cops were now calling The Witch Doctor— this smoked Irish son of a bitch... he was *trouble*.

Because he didn't seem to be tied to anybody or anything; and a man without ties, without a name, was a man that nobody could control.

7

Madame Marie supposed she should be concerned about Zakes's family, or his sweetheart, or whether or not anything could have been done to prevent his sudden and untimely death. But truth be told, her primary concern centered on the rest of the staff, who would start gathering in the main dining room in moments for one of the first and last all-staff gatherings before Aces & Eights opened its doors. It had been her idea to gather them—chefs, waiters, hosts, hostesses, chorus girls, bands members, and stage hands—for a single meet-and-greet; a pep talk, a statement of purpose, and a chance to see themselves as what she hoped they would become: a family.

And here they were, moments away from that meeting, when one of the electricians, a little, big-eared fox of a man named Zakes Mooring, had been electrocuted while hanging a light above the stage. Zapped good and proper, Zakes took a header—thirty feet, straight down—and collided with the immovable barrier of the stage itself.

Did the electricity kill him? Or the fall? Madame Marie had no idea. All she could see or worry about at present was the mess made by Zakes's collision with the hardwood stage floor.

She heard rumblings out in the foyer, beyond the dining room. Someone was coming. She looked to the nearest, wide-eyed stage hand—whose name escaped her at that moment—and snapped her fingers.

"Curtains down," she ordered, and the young man hurried to do as he was told. Just as conversation drifted to her ears, along with the footfalls of the first arrivals, the big plum curtain fell and the stage was cut off from the dining room. That was a start, at least.

She counted six of them: three stage hands; Walter, the stage manager; herself; Gideon. She and her second had been discussing her hopes for the place, standing on the thrust platform just before the proscenium, when they heard the hum, the grunt, and the flat, wet thud that marked the Zakes's untimely end.

Six of them, standing here, staring at Zakes's corpse, head broken open like an eggshell, blood and brain matter spreading every which way.

"This is bad," Gideon whispered beside her.

Marie looked to the stage hands and Walter. "Who was up there with him?"

"Wasn't nobody, Queen Bee!" one of the stage hands blurted. "We's all down here, workin' the fly rigs."

"Yes'm, miss. We just heard the hum and turned around, and there he went! Smack onto the stage!"

"I saw it all, Miss Marie," Walt added tiredly. "It's like they say. I saw the catwalk Zakes was up on. There was nobody near him."

The Queen Bee sighed. "We've got to get this mess cleaned up and Zakes seen to, quick and quiet. You boys, go shut and lock all the stage doors except that one, stage right. Walter, guard the stage right door and make sure nobody but one of the six of us gets in here, understood?"

Walter nodded. "And Z, miss?"

Marie looked to one of the wide-eyed stage hands. It was Beau, the kid who'd ducked hot lead in the hit two nights earlier. He'd come to the Queen Bee himself, saying that he still wanted to work for her; to be part of her crew; but street moves weren't his thing. He needed something legitimate; something with a future. So the Queen Bee, more than sympathetic to his plight and the fact that he'd been rattled, handed him off to Walter and told him to get Beau started back stage.

At the moment, though, Beau Farnes looked scared out of his wits. Still, the Queen Bee liked him. She decided to put him to use. "Beau? Think you can go fetch us a doctor, quick and quiet like?"

Beau nodded. "Yes'm."

"Do it," she said, and he hurried away. Then, she looked to all remaining. "The troops are gathering. I've got to speak with them."

"After this?" Gideon asked, suggesting poor, dead Zakes.

"We've got enough going against us," Marie answered. "Those people are my responsibility, Gideon. I'm not going to let Papa House, or Dolph Storms, or the cops, or even a whole pile of bodies take that away from them. We can see to this quietly, but we've got to keep them thinking happy thoughts, you hear me?"

Gideon sighed and nodded. He scratched the back of his head as he examined Zakes again. "Shit."

Marie nodded. *Shit*. Indeed. Then she composed herself, turned, and stepped out through the fallen curtain to address her troops. In the dining room, a sea of smiling faces stared back at her. She'd never realized just how many people she was employing here, but now that she saw them all gathered in one room, looking back at her... it was like addressing a family reunion, never having before realized just how far and wide one's blood had spread.

"Good morning, children," she said in her best school-marm fashion, and everyone laughed and greeted her, and already she felt the warmth radiating from them bringing her world back from the brink of a cold, windy abyss.

And she had them. She could see by all their bright eyes and glowing faces that they were hearing her words; feeling them; making them part of their own individual hopes and dreams, and Marie was on the cusp of forgetting that a dead man lay bleeding just a few feet from her, on the other side of the stage curtain.

Then there was the sound of shouted insults, breaking glass, shouts and screams, a scuffle. A young dishwasher came stumbling into the dining room, shouting at the top of his lungs.

"Birdie cut Del! Birdie cut Del bad!"

And then she lost them. Another scullion came stumbling out of the kitchen moments later, apron soaked with blood, a pile of bloody towels in his hands.

"Somebody call the doc!" he screamed. "Del's bleedin' like a stuck pig!"

This was bad. This was very bad.

XX

Dr. Dub Corveaux was enjoying a late breakfast at Pigfoot Mary's when Beau Farnes happened by, saw Dub through the diner window, and ducked in. The kid took a seat and leaned close. Dub sat in silence, a fork-full of ham and eggs hovering before his open mouth. He wondered if the visit had something to do with his evening with Beau's big sister last night.

"Doc, we need you," Beau said quietly.

"Something wrong with your sister?" Dub asked, and ate his ham and eggs.

"No sir," Beau answered, looking around, trying to fight an eyeful of panic. "Something's up over at Aces & Eights, the Queen Bee's new place. They asked me to get somebody and I just saw you as I was passing by."

Dub wiped his mouth. "Shouldn't you be in school, Beau?"

"Doc, please—"

"And what are you doin' in the Queen Bee's hive just a day after I patched you up? You lookin' to walk down the wrong street and get rolled again?"

"I ain't runnin' numbers," Beau countered. "They got me on as a stage hand, and my supe says he'll teach me the whole mess— lights, flies, management, even some stage tricks and such. But, look, this is important! Somebody's hurt bad."

That was all Dub needed to hear; and anyway, he wasn't the boy's keeper. He just enjoyed prodding him a little. He owed Fralene just that much. He put money on the table beside his half-finished breakfast. "Lead the way," he said.

Back at the club, Beau led him in through a side entrance, walked him through the maze of corridors back stage, and the two of them were finally ushered through a guarded stage door to the stage itself. Dub's first impression of what he saw of the club's back alleys was one of style and substance. It'd be a nice place; maybe worth bringing Fralene around to if she seemed so inclined. But even before they'd reached their destination, Dub started to feel something strange in the air as well; something untoward and incorporeal. It was a darkness he hadn't felt since some of his nastier days in the trenches; or his darker days on the plantation. It was evil: present, conscious, and completely malevolent. Even the *veve* pendant that lay under his shirt, against his chest, gave a tentative quiver—absolute proof that something in this place was *wrong*.

They emerged onto the stage. The curtain was down, and Dub heard activity on the far side—a commotion in the kitchens. But then he saw the dead man on the stage; the blossom of brain matter and blood beneath him, rolled out like a shapeless carpet; and Dub felt a terrible pity for Beau, having to see something like this only a day after the mess on 128th Street.

It put Dub in mind of the trenches. But it was clear this fella's head hadn't been broken by a bullet. He'd taken a tumble from the catwalks above. His melon connected with the hardwood stage floor and that was the end of it.

"What the hell am I supposed to do for this man?" Dub asked, kneeling beside the body. "He's dead as Jonah, Beau."

"You're the doctor?" a feline voice purred, and Dub turned to see Madame Marie, the one everyone called the Queen Bee, coming his way. She had a big, pantherish fellow in a fine suit at her elbow, and Dub figured he'd be Gideon Mann, the Queen Bee's first mate and enforcer. Dub knew them all by name and reputation, if not by sight. The Queen herself was a fine-looking woman—probably into her forties, but well taken care-of and still young of face and taut of body. Her skin was the color of café au lait with plenty of cream; her eyes two big marbles of onyx and ivory; her mouth wide, painted a deep, berry-dark red.

Dub stood and offered his hand to her. "Dub Corveaux, Ms. Merriwether."

She looked a little puzzled. No one ever addressed her by name, he supposed; especially not a stranger. But a moment later, she realized it was just a mark of her rank and reputation, and she smiled a little and nodded greetings. "Doctor," she said. "You're the soldier, correct? Your office is over on 135th Street? Family in rum?"

Dub was impressed; clearly, he, too, had a reputation. "You're a block off. 136th Street. I own the building. But you're spot-on with the rum. Family label. Triple distilled. My mother still owns the plantation and distillery back in Haiti."

Madame Marie suggested the corpse. "We thought to have you examine this poor fellow and help us see him off quietly, but there's been a complication in young Beau's absence."

Dub raised an eyebrow.

"Fight in the kitchens," Gideon filled him in. "Some nonsense about money owed or an old feud. Kitchen help. One man dead, one going to jail."

"But we still haven't made the authorities aware of *this* mess." She indicated the dead stage hand, then added, "Still, the cops should be here any moment."

Dub turned and studied the dead man. He wasn't in the habit of selling his advice to gangsters—even one so lovely and compelling as Miss Maybelle Merriwether—but nonetheless, the fella was dead, and now something worse had unfolded in the kitchens, and clearly the Queen Bee wanted to keep things quiet. He supposed he couldn't blame her; bootlegger and numbers queen or no, she probably saw what she did here as a sort of public service, and truth be told, she was right. These people needed their jobs; and they needed those jobs from a black employer, not a white one—especially not a white one with mob ties like Harry Flood over at the Jungle Room.

So Dub made a judgment call that he hoped he wouldn't regret. "That fella's dead," he said, stabbing his hat toward the broken-headed corpse. "You got trouble in the kitchens that stirred up attention, best use that as your cover story, and let it be known that this poor sap fell out of the catwalks after the kitchen mess exploded."

Madame Marie arched one well-sculpted brow. "Very cagey, doctor. Is that your professional opinion?"

"That's my friendly advice," he offered.

"And what's the bill for such friendly advice?" Gideon countered.

Dub smiled, placing his hat on his head. "First parcel's free, sir. But if you send Mr. Farnes here to find me in the future, the bill will be in the mail, I assure you."

"We're square, then," the Queen Bee said. "What about a token of gratitude?"

"Not necessary," Dub said. "Except, perhaps, special consideration if I happen to come round some evening for dinner and a show?"

Madame Marie glanced at Gideon. He reached into his coat and produced a little card—larger than a business card, but smaller than a normal party invitation. He handed it over to Dub, and Dub read the embossed copper writing on it quickly. It was a special invitation to the Grand Opening of the club on Saturday night.

"A special invitation," the Queen purred. "Feel free to bring a friend."

Dub threw a glance at Beau. The young man's face was still slack with puzzlement, as though everything that just unfolded had unfolded too quickly for his slow-witted young man's mind to fathom. Dub thought of Fralene. "I just might have to do that, Miss Marie."

"Madame Marie," Gideon corrected.

"Or Queen Bee," she added. "That's what I am to all my friends."

Dub grinned. "Well, I count myself lucky to be part of that very select social circle. Good day, Queen Bee."

"Good day, doctor."

As Dub moved for the door, he turned to Beau. "Keep those wounds clean, Beau," he said, suggesting the scratches on his face. "Come 'round next Tuesday and I'll take out those last stitches."

Beau nodded absently, and Dub left him to his shady company.

XX

All the way home, and through his afternoon appointments, Dub mulled over the peculiar feeling he'd had in Aces & Eights. Something was *wrong* in the place, and that wrongness boded none too well for the Queen Bee, her employees, or Harlem in general. Mixed with Dub's natural concern for a major employer and the people who counted on her, there was his more specified concern for Beau and his big sister.

So when the last of his neighborhood patients had left,

and Cecile had begged off for the evening, and the office doors were locked and Lady Night came on with her purple mantle and parasol, Dub climbed the stairs to his apartments above the offices on the ground floor. There, he took a shower—the ritual, cleansing sort, because he had work ahead for the evening...

Shower through, he slipped into a button-up shirt, black trousers, and suspenders and climbed another stairway—a secret spiral stairway at the southeast corner of his building—up to the fourth floor of his brownstone. There, in the attic, his special sanctum awaited.

In Haiti, such spaces were called *hounfors*, sometimes peristyles. They tended to be low buildings in untamed, out of the way places with dirt floors and few neighbors. Here, in the heart of Harlem, he'd had to improvise, adapt, and overcome to meet all the requirements.

The two toughest requirements were the earthen floor— through which sound and the energies of sacrifices were transmitted to the *lwa*—and the central pillar, the *Poteau Mitan*, by which the earth gave energies to the worshipers and the worshipers fed their energies to the earth. The latter had presented itself by accident—or perhaps by design: when Dub had toured the building, with an eye toward buying it, he'd noticed that the same, uninterrupted piece of iron piping led from the roof all the way down into the foundations. The real estate agent suggested that maybe it was some forgotten piece of conduit or plumbing. On most floors, it ended up being shut into a closet or lost behind a wall. But here, in the attic, it was right out in the open: almost in the very center of the room once a wall had been added to partition the aft third of the fourth floor. Thus, Dub had his umbilical connecting the fourth floor to the earth.

As for the former, the earthen floor: he'd overcome that with simple hard work, carting up bag after bag of soil and spreading it like a carpet throughout the peristyle, until it was finally more than an inch deep. It absorbed libations nicely, and it also dampened the sound of his horsed dancing.

Requirements of contact with terra firma and earthen foundations met, Dub had proceeded to decorate his *hounfor* like many of the others he'd seen in his youth—with a few added touches of his own, to personalize it. It was a solitary worship space, after all, not a public one.

The attic windows were covered with heavy crimson curtains to keep curious eyes from finding him and wondering just what he was up to. On the east wall, Dub had painted rough images of the *Rada lwa*, complete with their *veves*, or holy seals. He was no artist, but he reckoned he'd done all right. Beneath that mural stood an altar crowded with the accoutrement of *Rada* worship: an image of St. Jerome in honor of Legba; St. Joseph in honor of Loko beside a picture of Dub's own father; a faded St. Anne in honor of Ayizan; and an image of the Virgin to honor Erzulie Freda. Between the Virgin and St. Anne stood a picture of Dub's mother, Lenore, and at the center of the clutter, a statue of St. Michael slaying the Dragon, to honor Dub's *met tet*, or patron, Ogou. And candles—many candles—all surrounding offerings of loose tobacco, rum, cigars, dates, flowers and perfume. Rounding out the cramped little altar were Dub's weapons of choice: his twin Colt 1911 .45 automatics, and a long, serpentine scarf, the angry red of a fresh wound—a gift from Ogou himself.

Adjacent to the Rada altar was a shrine for the Ghede—the unnamed dead—and on the opposite wall were the signs and altar of the *Petro lwa*—the fiery, infernal spirits that Dub sometimes employed for more risky or ferocious pursuits. Tonight, though, only the *Rada* would be called.

For light, he had strung lengths of small, colored electrical bulbs—the sort used at Christmas time—all around the baseboards and the eaves. Aside from these, the peristyle was lit only by candles—hundreds of them—tapers, votives, and the large, slow-burning sort of many colors in glass chimneys. Most nights, like tonight, it took him a while to light them all. But as he took his time and summoned the light, he began a low hymn to the *lwa*, crooning evenly and melodically throughout, the sound of his own voice and the circular phrasing of the chant focusing his mind and spirit.

Afonga Alafia Ashé Ashé...
Afonga Alafia Ashé Ashé...
Ashé Ashé...

Ashé Ashé...
Afonga Alafia Ashé Ashé...

Soon the attic peristyle—with its heavy crimson curtains drawn, and all its doors and windows shut tight and locked—was ablaze with a soft golden light. At last, the real work could begin.

He put on a Victrola record that he had had specially recorded in Port-au-Prince, and the tri-partite beat of the wango drums and the cool, Creole tremolo of a vodou mambo filled the room. Dub poured offerings of his good family rum, lit cigars for Ogou and Legba and set them upright in an old trepanned skull, then burned dried sage and set some cones of frankincense smoldering. As the drums thumped and the mambo crooned, Dub let his body sway, and his feet stomped the earthen floor to keep time. He circled round his *poteau mitan* and little by little, he felt the doors between the worlds bulging; the locks and bars thrown back; the barriers ready to recede.

In his hands he held his *asson*—his sacred rattle, filled with *gris-gris* from the lands that had borne him and adorned with colorful glass beads and snake bones. He let the rattle hover above a trio of sand-painted *veves* he'd prepared on the earth floor—the symbols of his *lwa* patrons, drawn for the purpose of gathering them in. With his footwork and the chatter of his rattle and the song from the Victrola record, he called the *lwa*. In short order, he knew they'd answer if he invited them in.

Thus, he fell to his knees, kissed the earth, and knocked upon it three times. That opened the door. The *lwa* stepped through.

He smelled old Legba's corn-cob pipesmoke first; then Erzulie's Florida water perfume; finally, the bitter, brimstone tang of Ogou's hot iron mingled with the sting of gunpowder and stale tobacco smoke in his nostrils.

Dub knelt in their presence, in the place where answers could be divined and requests made. He considered offering a briefing, to bring them up to speed, then realized they already knew why they'd been called. Thus, while he spoke he moved to his Ghede altar to prepare himself for a long night's work.

"There's something wrong about that place," he said aloud, painting for them a picture of Aces & Eights in his mind's eye.

"I need to know what it is." As he did so, he slipped a cord round his throat, from which hung a trio of pewter pendants: *veves*, the seals of Legba, Erzulie, and Ogou, to protect him on his foray. Next, he slipped on a pair of dead man's socks swiped from an undertaker and a pair of indefinitely-borrowed grave-digger's boots that waited beneath the altar.

Somebody else's magic, Legba answered. *Somebody else's problem.*

"Wrong," Dub countered, now buttoning up a purple-and-black striped waistcoat gifted him by an *houngan* in Haiti. "Harlem's problem. *My* problem."

He heard ruffled pride in Legba's voice. *Who you think you're talkin' to, boy?*

"My sponsor," Dub said, "not my master."

Such a good boy, Erzulie purred.

You did good the other night, Ogou snarled around his cigar. *I had my doubts when I horsed you in Haiti, but for a saw-bones, you make a fine soldier.*

"Many thanks, Papa Ogou," Dub answered, though having to speak so deferentially—even to one as potentially dangerous as the *orisha* of steel and warfare—rankled him. He was in his long, coal-black trenchcoat now. Next he swiped a handful of bootblack and darkened the hollows of his jaw, his eyes, and his lips.

There's lots of doors already been opened, Legba interjected, *and it's been so long now, I don't know as I can say who opened 'em.*

"Just find me a trail and put me on it," Dub said. He planted a knotted, natty wig of dreadlocks on his head—dreads cut from the head of a hanged black prophet in Jamaica—then crowned it with his undertaker's top hat. Almost ready now: only the Baron's face remained.

Lots of doors still opening, Ogou added. *Bad doors. Locked doors. The sort with dark spirits and nasty juju on the other side.*

"Then I guess I better be ready to close 'em again," Dub answered. He drew on his black minister's gloves; loaded his guns and holstered them under his coat. "Or lay low whatever crawls out."

Ogou chuckled. He spoke to Erzulie, but Dub heard him clearly and knew Ogou meant to be heard. *Yeah, he's a good boy alright*, he said. *Good with the healer's wand or the smoking gun.*

"Can my questions be answered?" Dub asked, feeling the moment nearly upon him; knowing that tonight, there would be no rest—Ogou had work for him. He pocketed some govi grenades.

They were small, sealed clay jars about the size of fat oranges, holding inside the detritus of unquiet spirits the good doctor had discovered while wandering Harlem. Some were hot, like the *Petro lwa*. When they were loosed on a target, they worked his shame and his guilt, the venom in his veins, and the target thought they were burning in hellfire—though not a mark was left on them. The cool sort, akin to the *Rada lwa*, worked on the target's fear. They chilled them to the bone and left them in a terrified, fetal crimp—non-lethal, but clearing delivering a message.

I'll do what I can, Legba said, though Dub noted that he made no promises. *Thankee for the cigars, boy.*

Dub nodded. He dipped one gloved hand into the powdery mess that would give him the gravelord's countenance. Taking a deep breath, he closed his eyes and shoveled a handful of the bone powder against his face. He didn't have to look in a mirror. He knew that the magic would always mask him properly.

You ready? Ogou asked, voice now right in his ear; the sound of iron scraping iron.

Dub prepared himself. "Let's get horsed," he answered.

The *lwa* fell upon him.

The Dread Baron opened his black eyes.

XX

It was a Wednesday, so Angie's was slow, but the money and the booze flowed freely. Wednesday was the night for downtowners—white downtowners—the sort who wore tailored suits and monogrammed shirts to their workaday jobs, but came uptown to Angie's for a taste of vice and dark meat. Angie Ford, the handsome, high brown madame of the whorehouse on 129th Street, between Madison and Park, was happy to host the ofays from down midtown way; they were like little boys with too much time and money who came to Harlem for kicks and cooze but still found politeness almost habitual. They threw money around like confetti, kept the drinks flowing, and for all their brash talk and sneaky forays into kink, largely treated the girls with kid gloves and something like respect. Probably spooked that dark dames, being half-wild, would cut their throats in their post-coital dozes if treated too brashly.

So traffic in the sporting house was slow in terms of warm bodies on the floor, but rich in terms of dollars spent. That was Angie's favorite sort of business to do: high-density, low-volume. That was why her best girls—the chorus dolls and well-spoken secretaries looking to make an extra buck, not the wild, country sort that worked the weekends—worked Wednesdays. The 'fays wanted dark-meat, but they still wanted it well-seasoned and prepared with some panache. If they wanted something cheap—something dirty—they went to one of Papa House's flesh pots below 125th Street. Here, the Queen Bee ran a respectable, high-class pussy den, and Angie was her right hand, cool enough to keep the tricks and the customers happy, hard enough to keep the whole machine chuffing along and well-oiled.

It was getting on midnight when she did her walk-through. She started at the front apartment on the second floor and made a big horseshoe-shaped loop, down the length of the east wing, across the rooms on the aft end, back up the length of the west wing. The second floor was collectively referred to as 'the parlor'. There were a lot of rooms, but they were all wide open, separated only by lush purple or crimson curtains, well-furnished and decorated, atmospherically lit with candelabras and Turkish lamps. The second floor was where all the meeting, greeting, drinking, gaming, and courting went down. Girls gave the johns public dances, sat on their laps and listened to their boring stories, led sing-alongs or played cards or dice—the sort of stuff that men sometimes did in the company of strange women, as though there were some real and legitimate courtship unfolding between them.

The third floor—that was where the magic happened. After oiling the john up all night with booze and charming company, the twists would put the hook in: *Want some privacy, baby? Wanna go somewhere where we can be alone? You're so tense, baby-doll; mama needs to give you a massage. I got a room right upstairs...*

Angie would finish her walk-through of the parlor rooms, then she'd hit the third floor. She wasn't into kink, so it wasn't like strolling the halls and hearing the huffs and grunts and groans behind all those closed doors gave her any pleasure. She just wanted to keep her ears open for strangeness—a scream of real fear instead of feigned pleasure; a John's angry tirade; anything that just seemed wrong or out of place. These girls and their professional reps were an investment. The Queen Bee had placed her trust in Angie, and Angie wouldn't betray that. She wanted to keep the girls safe, and clean, and in circulation. That's what lined everyone's pockets, and that, at the end of the day, was all that mattered.

So here she was, doing her walk-through, smiling contentedly as she saw the same 'fay faces beaming the same smarmy grins at the same tarted-up tricks while the same smells of incense and tobacco and sweat and bathtub gin clogged the same close air in the same, decadently-appointed chambers and halls that Angie kept in working order, day after day after day. Getting on midnight meant some of the neighborhood beat patrolmen might be dropping in soon on their 'lunch hours.' They'd want quickies, suds, and maybe some sandwiches or coffee. Angie wanted to finish her walkabout before they arrived, so she could work them personally. It was good to keep the boys in blue happy, after all; they were community servants, bulwarks of order in a chaotic world; they deserved a little pampering.

That's when she heard the first scream, followed by gunshots.

Angie froze in the parlor room she was passing through. There were three johns and four tricks nearby—a pair of city councilmen and a Union steward—and their drunken revelry evaporated with the screams and punctuating gunshots from the rear of the building. Angie looked to the tricks: the girls were wide-eyed and gape-mouthed, stone cold sober; the muddle-headed johns sweated out their bugjuice and stared.

"What *was* that?" the Union steward asked.

Angie felt a sickening knot in her belly. There were really only two options: a raid by cops, or a raid by crooks. Neither made her feel safe, especially when shots had been fired so quickly.

"Up, move," she said, snapping her fingers. The white customers apparently didn't mind taking orders from a black woman in this case. All three were down to their undershirts and trousers, shoes, socks, shirts, and coats nearby. They snatched them up in hasty bundles as the girls shot past, and all seven of them fled the room, heading back toward the front of the house. Angie didn't like the thought of taking customers out the front doors, but if someone had stormed the back, what other choice did they have?

But that way was blocked too. As they reached the front room of the east parlor and stumbled out into the hallway in search of the stairs, they heard more voices, more screams, and the slap-bang of two more pistol shots. As a flock of tricks and johns crowded toward the stairway in the second floor hallway, Angie at their head, a group of men in long coats, low-dipped hats, and kerchief masks came thundering up the stairs. Angie saw flashes of olive-colored skin at their wrists and above their collars—guineas, more than likely, maybe ballsy Abes, cruising uptown for a little snatch-and-grab. The front two held pump shotguns with their barrels and stocks sawed off for close-quarters work. The men behind all stocked pistols. As the shotgunners drove the crowd in the hallway back, the third in line, a tall bandito with a long-barreled Webley revolver, stepped up between them and pointed his heater at Angie.

"You," he said.

She dared a glance over her shoulder. The hallway was corked at the other end too; more men with guns, men with masks, herding the clients and the hired hands into the center of the hallway like a sweaty human dam in a river. Angie turned back to the hood and tried her best not to show fear.

"Where's the safe?" he asked.

"What safe?" she asked in answer.

He swatted her backhand and cocked his pistol, shoving the barrel in just inches from her gaping mouth. Angie felt fury mixed with her fear. It was an innocent question: they had three safes in the house.

"These swingin' dicks don't get their rocks off on credit, and I'm guessin' you don't take checks. One more time, lady: where's the safe?"

She tasted blood on her tongue. She heard sounds through the whole house: more gunmen on the third and lower floors, most likely, holding everyone in place while the boss man here had located her to get them to what they were after. How many were there, then? A dozen? More?

She answered. "Safe's in my office, end of the hall on the left."

The gun-barrel hovered. "Move, then. Tick, tick, mammy."

Angie did as she was told. She turned and marched down the hall, followed by the lead tough and a couple of his fellows. The crowd of tricks and johns parted before her as she marched. It was just as she'd cleared the crowd and moved past the gunmen at the aft end of the hallway that she heard breaking glass above, followed by a quick storm of gunshots, and more screams.

"The fuck... ?" the lead hood muttered. Clearly, not part of the plan. He turned to one of the pair following him. "Go check it out and—"

Just then, the lights that lined the hallway—small, tasteful chandeliers and electric wall-sconces that looked like old-fashioned gas lights—all dimmed, threatening to go out. The darkness in the corridor was oppressive when it pulsed and threatened to swallow them all. The crowd in the center of the corridor, still held at gunpoint, all cried out in unison, not sure what was happening. Angie shot a quick glance at the lead hood who held the gun on her. Above the bandito mask that covered the lower half of his face, she saw wide, wondering eyes and a knitted brow.

Definitely not part of the plan.

Then, there were voices above: the toughs; the robbers. There were orders bandied back and forth; the thump of feet on the carpeted floor-boards, then a rumbling, rending crack, screams, and a storm of gunfire; fast, thick volleys whose violence and fury bled right through the floor to meet them.

Then the lights all dimmed again, pulsing twice this time before finally staying lit.

Angie felt the hood's hand on her arm, the press of the warm gun-muzzle between her shoulder-blades. "The safe, lady. Now."

Angie nodded and moved forward again. They'd only made it three steps when more gunfire and screams gave way to curses and a persistent, thumpety-thump-thumping as two bodies came rolling down the stairs from the third floor.

Again, the knot of tricks and johns in the hall all screamed. They fell against the walls and one another, not believing what they were seeing, nor understanding it.

The men who rolled down the stairs screamed and writhed, engulfed in flames. But the flames on one were crimson red—redder than any fire Angie had ever seen; and the flames on the other were ice blue. The hoods tumbled end over end, over one another, then finally came crashing to a halt on the landing. Both flopped and twisted so violently that Angie thought they might break their own spines.

And they kept screaming. Oh, how they screamed and screamed. And from where she stood, she noticed something else strange: the flames licked at their victims, but they didn't seem to burn anything.

What the hell was going on?

"Sammy!" the head tough shouted, pointing to one of the shotgunners, then suggesting the hoods on fire. "Douse those two and—"

The lights dimmed again, pulsing, fighting the power of some unseen darkness that hated them and wanted them out, out, out. In the flickering light, Angie's eyes started toying with her. She saw snatches of frightened faces; saw one of the shotgun hoods shuffling over to the pair of blazing men in the shuddering dark, laying down his sawed-off, whipping off his coat, and trying to beat them out; saw the other gunmen in the corridor—she counted seven in all—whipping their guns and their wide, rolling eyes from side to side in the strobe of the failing light, trying to make sense of what was happening.

Then the devil arrived, and Angie thought she understood, even if the rest didn't.

He swung in through the window at the street end of the corridor, arriving in a spray of shattering glass and blasting away with a pair of .45's before his heavy boots had even hit the floorboards. The shotgunner trying to douse his comrades took a full barrage in his chest and went sprawling. As two more hoods with pistols lunged forward on opposite sides of the stairwell and took aim, Angie lost sight of the shadowy attacker for a moment as he ducked sideward, behind the third-floor stairs. Then he emerged on the far side, tossing small spheres that shattered when they hit the gunmen square in their chest. More flames burst forth and engulfed them—the crimson sort—and the gunmen fell, writhing and screaming and begging mercy, just like their comrades hunkered on the landing.

The nearest hoods opened fire. The shadow man didn't stop moving. As bullets punched holes in the plaster walls and riddled the underside of the third floor stairs, the attacker dove, snatched up the cast-off shotgun from the first hood he'd taken, rolled into a crouch against the west wall, and fired. The spray went wide and tore the nearest gunman wide open. As the gunman opposite the stranger kept firing from across the gulf of the stairwell, the stranger shot to his feet, skated sideward, pumped, and loosed another blast. The wall went dark red with a crazy floral pattern of blood and buckshot.

The lights still flickered, as if the stranger's very presence affrighted them. The corridor was ablaze with curses and gunfire, the johns and tricks on the deck, faces down, holding one another as shields and as comfort, the hoods all rushing forward to meet the newcomer.

He tossed two more of his strange grenades. The flames of one actually took two close-spaced gunmen and down they went, writhing and screaming. The other hit a hood in the face, broke his nose, stunned him, and sent him reeling, but didn't actually break. Angie caught the look of frustration on the stranger's face at that, but he carried on, finding some cover where the corridor narrowed to reload and prepare another charge.

His face: a broad face, under a top hat and a nest of island dreads, painted like a skull.

Angie's knees went out from under her. She was on the floor now, head and body low, but still watching. A vodou baron? Here? In a gunfight with hoods in her cathouse?

How the hell did she rate?

The Cemetery Man and two more gunmen exchanged volleys

at close range. The Cemetery Man took hits—Angie saw them—but he shook off the shock of them and kept going, as if they were no more than annoyances, not mortal wounds. The hoods that made them went down with new colonies of .45 slugs in pulverized chests.

Someone grabbed a handful of her hair and yanked her to her feet. Angie screamed, the pain searing through her scalp. It was the lead hood, the one who'd been taking her to the safe. He drew her up in front of himself and leveled his pistol over her shoulder. She was a shield now. She felt his hot breath on her shoulders.

And now she was staring down the barrel of the Cemetery Man's smoking .45's. The hungry, empty darkness of those gunbarrels and the look in his eyes suggested he'd be at ease shooting right through her. She was just some Harlem whore-monger, after all; not an innocent woman by any stretch, and not exactly a community light.

"What're you dressed for?" the hood growled behind her. "Halloween?"

"Dressed for a funeral," the Cemetery Man replied.

"Yours," the hood sneered, and fired.

The shots took the Cemetery Man square in the chest and he sprawled. The tricks and johns nearest him went skittering away as he fell, as if terrified even of touching him in death. He landed with a thud on his back and didn't move. Angie waited. The hood that held her pushed her forward. No one made a sound. They were all watching the dead hoodoo man, waiting for some sign of life. He gave none.

Angie and the hood that held her inched closer. He kept his gun levelled around her, still used her as a moving shield. Angie was too terrified to fight him.

She studied the Cemetery Man in the still-flickering lights of the corridor: dressed all in black except for a purple and black striped waistcoat underneath his ratty old black trench coat, and a long red scarf around his throat. As they neared, Angie noted that the scarf still moved on the dead man's chest, snake-like, alive.

The hood pushed her aside a little, to get a better look.

That's when the Cemetery Man moved. He snatched up the unbroken grenade and hurled it from where he lay. Angie saw the little clay sphere streaking toward her and tried to duck it. It took her captor square in the chest and shattered. Red flames engulfed them both.

Then Angie felt herself falling, felt the flames licking at her skin and bones and her very soul, and heard a hundred fierce and furious voices in the center of her brain and knew a pain and a shame and a sorrow and a suffering like none she'd ever imagined on earth.

Only in hell was there suffering of this sort.

Then her mind couldn't take any more, and everything went out like the shuddering lights.

XX

The night was filled with frightened faces, fleeing crooks, and pleas for mercy, but finally, even the Dread Baron had to call it an eve and head back to his sanctum.

He had one more stop to make along the way, though. The Baron needed to give Aces & Eights a quick once over to see if he could root out the source of that sickening vileness, that undertow of dread that had coiled in his guts like a clammy snake, the terrible foreboding he'd felt that afternoon, just after that poor sap in the flies had taken a header onto the stage; just before Birdie cut Dell and got him bleeding like a stuck pig in the kitchen.

It was four in the morning and the place was deserted. Doors were no bar to him, and soon enough, he was inside, puffing on his cigar as he wandered the back corridors and stairwells, letting his gut play dowsing rod to the bad juju that the building held. Sure enough, he found what he was after: that sinking feeling overtook him when he stepped onto the vast, empty stage, seemed to pull at him through the floor, sure as gravity. Just to be certain, he drew one of a number of small brass pendants from around his neck, this one bearing a Saint Sebastian icon on one side, Papa Legba's *veve*—his vodou seal—on the other. Papa Legba being the keeper of the crossroads, a doorman to the back alleys of the otherworld, his sign should be drawn where the evil was most concentrated.

It hung plumb straight at first. As the Baron moved toward the front of the stage, the pendant cord bent backward, and the pendant hung at a crazy angle impossible by all the laws of physics. Circling the spot brought the same result.

It took him a few minutes—the club was quite the labyrinth —but at last he located the stairwell to the basement and descended. The basement was vast, with high ceilings and wide open spaces, towering, sentinel rows of industrial shelving and clanging, chuffing chambers where the furnace and the water pipes waited like penned-up beasts of burden. The Legba *veve* bent before him on its cord, leading the way, and the Baron followed it, passing through criss-crossing corridors, slipping round shelves rife with mislabeled (that is, disguised) bottles of booze and wine, canned goods, and unemployed kitchen tools. Finally, he came to a dead-end alcove near the rear of the largest basement chamber, and there, between high shelves loaded with spare place settings yet to be unpacked, the pendant pointed straight down, suggesting a rusted old manhole cover in the dusty floor.

The Dread Baron knelt, replaced the *veve* round his throat, and lit a match off his calloused thumb. In the yellow light, he saw clear indications of movement round this dusty span of floor. Likewise, the manhole cover bore handprints on its rim.

The match flame nearly burnt his thumb and he blew it out. In the dark, he pried his fingers under the edges of the manhole cover and heaved it up and over, the iron bulk of the thing straining his muscles. It made a loud clang on the cement foundation. Instantly, an invisible but palpable vileness wafted out of the empty space beneath: not a smell, exactly, just a *feeling*, deep in his nethers, up his spine, down to the tips of his fingers. He felt blood thundering in his ears and the warmth of a flush in his white-painted cheeks.

Even Ogou—horsed to him, part of him—stirred and recoiled from the malignancy that billowed like smoke out of that gulf. *Good God*, the Baron wondered. *What could it be?*

He drew another match from his coat, popped it on his thumb. The sulfur flared and the darkness receded.

He peered down into a shallow well, at the bottom of which was a strange sculpture of human bones—four skulls upon a flat pair of crossed fibulas, adorned with strange symbols, animal talons, crow-feathers, and tiny skulls.

He stared, reading the thing, trying to drink in the sight of it and burn it into his memory before the match burned out. It was strangely familiar—not so unlike a million vodou altar-pieces he'd seen in some of the more fearsome, benighted Petro peristyles he'd visited—and yet, the symbols painted roughly upon it and something about its construction were alien. It was modeled out of the same black recesses of consciousness and ancient worship that vodou sprang from, but it was *not* vodou. Its origins were completely unknown to him.

Then he heard the low, guttural snarl of some beast in the dark, and turned toward the sound. The match still glowed in his left hand, nearly burned down to his clutching fingers. His right dove into his coat and drew out one of his .45s, training it toward that loathsome sound from the darkness.

Suddenly, the manhole cover slid across the short span between where it lay and the well it had covered. With a cacophonous clang, it fell back into its seat. Before the Baron could decide what he'd just witnessed, the beast in the darkness snarled again, seemed to huff and heave, and one of the great, heavy shelves that towered over him pitched sideward with a groan, falling right toward him.

The Baron leapt and the shelf unit—easily four times his own weight—came crashing down against its neighbor. That neighbor toppled, setting off a clamorous domino effect, filling the vast cellar with the thunder of chaos crashing down, row upon orderly row.

He didn't wait to find out what had brought the shelves down. He turned and ran.

That charm in the well was bad news. But, the Queen Bee was a big girl—and engaged in dirty business, to boot. If she had enemies powerful enough and determined enough to put a hex that heinous upon her—well, who was he to interfere? There were plenty of innocent people in Harlem who needed his help, after all. The Queen Bee would just have to reap the bitter harvest of a fortune made on running numbers, bootlegging and turning tricks.

As he hurried away over the rooftops from Aces & Eights, he silently wished her luck.

She'd need it.

8

Gideon Mann sighed, but it sounded like a temperamental tiger's snarl. It was too early in the morning for b.s. of the present sort: first, word in the wee hours of a raid at Angie's 129th Street brothel and a debriefing that left everyone more baffled than not; then, a terrible mess in the club's basement, courtesy of a late-night prowler; and finally, the late arrival of a delivery truck from the harbor loaded with crates marked DUTCH PORCELAIN – FRAGILE! that *should have* contained cognac and champagne, but that actually turned out to contain Dutch porcelain.

As the boys opened crate after crate, verifying that each did, indeed, contain what they were marked to contain and not the contraband that they should have, Gideon mulled over his talk with Angie. She was an old hand at the business: cool, collected, equal parts actor and observer. That's what made her trembling, nervous recounting of the events in the brothel so troubling: the frightened, shame-faced woman that Gideon spoke with at four in the morning was merely the ghost of the shameless, pleasantly profane Angie he knew.

"It was the Cemetery Man," she kept going on. "Baron Samedi. Packin' heat. Throwin' fire."

Gideon had drawn a long drag on his cigarette. "So Baron Samedi knocked over the joint?"

"No," Angie said. "He came after. It was white men knocked us over; ginzos if I had to guess, but I couldn't see their faces too well. Masked. All of them."

"So you think some Italians rolled the joint," Gideon said. "Then came the Cemetery Man?"

Angie had nodded, eyes wide in her dark face. "That fire he

was packin'—it was hellfire, pure and simple, Gideon. The sort that burns the poison out. Digs up all your sins and sets them to tearing at you."

Gideon had been confused then. "Fire? What are you talkin' about?"

"Grenades, like," Angie said, frustrated. "Grenades full of red and blue flames. Some burn hot and some burn cold. I took the hot sort and it burned me, Gid. Burned me clean to my soul."

"There ain't a mark on you," Gideon said, suggesting that maybe Angie was misremembering, having snapped and gone plain loco.

"Ain't that sort of fire," she had said. "It ain't after your flesh, Gid. It's after your soul."

"Enough," Gideon said, back in the moment, tired of watching the boys open crates on the loading dock that only contained porcelain knick-knacks. They all stopped their work and stared, wondering what came next.

Gideon's eyes caught sight of movement in the foggy alleyway beyond the loading dock. Before he could even have suspicions as to who, or what, he was seeing, they came out of the fog and closed a little cordon around the truck and the dock.

Cops. First they appeared on foot, then three cars rolled slowly into the alleyway, blocking all exits. That cinched it. This whole mess with the porcelain was a set-up. Someone had bait-and-switched them, and Gideon just hoped he'd have the chance to find the man or woman who'd done it.

But for now, he had to deal with the situation at hand. He looked to the truck driver, a fat fool named Calvin who'd driven for them a hundred times. Calvin's pudgy, slack face gave his answer: he was just as surprised to see the cops as Gideon and the boys were. Ditto the crates.

Shit.

The cops fanned out across the mouth of the loading dock, led by short, fat Officer Heaney, the same cherry-nosed papist son of a bitch who'd harassed them just two days before for a grease. The bastard smiled broadly: clearly, he was in on the joke.

Gideon put it all together fast: they'd insulted Heaney the

other day; he'd reported to his superiors, who'd reported in turn to theirs—the Irish or the Italians or the Jews or all three. They'd applied some thumbscrews, greased some palms, intercepted the shipment somehow, and made sure that the booze crates disappeared and these dummy crates loaded with porcelain angels and saucers arrived.

Double shit. They weren't here to make arrests. They were here to blackmail the Queen Bee.

"Top o' the mornin', Mr. Mann."

Gideon scowled. "Officer Heaney."

"What'a ya got there?"

Gideon made a big show of reading the crate's stenciling. "Dutch porcelain. Fragile, apparently."

"It *is*, at that," Heaney answered. "Take many shipments of porcelain in the wee hours of the mornin', do ye?"

"Madame Marie's a collector," Gideon offered.

Heaney marched forward, mounting the steps onto the raised loading platform and standing an arm's length from Gideon. He peered into the open crate, studying the contents. As Gideon took two steps back, sickened being so close to the little fat fuck, he noted new faces just inside the loading dock, in the shadows of the ground floor storeroom.

White faces. More cops. They'd come in from the front too.

Big show of force, Gideon thought, *and no booze to arrest us with. It's a message. It's a threat.*

"Now, Mr. Mann," Heaney said, cocking his hat back on his melon head, "I hope ye don't take me for a fool."

"And I hope you don't take me for a queer," Gideon said.

Heaney stared, not grasping Gideon's meaning.

Gideon should have bitten his tongue. He didn't. "I don't feel like getting fucked by you this early in the morning."

His next thought was to tell the boys to stay cool; to keep their hands in the open, let *him* talk tough; but they were not, under any circumstances, to challenge the cops.

But he heard a thunder of footfalls and felt something hard and solid—a billy club, no doubt—connect with his skull, and down he went, without getting a chance to say any such thing.

The world went black. Vaguely, he heard a lot of voices raised in threat; the *ka-chak* of scatterguns pumped and shells filling empty chambers. Then, cutting through the gradually-clearing haze, Officer Heaney barking, "Cool off, the lot'a ye! You black bastards, you drop those smokers, here and now!"

Gideon blinked. He was on his knees. He looked around. Heaney's red face showed fury not only at Gideon's men, but also at the cops themselves. No doubt, he'd told them to play it cool; hadn't meant for Gideon to get whacked before he'd given an order. Sense was returning. Gideon's head throbbed. He stared at the cement of the loading dock between his two hands, which held him up on his knees.

Heany bent over him. He smelled sour old whiskey on the spud-eater's breath. "I'll not take such talk from *you*, you black bastard. You're just lucky I'm not queer for your dark sort, else I'd have already rammed this billy bat of mine up your puckered black arsehole."

"Get to the point," Gideon growled.

"You were expecting somethin' else in those crates, weren't you?"

Gideon drew a deep breath. "Mayhap."

"French brandy? Bubbly from the old country? Oh, such a great quantity of contraband probably set your precious colored Queen back a heft, didn't it?"

"But I'll bet you'd be willing to find our missing contraband for us, wouldn't you, Officer Heaney?"

"That's what we do, lad. Serve and protect. Dole out justice, and see wrongs righted."

"For a price."

"Call it a retainer. There are a great many nefarious sorts in this city, boyo. Could take us some time—our own personal time, off the clock, mind ye—to find the blackguards that absconded with your very *illegal* crate full of very *illegal*, and *expensive*, booze."

"You're wasting my time," Gideon snarled, finally raising his eyes to meet Heaney's watery gaze, though he still couldn't quite focus. He felt a knot rising on his skull; felt warm blood staining his collar. "What's your price?"

"Twenty five percent of your shipment—the goods themselves—along with, say, one hundred dollars for each crate recovered and delivered."

Fucked, good and proper. The price was just high enough to hurt, but just low enough that *not* to pay it was foolish. They had a gin joint to run here; a classy place; they needed booze or they'd never be able to compete.

"I ain't the Queen," Gideon said. "I can't give you an answer."

"Excuse me if I cry bullshit, boyo. If you ain't keeping your queen's twat happy with your big, black dick of yours, I know you've at least got her trust, elsewise you wouldn't be out here, in the early dawn, waiting for such an important delivery. You can speak for her, to me, man to man, and I'll wager she'll accept it."

Gideon wanted to gouge out the bastard's yellow, besotted eyes; he wanted to close his hands on Heaney's soft, double-chinned throat and squeeze until the Finn's eyes rolled like marbles and his tongue wagged like a stray dog's tail; he wanted to shove the barrel of a heater down his throat and pull the trigger, again, and again, and again...

"What'll it be, lad?"

Gideon sighed. Once again, it sounded like a temperamental tiger's snarl. "No delivery in twenty four hours, no pay. After that, you can jar that cognac and pickle your sick old Irish liver in it, for all I care."

Heaney stood tall again, looming over the still-on-his-knees Gideon. "You give good lip for a nigger, boyo. It's been a pleasure doin' business with ye."

And with a sickeningly polite cock of his hat, Heaney dismissed himself and gave the signal to his men to fall back. In moments, the cops had receded, withdrawn back into the club or into their cars, and scattered into the foggy early morning.

Two of the fellas helped Gideon to his feet. He shook them off, sick at himself, and did the only thing he could do.

He toppled the nearest crate of porcelain off the loading dock with a swift kick and roared like a caged lion as the myriad contents shattered on the concrete.

XX

While Gideon brokered trade with Officer Heaney aboveground, two stooges named Maurice and Abe were stuck in the basement, cleaning up the mess of toppled shelving left over from the prowler the night before. They would've preferred a task up top because the cavernous basement of Aces & Eights creeped them both out fierce. If they had been on booze duty, they would've had their hands on bottles of fine hooch, and could maybe pocket something to take home. Ditto if they had been relegated to the kitchens: at least there they would've been trying the recipes the new staff of chefs and line cooks were whipping up. Hell, even if they were put on the stage or the floor, they would've been free to roam, and it wouldn't just be the two of them.

But Gideon, by way of the Queen Bee, put them on cellar duty; so here they were, rebuilding and erecting, one by one, the toppled battalion of enormous shelves that made up the huge larder and storage pantry underground. They were to put the racks back up—and this time, to bolt them to the rafters. So right now, it was just the two of them, setting up the steel girders that made up the bones of the industrial shelving, bolting the reinforced wooden shelves in place within the girders, then securing each construction to the cement floor and the oak rafters in the ceiling above.

It was slow, it was boring, and no matter how many lanterns they cribbed from above, or how high the morning sun got outside, the darkness in the cellar never seemed to recede. Truth be told, Abe felt a weird chill in the air, too; something untoward and unnamable that tickled the nape of his neck and tensed his nuts. But he just chalked that up to the shadows and the dust and the smell of the old cellar and tried to concentrate on moving their task along and being done with it.

So here he stood, spotting Maurice as the younger man climbed his ladder to put the topside bolts in the rack they'd just finished—their fourth, of a projected eight. Just their luck. They'd be down in this goddamned basement until lunch.

The ladder swayed a little. Abe held it, but it was Maurice who steadied it. The kid had good balance, and the height—

the basement had twelve foot ceilings—didn't bother him. He went to work with a crescent wrench on the rafter bolts that would hold the top end of the rack in place.

"I'm gonna bring Maisey up here some night," Maurice said for the umpteenth time. "Yessir, she'd roll over and stick that bucket of hers in the air after a night upstairs."

The ladder swayed again. Maurice corrected and Abe tightened his grip. "Don't lean out so far, boy," Abe said. "You hit this concrete floor from where you at, you'll crack your goddamn head."

"I'm copacetic," Maurice tossed back. "Just hold it. Shit, Abe, you sound like my mama."

Abe studied the shadows in the darker recesses of the basement around them. What was it down here that gave him the creeps? He wasn't some country cane-break nigger just up from the Old South... he'd been born and bred in a Detroit tenement; moved to Harlem just after the turn of the century, word getting out that this was where all the Negroes were headed; where all the opportunities would be. He'd tired of Detroit and he wanted to see what a Negro metropolis might look like, so he landed here, and he fell in love with it.

But the point was, he didn't go in for that superstitions old-world hoodoo bullshit that so many of the down-South fellas and their gals went in for. So what had him so on edge? What was it about one musty old basement—no matter how dark, how large, how hungry it seemed—that so distressed him? He was starting to feel the edge on his nerves seeping into his bones, humming like electricity in his joints and fingertips.

And why the hell was it so cold down here? The boiler was just yards away, after all, squatting like a fat old iron toad in its hollow log. If anything, it should be warmer down here than anywhere else in the building.

"You ever had a girl got hot on dancin', took you for a roll all night long with the sweat still on her, then woke your ass up Sunday mornin' tried to make you go to church? Maisey does that shit and—"

"You done yet?" Abe interrupted. "Shit, boy, if you'd just do what you gotta do and stop beatin' your gums—"

Maurice looked down at him from his perch atop the A-frame ladder. "Damn, Abe, what got into you?"

"We got a lot of damn racks to raise, Reesey, and we barely started."

"Well hand me that other crescent. I gotta brace this bolt from both ends while I get it tight."

Abe shook his head. It was gonna be a long day.

He left the ladder, took exactly three short, shuffling steps toward the tool box, and bent to grab the very crescent that Maurice was suggesting. What happened then happened fast, and Abe would never stop being confused and puzzled by the whole mess.

He bent. The nearest kerosene lamp was at his back, about three feet away, and as he bent, lamp behind him, a shadow darted, quick and fleet, across the ghostly light spilling forth from it. The shadow crossed his peripheral vision just as Abe laid hands on the wrench, and he shot upright and spun around, thinking that one of the jokers from upstairs had arrived and was trying to sneak up and spook him while his back was turned.

Then he heard the scoot of the ladder. As he turned full round, he saw the whole mess teetering, as though someone had given it a heavy shove from the floor. Maurice started to curse, and Abe got a quick glimpse of his face—enough to know that the kid didn't even realize Abe wasn't below him anymore.

Then Maurice and Abe's eyes met across the space between them. Abe saw it in the kid's piebald gaze: *What are you doin' way over there, Abe?* he seemed to ask. *Who just shoved this ladder I'm standin' on?*

Then the whole mess toppled, and Maurice gave a loud, hoarse cry, and down he went, head first, toward the bare concrete floor.

Abe had time to lunge forward, but his front foot didn't even move. Maurice's brown melon head impacted with a hollow *thwack* on the concrete and a warm, wet flower of blood shot every which way, painting Abe's clunky old work shoes and the cuffs of his dungarees.

And then it was all over. There wasn't a sound to be heard

except for the slow burble of Maurice's blood, shooting out of his cracked head in hitching streams, spreading in an ever-widening pool across the concrete floor.

Abe ran for help, leaving his young companion where he lay, body still twitching as the last light crept out of his half-open eyes.

XX

It was barely eleven o'clock when Madame Marie arrived at Mambo Rae-Rae's Voodoo Botanica on 135th Street near 8th Avenue. The place was a hole-in-the-wall, barely the size of a newsstand, but it was chock full of the tools of the trade: *veve* flags and medallions, *gris-gris* sacks, fresh and dried botanicals, magic water, perfumes, oils, statues and lithographs of saints, and glass-chimnied, slow-burn candles. There was barely room for two or three customers to enter the store and linger beside the littered counter. Knowing how such places operated, Madame Marie assumed there was probably a back room where the mambo kept the good stuff: *namh*-charged reliquaries, *govis*, *assons*, mummified animals and more powerful magicks that only the most desperate or well-to-do *vodouisants* might come seeking or know how to properly employ.

The lady of the house leaned behind the counter, one foot propped on a stool she usually sat perched on. She was smoking a clove-spiced cigar and staring at Madame Marie like the Queen Bee's presence was both the most amusing and most banal thing she'd ever seen. The Queen Bee had no direct experience with this woman, but she'd heard plenty of talk about her, and knew her to be one of the more trusted mambos uptown.

Rae Gooden was her name, and the Queen Bee could already tell that the mambo knew who *she* was.

"Here come the Queen Bee," Mambo Rae said, "buzzing into my hive. Harlem's Miss Anne in linen and lace. What you doin' in my *botanica*, Queen Bee?"

"I've got a problem," Madame Marie said.

"Everybody got problems," Mambo Rae countered. "What makes you so special?"

Madame Marie lost her patience. Her hand dove into her purse, dug out a wad of bills, and laid them on the counter. "I need a cleansing."

Mambo Rae's eyes were alight at the sight of all that green, but she fought to play it cool. She might be a businesswoman, but clearly she wanted to make the Queen Bee sweat and relish her newfound power. "Hire a housemaid," she said.

"Cut the crap, Ms. Gooden," the Queen Bee snarled. "There's something nasty in my club, and I need it gone. Yesterday."

"Call the preacher."

"I may have to," the Queen Bee said. "But I'd like to start with you."

"Why you wanna do that?"

"Because maybe it's one of *yours*," the Queen Bee said.

"One of mine?" Mambo Rae asked, eyes widening. "Queen Bee, they not *mine*. They *ours*. 'Less you lily white under all those pretty, bloomin' vines."

"You know what I mean," the Queen Bee snapped. "Maybe it ain't just a devil that runs at the first cry of Jesus Christ. Maybe it's something older. Something meaner. Something only folk magic's gonna pry out."

"*Folk magic,*" Mambo Gooden said, and drew a long drag from her cigar. "How quaint. That must amuse you to no end, watching all us little darkies scurry round and say our funny blessings in funny tongues to funny gods. Must be nice, being so modern and civilized and all."

The Queen Bee swept up her wad of cash and headed for the door. "I don't have time for this. Good day."

"Cool your heels, Queen Bee," the mambo said. "Can't you take a joke?"

"At a time like this?" Madame Marie said. "No, miss, I cannot."

"Come in the back," the mambo said. "We'll gather some mojo and be on our way."

XX

House, despite his size, felt remarkably vulnerable surrounded by all these spaghetti-eaters, even with Wash and Timmons by his side. Nasario had sent a car, saying Soccorro wanted to talk about the hit on the cathouse the night before. House already had some inkling of what the old don wanted to discuss, and he wasn't disappointed.

"Who was he?" the wheezy old bulldog said.

"Who was who?" House asked.

"Don't crack wise," Nasario answered, standing at his rotund master's side. "The spook in white-face. The one that fritzed the roll. Who was he?"

House lowered his eyes and sighed. "Fella in a top hat and braids, sporting a skull face and pistols?"

Nasario pressed. "One of the Queen's?"

House shook his head. "She says no. She's got no reason to lie."

The old don looked completely befuddled. "Who is he then?" he rasped, looking for the first time like something really, deeply troubled him. "This is no good, Papa. This is a disaster. When we made alliance, we had no inkling that you had personal enemies who might interfere—"

"How can he be my personal enemy if I never met the man?" House countered.

Nasario didn't like that. "Don't crack wise, sambo. You're a hood, same as everyone in this room. You should know, same as we do, sometimes we make enemies we don't know."

"Well, then," House said. "Clearly, I've done just that. Gimme some time, I'll flush him out."

"Time?" Soccorro asked, leaning forward. "There is no time. My men are dead. They died on your turf, doing a favor, we thought, for you, at your behest."

"That goes on the bill," Nasario said.

House smiled in spite of the seriousness of the situation. "Start me a tab."

"You think this is funny, sambo?" Nasario growled. "Our men, dead on your turf, on your errand. Your problem. We need a solution, and we need it fast."

House nodded. "We'll flush him out. Didn't I say so?"

"Flush him out," Soccorro said quietly, a mandate of the highest order.

"Flush him out," Nasario added, "and put him in our hands. This spook son of a bitch made this business personal now, especially if he ain't with a crew. You lay hands on him, you deliver him to us, preferably alive."

"Harlem's *mine*," House snapped. "That makes the Cemetery Man *mine* to deal with."

"If Harlem's yours," Nasario said, "it's cause *we* say so. Cause *we* made it that way. So by *our* good graces, Harlem's yours— but the Cemetery Man is ours. Capiche?"

"Bene," House said, trying to smile even as he scowled.

XX

Most days and nights, Madame Marie lost no sleep and thought of herself as a fine, upstanding pillar of the community. She knew she dealt in black market trade goods and contraband thrills, but what of it? And if she spilt blood, it was only to protect herself or her employees.

But sitting face to face, as she did now, with the Reverend Barnabus Farnes of Harlem's Mother Zion African Methodist Church, made her feel like quite the blood-drenched sinner. Maybe it was his sterling moral reputation or his dour face—both added up to a decidedly Old Testament feel about the man. Either way, his severe gaze and stony countenance shrunk her and made her feel like a naughty little girl about to get a spanking.

"You want me to bless a house of sin, gin, and jazz?" the reverend said, wizened old baritone rumbling from his rather thin, bony chest.

"I'm not just looking for a blessing, reverend," Madame Marie said, trying to maintain her dignity. "I need an exorcism."

"You could start by closing its doors and opening a real business establishment. One that *helps* this community: a manufactory or some such, but—"

"Reverend," she said, losing her patience, "this is serious."

"So am I, miss," he said, and he meant it. "Despite my reputation, Miss Meriwether, I am *not* a teetotaler or a prude. I have no objection to good men and women enjoying an evening's repaste with wine or liquor, or dancing out their curdled dreams and workaday frustrations. But, by God, woman—Harlem doesn't need *another* gin joint with a gangster's grubby hands in the take!"

"Now see here," she started, not even sure what kind of defense she could offer. That she *wasn't* a gangster?

"No, *you* see here!" the reverend said, and his voice rose and boomed in the cavernous, now-empty church like thunder on a mountaintop. "You're sowing jobs and putting money in black pockets; for that, I cannot fault you. But your brand of business, Miss Meriwether, draws violence, and graft, and corruption, and sows its seeds in this community as well. If your most recent endeavor seems somehow poisoned, I daresay you should not first speak to a preacher, but to a policeman."

"This ain't the tangle of graft or booze or gambling or numbers, reverend!" Madame Marie shot back. "I've had deaths! I've had terrible chills and passed through what seemed like clouds of malignancy, sure and settled as a fog! There is something *wrong* in that place, reverend! And for the well-being of my people and myself and this community that you say you care so much about, I need the hand of God!"

"You need to expiate your guilt," the reverend said, lowering his eyes.

Well, he was at least partially right about that. But what, precisely, was she guilty about? Going to a vodou mambo *before* coming to a man of God? Leading that vodou mambo into a sparring match with powers that she wasn't equal to meet? The Queen Bee was still haunted by Mambo Rae Rae's exasperated, shameful scream as the protective *veve*'s she tried to lay burst into smoking flames and some invisible, but very solid phantom had bolted from the dark and lifted the woman a full twenty feet into the air. Rae Rae had struggled, floating there for some moments, then been released and tumbled again, her fall, and her tail bone, broken on one of the dining room tables.

The Queen Bee had sent that Farnes boy with Rae Rae to

Harlem Hospital. And the Queen Bee had decided that where hoodoo failed, God Almighty might succeed.

"Come down there with me," the Queen Bee begged. "Walk inside. Let me give you the two-bit tour. I promise you, reverend, you'll feel it too—and I'm guessing whatever it is will feel you. If I can convince you this isn't a figment of my imagination, will you help me?"

The reverend considered this, long and hard, picking at his nibbled old fingernails. "This is not an endorsement of your establishment."

"I ain't askin' for it. And I ain't even askin' you for a blessing. I'm askin' you to chase something unnatural out of that place. Whatever it is, it doesn't belong there. A man of God should recognize that much, at least."

He sighed. Checked his watch. "I need to be back here in two hours."

"I could make a donation to the church, reverend."

He stared at her as he rose. "This church doesn't want your money, Queen Bee. Let me get my things."

9

The Queen Bee's Lincoln pulled up to the rear entrance of Aces & Eights, and out came Madame Maybelle Meriwether and the Revered Barnabus Farnes. Over his long coat he wore a purple mantle—an official raiment of his office—and he carried in his hands a Bible. Madame Marie also knew that he carried more accoutrements in his pockets: a small wooden cross, a flask of blessed water, and a flask of blessed palm oil. Thus the Queen Bee led the Reverend Farnes into her den, and began the business of showing him around.

They entered by way of the loading dock in the alley, so their first stops were the storerooms and kitchen. For a moment, the reverend paused in the loading dock hall and turned, staring back toward the stairwell at the end of the hall that led down to the cellar. The Queen Bee waited, finally asking him what he thought he'd seen or heard.

"Nothing," the reverend said. "Carry on."

So they moved through the kitchen; took the stairs used by the wait staff up to the second floor and emerged into the dining room. The reverend gave the place a long, slow look, then suggested the stage. Dorey and Croaker followed them without a word, staring wide-eyed at the reverend, as though he might damn the two of them at any moment for even associating with the notorious Miss Meriwether.

Then they passed from the stage into the long backstage corridor, and there, in the dusky light beneath a long line of swinging drop lamps, Madame Marie felt a cold embrace, and saw her breath plume in the half light. She spun around to speak with the reverend.

Reverend Farnes had stopped in his tracks, halfway up the length of the hall ahead of them. He raised his eyes and seemed to search the darkness above them and around them; watched the plumes of his own breath in the harsh, dim light of all those weak, hooded light bulbs; almost seemed to smell the evil at work. Finally, gravely, he reached into his pocket and drew out the small wooden cross. He moved further away from them, searching the shadows and the peripheries, the cross held out before him as if it were a shield. He was feeling it out, the evil; eager to flush some fleeting sign from the shadows. Marie didn't know what he was searching for, precisely, but whatever he was doing, he seemed to do it with authority. Then, the reverend spoke.

"I'd like to apologize, Madame Maybelle," he said, voice catching in his throat.

"For what, reverend?"

He turned, slowly, deliberately, suspiciously. "There *is* something here, and it bears a terrible, ill will to *all* who would cross its path..."

Madame Marie looked to Dorey and Croaker, her bodyguards. They were each nearly a foot taller than she, but both looked like wide-eyed, scared children dreading a visit from the Boo Hag.

The reverend continued his slow march of the long, high corridor, peering myopically into the darkness surrounding him. Finally, reaching a point some distance from Madame Marie— the crossroads of the stage right corridor and the long backstage corridor they were traversing—he stood tall, slowly opened his Bible, and settled on a certain passage. He squared his shoulders, and addressed the empty air about him.

"'O lord God of my salvation, I have cried day and night before thee! Let my prayer come before thee; incline thine ear unto my cry! For my soul is full of troubles, and my life draweth nigh unto the grave!'"

He paused, turning the page to seek another passage. As Madame Marie watched, the lights in the corridor seemed to flicker, as if preparing for a surge of power.

The reverend continued. "'He that dwelleth in the secret place of the most High shall abide under the shadow of the Almighty!

Thou shalt not be afraid for the terror by night!' Now tell me, devil, what is your name?"

Madame Marie's belly dropped into her knees. A deep rumbling, like the moving of great machinery or the hungry snarl of a predatory beast, rose up from beneath her, as though the foundation of the building itself were answering the reverend's challenge.

"What is your name?" the reverend demanded. "If you don't answer me, I'll be forced to call the Lord down upon you, and you *will* be sorry!"

Again, the foundations creaked. Dorey uttered a little sound, like a child in the throes of a nightmare. Croaker choked and coughed.

"You boys stand fast," Madame Marie said. "Be brave now... whatever happens."

"I *will* know your name!" the reverend boomed. "I *will* draw you out like poison and see you banished from this place! There is *no* power here to withstand the power of God! The might of the light of our Lord and Redeemer, Jesus Christ!"

At the invocation of Christ's name, the lights in the corridor darkened, as if their power supply strained under some terrible weight.

The reverend seemed to smile. "You don't like that, do you? The name of our Lord and Redeemer! Jesus Christ!"

Again, the lights dimmed. Behind Madame Marie, a bulb exploded with a sound as strident as a gunshot, and Dorey and Croaker both fell upon her, crushing her in a bear embrace, and she fought to shrug them off. "Ain't a gun!" she screamed. "It's the reverend! He's drawin' it out!"

"What *is* it, Queen Bee?" Croaker hissed.

"Just be brave now, Croaker. Stand for me."

"I draw you out!" the reverend cried. "I draw you out, Satan! I draw you out, Lucifer! I draw you out, you who are Legion! You who are damned! You, who our Father cast out from Heaven at the dawn of Time!"

The floor beneath them buckled and thrummed. The lights in the corridor dimmed and flared at mad intervals. The rumbling of the earth beneath them and the creaking of the walls above and around them filled their ears. Madame Marie shrank into Croaker's and Dorey's still-tight embrace, coming to think of the two scared boys now as her only shelter. What was the reverend drawing out? What was it that had poisoned this place?

He turned and called down all the four legs of the back-hall crossroads he now stood at, as if addressing adversaries in each. "I draw you out, Fallen Star, like poison! I spit you out, Satan, like lukewarm water! Like sour wine! Like the water from the tainted well that sickens and gives no life!"

The lights in the corridor all danced on their hanging cords, and the shadows tilted crazily and the whole world seemed to be hitching and toppling, this way and that.

"Give me your name or I shall see you lifted up and humiliated before all the Heavenly host! In the name of God, and His son, Jesus Christ, and with all the force of the Holy Spirit, I bind you and draw you out of this wounded house! *Like shrapnel from a wound! Like poison from a serpent's bite! Like the pus of infection, I call you forth and bid you, NAME YOURSELF!!!*"

The lights in the corridor exploded in rapid succession, and the whole world was plunged into darkness.

XX

Dr. Dub Corveaux turned the corner in front of his brownstone just as the last light of the waning day turned everything on the block deep, smoky shades of purple and gold. He'd just eaten dinner—his only decent meal all day—but the food sat in his stomach like a bag of bricks. It'd been a hell of a day, full of desperate patients and ill tidings, one after another. The only thing worse than the weariness he felt was the realization that none of the troubles he'd faced that day were mere bad luck or coincidence.

It started before he'd ever left his apartment. While still dressing, he'd heard a frantic pounding on the front door downstairs, and voices raised, calling out again and again for a doctor. He'd hurried down to see what the commotion was about and found a pair of young men in kitchen aprons, wide-eyed and frantic. One of them had his fist balled up in a bundle of towels, soaked through and dripping blood. The other carried a wax sandwich bag with his friend's two fingers in them. Apparently they worked at a delicatessen, and the bloody one had surrendered two of his fingers while slicing some country ham.

Before he'd finished sewing the young man's fingers back onto their nubs, Cecile had arrived with terrible news: some fellow in the apartment building just a block from her own had gotten into a heated argument with his wife in the night, beaten her within an inch of her life, then stabbed her repeatedly to finish the job. There had been a thick crowd outside the building when she'd passed by, all clucking about the noise and the mess.

Later in the morning, a short, thick-set Jamaican drycleaner had barged in with one of his employees in tow—his own son, barely out of his teens, face scalded horribly by a burst steam hose on his pants presser. Dub did what he could, but suggested that the drycleaner get his son to the hospital once they'd left his office.

Finally, in the afternoon, after a string of folks complaining of headaches, nausea, and 'the general willies' as one old woman put it, a sobbing mother had swept through his door with her eight year-old in her arms. The boy was still breathing, but he'd been beaten badly. More than a few of his teeth were gone.

"Animals," the woman kept hissing as Dub examined the boy and tried to stabilize him before sending them, too, to the hospital. When he asked who'd done this, she offered a hysterical re-cap: her boy had been playing marbles with some friends on their favorite stoop, just around the corner from her own apartment. An argument erupted. Before anyone knew what was happening, the other three other boys had ganged up on her son, and they laid into him without mercy.

"Over marbles?" Dub asked, amazed.

"It's that boy Jerome," she spat. "He's jealous. My baby had a big ol' glassy with an American flag in the middle. Jerome wanted it all for himself."

Dub didn't know much about marbles, but he knew they generally weren't worth beating a playmate to death for.

The string of terrible injuries and upsets seemed to throw a pall over the whole day. It wasn't until he was nearly out the door that it had all come together, and all because Cecile had made an offhand remark.

"Terrible," she said, shaking her head. "Such a mess, all in one little block."

"One little block?" Dub asked.

Cecile, who was filing away the day's paperwork, nodded but did not bother to face him. "Yes, sir. Right over round 137th and Lenox. That fella lost his fingers... the drycleaner... the fella stabbed his wife... them kids... the whole mess from the same block. Most of our other patients come from up that way, too. Somethin' in the water, maybe?"

Dub didn't offer an answer. He'd simply shrugged and taken his leave. He needed something to eat, badly. All through his dinner he'd mulled over Cecile's musings about their busy day. *All in one little block... right over round 137th and Lenox.*

The same block as Aces & Eights.

That revelation had haunted him all the way back to his brownstone. When he made it there, weary and filled with a terrible forboding, Fralene Farnes waited for him on the stoop. He was delighted to see her, but the cloud of worry in her eyes and the way she moved to meet him the moment he appeared and led him away by the arm without explanation left him a little puzzled.

She explained on the way. Her uncle, the Reverend Barnabus Farnes, had returned home just an hour or so before, muddle-headed, muttering, and generally bearing an air of wrongness about him. Fralene had tried to get an explanation from him, but her uncle Barnabus just shrugged her off, advised her to keep herself to herself, and disappeared into his study. Before Dub could even ask what part he could play in this turn of events, Fralene offered that her uncle had seemed to like him when they'd met and talked the other night; perhaps if Dub came around, her uncle would emerge; or, at the very least, invite Dub in for a pow-wow.

So, he went along, and within a block or so, even though Fralene was still trembling with worry, her arm in his rested almost casually, as though they were just out for a sundown stroll.

When they reached the parsonage, Dub knocked on the door of the reverend's study and offered the only words he could come up with. "Reverend, sir? It's Dr. Dub. Heard you had a rough day and thought maybe we could talk."

No answer. Fralene urged him on silently. Dub tried again.

"She's worried, reverend. You wanna at least show your face, make sure she knows you're safe?"

The door opened then and the reverend did indeed show his wrinkled, wizened old face. To Dub's surprise, he looked more annoyed than troubled or crazed. The reverend looked at Fralene.

"See?" he said. "I'm alive. Now go make yourself useful and stop worryin' over me, girl!"

Fralene balked. Dub felt a fury coming on. "Uncle!"

The reverend looked to Dub. "You hungry? I'm hungry. Fralene, go rustle us up some supper. I think there's some leftover beans in the icebox and some of that ham, too."

"Uncle Barnabas!"

"Doctor, come on in," the reverend said, ignoring her. "I got some distemper you may be able to diagnose." He yanked Dub into the office and shut the door behind them.

The office den was small but cozy. There were many books, magazines, and journals, a Victrola in one corner along with a wooden box of records in paper sleeves, and two chairs. The reverend bid Dub sit, and Dub did as he was told. The reverend slumped into a rocking, rolling desk chair and stared at the doctor with weary eyes. He sighed, but his pursed lips almost made it sound like a whistle.

"Long day?" Dub asked, suddenly very curious as to the cause of the reverend's troubles. He also noticed a bottle and small tumbler sitting out on the reverend's desk: brandy, if he guessed right.

The reverend saw Dub eyeing the bottle, went rooting in a drawer, and brought out another small tumbler. He poured some for the doctor without asking if he wanted it, but Dub took it happily and gulped it down.

"What's your story? You've got Fralene scared half to death."

The reverend poured himself a shot of brandy and drank it down. He shook his head. He seemed loath to meet Dub's eyes, as though he were afraid he might be taken for a lunatic.

"I'm a reasonable man, doctor. But today, I saw some unreasonable things."

Dub leaned forward, clutching his empty glass. "Such as?"

The reverend met his gaze now. "I need to know you're equal to listening, and making no judgments."

"Reverend," Dub said, "did you touch an adjacent plane? Is that what this is about?"

Dub was afraid that the statement might as easily close the reverend off as open him; he might think—quite wrongly—that Dub was sporting with him. But Dub was dead serious, and the reverend saw that, and he nodded. "I believe in God, doctor, and I believe in the devil. I believe Jesus Christ was born from a virgin and I believe he rose up, bodily, after dying and resting in a tomb for three days. But until today, I never once, with my own eyes, saw evidence of the supernatural in this world of brick and mortar and steel and electric lights. It ain't the end all and be all. I'll go to sleep tonight like always and wake up tomorrow and go about my business, and after awhile, the pall of what I saw may recede into some dark, forgotten corner of my mind. But right now it's still fresh, and I'm still puzzled and scared."

Dub felt his face harden; his eyes narrow. He needed to do his best not to give too much away; not to tip his hand or reveal more than necessary about his interest in the matter.

The reverend misunderstood Dub's hardened face. "You think I'm crazy, boy?"

"No sir," Dub said. "I've seen two or three strange things in my life too. Grew up in Haiti, remember? Traveled in Europe, too. There's a lot of strange things in this world. Some folks see 'em and dismiss 'em. They choose not to believe their own eyes and ears; choose to forget they ever saw such things, and deny they're real when others do the same. But that ain't me. I know you're straight. The way you're scared by the whole mess tells me you're straight. If you weren't scared, then I'd be worried."

"You ain't gonna tell Fralene," the reverend said, and it wasn't a request; it was an order. "She'd think I was crazy and she'd start watching every move I make; judging every little thing I do; thinkin' I'm goin' senile or crackers or some such."

"Where was it?" Dub asked. "What did you see?"

The reverend sighed, whistling again. "Started in the afternoon, when that Merriwether woman, the one they call the Queen Bee, came to me for an exorcism."

Then the reverend unfolded his tale and Dub listened.

XX

It took some fancy talk about shell-shock and the weight of a clergyman's position and such, but Dub eventually convinced Fralene that her uncle was safe and healthy, just suffering a little work-related stress, and that he should be back to normal in a day or so. He offered that she could call him again on the matter if he didn't seem to sleep well for more than a night or two, or if she saw him being forgetful or suffering fugues. But otherwise, he lied, it was just the normal weight of a position of influence and responsibility, and all the reverend needed was a talk with a fellow man about the weight of such things.

Fralene rankled at that, wondering if her uncle needed to talk so damned bad, why he didn't just talk to her. Dub almost gave her a few words about the bonds that men shared as the bearers of weight in the world, but he figured that wouldn't fly, so he just shrugged off her protests with smiles and dismissals designed to deflate the whole issue.

"He'll be fine," he said to her at the front door. "Just give him some time. And thanks again for the ham and beans."

Fralene nodded and slipped into a quiet reverie, still leaning on the half-open door. Dub decided to mix pleasure with business. "When do I get to see you again?"

That snapped her out of it. Fralene smiled a little. "Maybe this weekend? I'd like to stay close to home for a couple days."

"Sure," Dub said, and put his hat on, signaling that it was his time to go. Part of him wanted to lean in and give her a little peck on the cheek or forehead; nothing predatory; just an indication that he cared. But he didn't manage, and simply nodded his goodbyes and headed home. It was well after dark now and he had a lot to mull on the way.

The reverend had told him a fantastic story. The Queen Bee had come to beg a cleansing at Aces & Eights, and the reverend had been intrigued by the request and done as asked. Once inside the club, however, he'd been immediately aware of something wrong about the place; a lingering, almost palpable darkness; strange drafts and phantoms at the periphery of his vision; movements in the load-bearing members of the structure and terrible, belligerent manifestations in the light and shadows. He'd done his best to do battle with whatever laid in wait there, but the force alive in that club had fought back, violently. After losing the light and nearly being crushed by a falling piece of scenery, the Queen Bee's bodyguards had ushered their regent and the reverend out into the light, and forbade either to go back inside. The Reverend Farnes had confessed to Dub that, even though he'd put up a fight and pressed to be taken back inside to keep fighting with the beast hiding there, he'd secretly been pleased that the bodyguards held their ground. He'd fought to go back in because he thought it the right thing to do; but he really did not want to go back. If he never saw the inside of Aces & Eights again, he confessed, it would be too soon.

Dub absolved the reverend of any shame—who wouldn't be terrified and find themselves unequal to such a task, especially when they'd never encountered such a thing before? That seemed to settle the reverend a little, but Dub could still tell that the old man felt like a failure somehow. Dub couldn't tell him that the truth was, it would take more than just the reverend's faith to pry the malignancy out of that club. No doubt, it would take full-bore magic of a sort the reverend would have been loath to acknowledge as potent, let alone useful in pursuit of a virtuous end.

But that's why Dub bore his burden, wasn't it? That's why he was a horse for the *lwa*: so other people—better people—wouldn't have to be.

XX

He was tired and he wanted to go home, but he had one more stop to make before doing so. Thus, he marched a few more blocks eastward, and found himself skulking in a shadowy alleyway directly opposite the front façade of Aces & Eights.

There were lights burning within and the shadows of movement on the few illuminated windows. The Queen Bee's drones, no doubt, burning the midnight oil in preparation for the big opening. Were they changing out the light bulbs that had burst that afternoon, even as he watched? Whispering among themselves about the drafts, the accidents, the sense that often pervaded one in solitary moments in those darkened corridors, or in the labyrinthine basement?

Being familiar with the bad juju that the place exuded, Dr. Dub Corveaux felt it even from this distance. No doubt, his senses were sharpened by Legba's pendant. But he imagined that even if he didn't have Legba's mojo for *maji* helping to sensitize him at the moment, he might still get the same sense of dread and foreboding that he now felt as he lingered in the shadows and studied the non-descript brick building opposite him.

Using the sensitivities bestowed upon him, he reached out, extending the gaze of that sixth sense he now wielded into the lease spaces on either side of the club. One was a dry-cleaners; the other a neighborhood grocer. Luckily, the owners didn't live in the apartments above the mercantile spaces—his sixth sense told him that the upstairs spaces were all used for storage and the like. But already, Dub could feel the shadows in each of those spaces deepening. The dry clean presses were getting hungry, like long un-fed lions at a zoo. There would be more accidents soon; malfunctions; the destruction of property on loan for cleaning. At the grocer's, Dub could already sense that some of the canned products were souring long before their appointed time; some of the shelving sagging, eager to snap and dump heavy contents onto unwary clerks or customers; that there were eggs in the big icebox that might suddenly have live, misshapen little chicks inside them.

The pall from the curse engine in the basement of Aces & Eights was spreading like vapor from its proper domain toward its unwary neighbors. Pretty soon, it might infect some of the blocks adjacent, if the flowing waters of the sewers beneath the paved streets couldn't provide suitable magical barriers against it. Bad happenings would follow soon—tomorrow, maybe the next day. How long before the sickness reached into the street? A shoot-out that killed innocent bystanders? Some hapless kid getting run down by a speeding car? Seeds of vileness, hatred and malignancy growing right up out of the sick waters in the sewer pipes below them?

The curse engine wasn't just mucking with the Queen Bee's business. It was on its way to being a blight on all Harlem.

Dub breathed deeply, exhaled, felt just how tired he was. How alone.

He'd have to get some sleep tonight. There would be legwork tomorrow, while the sun was shining.

And, most likely, bloody business when the sun went down.

10

Dr. Dub Corveaux rose early and wrote Cecile a note instructing her to reschedule all his appointments and turn away all walk-ins. He'd be out of Harlem for the day, on some personal business. Then, hat on his head, he snatched an egg sandwich at a corner greasy spoon and hoofed it toward the train station at Lenox and 125th Street.

He kept a growing list of the names of various specialists in and around Manhattan; folks whom he may never have met or spoken with, but who he heard of by reputation or encountered through research; folks with odd specialties and past-times.

Folks he might need to dig up when questions abounded and answers eluded.

One of these specialists was a fellow who'd hung out an investigator's shingle in the Red Hook section of Brooklyn two or three years back; a young misanthrope from Rhode Island named Howard Randolph. His reputation as poor company preceded him, but by all accounts, he was also a bookworm of the first order, well-versed in all sorts of major and minor arcana because he made a little money on the side writing chillers for the pulps. Dub still remembered the strange symbols he'd seen on the skull talisman in the Aces & Eights basement the night before—he'd even managed to write down an approximation of one sequence. Maybe this Randolph character could give him some clue as to where the symbols came from or what they meant.

So, egg sandwich devoured, he took with him a bright green apple as a snack and a copy of a new literary journal that was just making the rounds, called *Fire!!*, and set out on his long journey. By mid-morning he was on Canal Street, and an hour after that, he'd made it to Brooklyn Heights. From there, he began the long walk out to lonely Red Hook on its peninsula at the ass-end of the borough.

Red Hook itself was a labyrinth of squalor. It lay near the old Brooklyn waterfront in sight of Governor's Island, its crowded, grubby streets carving a tangle of Dickensian alleys and byways between its brick warehouses and tenements that made him instantly long for the neat, gridded streets of Harlem. The population was a miasmatic mishmash of immigrants—Mediterranean sorts, mostly, with some Anglo and Negro elements thrown in like dashes of salt and pepper for texture and flavor. Suddenly, Harlem, even its darkest corners, seemed a glittering modern metropolis. Red Hook, by Dub Corveaux's reckoning, was all noise, clutter, and filth, its chatter a counterpoint to the lapping of turgid waves at its piers and the intermittent groans of tug and barge whistles from the harbor.

He heard the tongues of a hundred different nations spoken; smelled smells that he'd never imagined and hoped were accidents, not purposeful concoctions; and generally, felt like the one angel set loose in a forgotten corner of Dante's hells. The foreign longshoremen and immigrants who populated the little borough-within-a-borough gave him the evil eye, seeming to will him away with belligerent glares and breathy mutterings to their hoary old saints or forgotten gods. Dub just kept walking, clutching the piece of paper in his hands bearing Randolph's address like a talisman of good fortune.

Finally he located the place, though he saw no indication that a private investigator lived or worked there. Instead, the address was home to a little hat shop, crammed in between a Kosher bakery and a Turkish tobacconist. The numbers matched, though.

There was a little bell above the door that tinkled merrily, and his first impression of the hat shop was of coziness and cheer. It was a little dark and cramped, but the proprietor had scented the place with jasmine, and the hats themselves—mostly for ladies—were of all sorts of gay colors and designs.

There were only two people in the shop besides Dub. One was a small, compact old woman, probably of Jewish descent, dressed all in drab black and purchasing a funereal bonnet to match. The other Dub supposed was a shop girl, a handsomely pretty, hearty woman of about his own age with strong but not unattractive features and quick, dark eyes. When she saw Dub, those dark eyes seemed to flash suspicion followed by a strange sort of hope. Dub couldn't imagine what was going through her mind.

He stood and said nothing as she wrapped the bonnet for the old woman (whose expression suggested that Dub had brought a stink into the shop with him), and finally the old lady waddled out on her way and Dub was alone with the shop girl. She folded her hands on the little counter beside an ancient cash register.

"How may I help you, sir?" she asked.

Dub brandished the paper bearing the address. "Pardon me if I've made a mistake, miss. I was looking for a Mr. Howard Randolph and I—"

Before he could finish, the woman had turned, snatched up a broom, and thrust the handle against the ceiling, making four solid thumps before putting the broom back where she'd found it. Dub must have been staring, for the woman smiled, and he decided that he liked her instantly. He liked that crooked, knowing smile. "Howie's upstairs, sir. He'll be right down."

"So I'm in the right place?"

She studied him. "*That's* debatable. But if you're looking for Howard Randolph, yes; you're in the right place."

"Your brother?" Dub asked.

"My husband," she said, and offered her hand. "Mrs. Sonya Randolph."

"Dr. Dub Corveaux," Dub said, taking her hand lightly and shaking it. A moment later, he heard quick footfalls on a back staircase, and another moment after that, a curtain hiding a narrow back corridor was drawn aside and a thin, wan fellow with a receding hairline and a pronounced under bite appeared. His eyes almost leapt out of his long, horsey face when he saw Dub, but after just a moment of fear and wonder, the look subsided, and the fellow turned to Sonya.

"Is there trouble?" he asked, as though Dub couldn't hear him.

"No, Howard," the woman said. "This nice gentleman is looking for you."

Howard Randolph looked at Dub again, suspicious, furtive, then once more spoke to Sonya in barely a whisper, as though Dub were not even present. "What does he *want*?"

Dub decided to cut through the red tape. He offered his hand. "Forgive me, Mr. Randolph. I'd heard you were an investigator and that you specialized on the side in... curiosities."

Randolph stared.

"Occult matters?" Dub offered.

Randolph looked fully thrown for a loop now. He seemed to weigh a number of thoughts in succession, without offering a word, then finally cocked his head toward the back hallway. "Come in, then. We'll talk."

Dub, his hand never taken even as a courtesy, nodded and followed the pale, thin figure through a hallway barely wide enough to pass, and up a cramped back staircase. As he went, he heard Sonya Randolph speaking from the shop to her husband.

"Don't be rude, Howard!" she called, and Dub detected a note of sarcasm in her voice. "Offer the man some tea!"

The apartment was directly above the hat shop, a cramped little cell in an urban hive consisting of a miniscule sitting room, a little kitchenette with a hot plate and a sink, and a bedroom jutting off to one side. Though tiny, the place was crammed, floor to ceiling, with books old and new, and strewn with hundreds of magazines. Collections of Leftist essays and old, yellowed National Geographics reposed beside issues of *Weird Tales*. The books on the sagging floor-to-ceiling shelves were a puzzling mixture as well: collections by Dunsanay, Blackwood, Poe, and Baudelaire beside dry scholarly texts on geology, architecture, and New England history. Dub saw a few books in Russian and supposed those might belong to Mrs. Randolph, since she had the look of European Jewry about her, even if her accent was pure Brooklyn slum. As Dub finished his study of the cramped shelves and their contents, he noted that Randolph had withdrawn into the bedroom, and now emerged again, tying a tie round his neck and working his narrow, stooped shoulders to settle a suit coat upon them. With a great air of officiousness, the pale, horse-faced little man swept a chair away from a small writing desk poised by the front window and offered it to Dub, setting it right in the middle of the only free space on the floor of the room. Dub sat. Randolph studied him for a moment.

"Do you have money?"

"If you can help me," Dub said.

"Let me see it," Randolph answered.

Dub produced his wallet and fanned it open, revealing a parcel of bills therein. Randolph's eyes flashed in disbelief and incredulity. Then, he swept back a stray lock of his thinning hair and cleared his throat.

"Who are you?" he asked.

Dub offered his hand again. The little man still didn't take it. He withdrew it. "Dr. Dub Corveaux. Practice up in Harlem. I'm looking into some strange matters thereabouts and I heard you were well-read and possessed of some"—he studied his book-laden surroundings—"peculiar research interests."

"Who sent you?" Randolph asked.

Dub shook his head. "Nobody, Mr. Randolph. I came here to solve a personal problem of my own accord."

"What sort of problem?" Randolph asked.

"That's none of your business at this point," Dub answered. He reached into the inner pocket of his suit coat and produced the paper on which he'd scrawled the strange symbols he remembered from the mojo in the cellar of Aces & Eights.

ꝏƷ℀†Ƹb†

"I need these symbols identified," Dub said as he handed over the scrap of paper. "I'll be happy to reimburse you for your time."

Randolph snatched the paper from Dub's hands and studied it. Immediately, something changed in his countenance: the suspicion was gone; the furtiveness vanished. The bookworm had a problem to solve—a *real* problem, suited to *his* peculiar skills!—

and he surrendered himself to it. Dub even thought he saw something resembling happiness and ease on the man's pinched face and narrow, pursed lips.

Without another word, he pushed past Dub, bent over a hip-high pile of books and magazines teetering against one of the high shelves, and reached for a tome above him. When he'd eased the dusty old book and its yellow pages down, he turned to Dub and waved him out of the chair.

"Move," he said. "I need to sit down."

Dub moved, and Randolph took the chair. He placed the book in his lap, fanned it open, and started searching its pages, all the while clutching the scrap of paper in his right hand.

"I could give you some time, if—"

Randolph raised a finger. "This won't take long, I assure you." Then, he raised his dark eyes and skewered Dub with them. "But I'll have to charge you for a full hour's work, I'm afraid. Can't charge in quarter-hours, after all."

"Can you identify it?" Dub asked impatiently.

"If you leave me be for five minutes," Randolph said with notable prickliness, "I can most likely translate it. Was this a particular sequence, or just random symbols you copied?" He lowered his eyes to the book again.

"That was a particular sequence," Dub said, stepping away to give the fellow some room to work. "There were more, but that was the only one I could remember."

"Where on earth did you find it?" Randolph asked, nose still in the book in his lap.

"It's hard to explain," Dub said, voice trailing off, settling into a slow perusal of Randolph's book collection as the strange little man went to work identifying the symbols. In the midst of his perusal, his eyes fell to another haphazard pile of pulp magazines, specifically, *Weird Tales*. Dub fanned out the pile a little, noting that the publication dates were all from the past year, and that nearly every cover to every issue bore the same name.

Howard Randolph.

In this issue: *The Festival! The Unnamable! The Temple! The Vault! The Outsider!*

All by Howard Randolph.

Dub might have dismissed the fellow's work as the product of an overly-fanciful or diseased mind, but there was still the great intellectual weight and eclecticism of the books on his shelves: Sir Richard Burton's translation of the *Arabian Nights*; Paracelsus; Cornelius Agrippa; Eliphas Levi; Carl Jung; Nathaniel Hawthorne; William Blake; Edgar Allan Poe; George MacDonald; Lord Dunsanay... and all of those puzzling tomes on subjects that people weren't known to read of for mere pleasure: history and geology; the *Chaldean Oracles*; the *Apocrypha*; the *Book of Enoch*; the *Enuma Elish*; the *Sephir Yetzirah*; and some narrow but well-worn little leather-bound folio called the *Necronomicon*. Quite the heavy handle for such a slim volume!

"You've got varied reading tastes, Mr. Randolph," Dub said.

"That's why you came to me, isn't it?" the little man muttered.

Dub shrugged. Yes. He supposed it was. He turned. Randolph was making some pencil notes on the scrap of paper that Dub had given him.

"Well?"

Randolph raised his eyes, now alight and downright proud; clearly the work of solving a mystery, however briefly, had brought the sickly little man to life. "Glagol. That's the alphabet. Slavic. Ninth century."

Dub stared, as though he could not believe what Randolph told him. Randolph, seeming to sense Dub's incredulity, stood and offered the book in his lap. Dub took it and studied it. It turned out to be a survey on the history of European linguistics. There on the moldered page was a chart showing the Glagol alphabet, clear as day, though the shape of the letters, as Dub remembered them, clearly reflected a more primitive, less refined version of those letters.

Dub looked at Randolph, duly impressed by his investigative abilities. "Well, that wasn't so hard, was it?"

Randolph smiled crookedly. "I suppose for someone who didn't know what they were looking for, it might have been. But I was just looking at this book a week or two ago—research for a story I've in mind—and so it was fresh."

Dub suggested the scrap. "You translated it?"

Randolph nodded and presented the scrap. "That's the really puzzling part. The alphabet is Glagol—Slavic—but the translation I get is a name out of Greek myth: Megaera."

"Megaera?"

"One of the Furies," Randolph continued. "Nemesis, Alecto, Megaera, and Tisiphone. Some say there were only three, but Nemesis was clearly associated with them; some say there were many more. But those are the central four. Now, then—would you like to tell me why anyone in Harlem would be using ancient Slavic letters to invoke a chthonic Greek deity?"

His tone implied that no one in Harlem could possibly have a working knowledge of, let alone an interest in, either. Dub licked his teeth, his patience at an end. After a moment, he shook his head and held out his hand for the little slip of paper. "No, I wouldn't," he said. He'd had enough of the fellow's impertinence. "How much do I owe you, Mr. Randolph?"

The pale Mr. Randolph narrowed his eyes and pursed his thin lips, clearly frustrated. "You can tell me what you saw," he goaded. "I'm prepared to believe you."

Dub raised an eyebrow. "Are you?" he asked. "Because if I see even a hint of condescension in your face, or if I hear words like 'quaint' or 'superstitious' come out of your mouth, I can promise you, Mr. Randolph, this meeting will not end well."

Randolph seemed insulted at first—then something else came over him. A strange sort of determination; a quiet acceptance. He nodded and folded his hands before him. "I apologize for my rudeness, doctor. Clearly you're a man of learning. Once I heard the nature of your request and bore witness to your interest in my books, I should have respected that fact."

Well, here was progress. Dub was duly impressed by the fellow's willingness to apologize. And he was knowledgeable. Perhaps storming out over a case of bad manners was an overreaction.

Besides, a man who lived in such a cramped little hovel, wrote spook stories for fun, and found occasion to casually research Slavic alphabets might not think him mad when he offered a frank explanation. Dub sighed. "It was inscribed on a skull; part of sculpture of sorts; sort of a talisman."

"Like the skulls employed in vodou?" Randolph offered.

Dub nodded. "Something like that. There were four skulls, each with a different name, in those letters, written on its forehead. They were arranged in a cluster, each facing outward, and beneath them were a pair of crossbones, along with some other stuff: crow feathers and animal skulls, teeth and nails and whatnot."

Randolph stared, almost as though Dub's words were winning his heart of hearts. "That's extraordinary," he said breathlessly.

"It *was* that," Dub said.

"Do you mind if I use that?" Randolph asked.

"*Use it?*"

"In a story?"

"Do what you like with it when I'm gone, Mr. Randolph. But here and now, I need your best guess on what such a thing might be, and who might have made it."

"Where did you find it?"

"Hidden in a place of business. In the cellar. Under an old, plugged manhole cover."

Randolph considered this. "Does the proprietor have enemies?"

"She does," Dub said. "Most assuredly."

"Then it's a curse engine," Randolph said. "Someone wanted the owner of this place of business to fail miserably and planted that talisman, as you call it, to curse the place. Have there been strange events of late? Discord? Violence? Deaths, perhaps?"

Dub nodded. He'd heard all he needed to. "All three. Guess I need to get that thing out of there."

"You mustn't! It's a curse *engine*, Dr. Corveaux! It spews malignity like a still drips liquor. It's probably already infected the place, and will continue to, regardless of its physical removal. And if *you* lay hands on the thing—you didn't, did you?"

"I wasn't able to," Dub said. "Just as I found it, there was a... disturbance. I wasn't able to touch it—"

"And best you didn't!" Randolph said. "No, sir—the only means of lifting the curse now is either to employ the engine's maker, or some powerful, apposite magical rite to clear the air."

"Any ideas on whom might have made such a thing?" Dub asked.

"Glagol," Randolph said, shrugging and indicating the scrap with Dub's notes on it. "Slavic. Invoking the name of an ancient, chthonic Greek deity. I'd say your mage is Eastern European... probably very old, and very *Old World*, if you get my meaning."

"I think so."

"Likewise, there's the *subject* of this curse to consider. Who is he? One of *your* kind?"

Dub felt his teeth grind. "Yes. *She* is."

Randolph seemed puzzled by that. "A Negro businesswoman? How extraordinary."

Dub didn't know how to read the thin man. He seemed to alternate between being an egg-headed, arrogant, bigoted know-it-all and a wondering, wide-eyed babe in the woods. And his *astonishment* at both Dub's monetary means and the notion of a Negro businesswoman was nothing short of infuriating.

Still, he now seemed willing to help—more focused on the problem itself than on his apparent disdain for the Negro seeking aid. Dub supposed that was a step in the right direction. The horse-faced little prick could just as easily have refused him outright... or sent him packing with nothing more than the alphabet, sans translation, his wallet lighter and the mystery he was pursuing still no closer to being solved.

Randolph interrupted his moment of cynical introspection. "I take it the place of business in question is in Harlem?" he asked.

Dub nodded. "Correct."

"In magical terms, Harlem has its own gods and its own pagan protectors, like any minority enclave."

Dub felt a little flush of pride. *Pagan Protector, at your service, Mr. Randolph.* Dub shrugged, trying to remain noncommittal. "I suppose."

"Then clearly this magic isn't African or even Caribbean in origin. The one who contracted it might be, but they would've gone far affield, to try and fetch some means of cursing a fellow Negro that Negro folk magic would have no means of countering."

"Could there be someone out this way, capable of—"

"No no no," Randolph said, waving away Dub's suggestion, annoyed. "These are all Mediterranean sorts hereabouts—and Jews, who you can probably discount, because the letters would be in Hebrew and the gods invoked would *never* be Greco-Roman. Were your cursor Jewish, they'd most likely invoke some Judeo-Persian angelic or demonic name. No, the script is the key. Clearly, you're looking for someone with *very* ancient knowledge, most likely of a Slavic descent."

"The Lower East Side?" Dub offered.

"Magda!" Randolph breathed, suddenly seeming to discover the name of his own accord.

"Excuse me?"

Randolph looked around, found a slip of paper, and scrawled some hasty directions upon it. He offered it to Dub. "I've heard of her, but never seen nor spoken to her. I'm not even sure where she lives, exactly. But she's well known below Canal Street. There's a fine old Moldavian Jew thereabouts. Owns a pharmacy. Tell him I sent you, give him the thinnest of explanations—please leave out your rather vivid description of the engine itself—and ask him to point you toward Old Magda. If he refuses to help, there's nothing more to be done, save wandering the Lower East side and asking strangers. One of them might take pity on you."

Dub took the paper and studied the little man. Randolph held out his hand. "Twenty-five dollars, please."

Dub gave the strange, thin fellow with the horse face a full thirty, then hurried on his way.

XX

Come late afternoon, Dr. Dub Corveaux found himself in a dishwater corner of the Lower East Side, wondering just how stupid one black, college-educated physician was capable of being. If he had come down this way in the dead of night, horsed and armed, he *might* have felt safe. But here and now, late in the day with the sun hidden behind the glowering tenements and the populace staring at him like the devil incarnate or fresh meat or both... well, he had to question his own judgment. Dr. Dub Corveaux could talk his way out of most trouble and scrap his way out of the remainder, but given his druthers, he didn't want to see which would be necessary to get out of the Lower East Side alive.

Yakov Spiel had been the Moldavian pharmacist whose name Randolph had offered. Spiel had looked Dub up and down with respect and pity: he didn't give him the normal cold shoulder that a lot of Old World mocks gave a Negro in a decent suit, but neither was he eager to help.

"You look for Magda," he said, after Dub had introduced himself and explained his presence in the briefest manner possible. "Why you seek Magda?"

"I'd just like to talk to her," Dub answered. "Ask her some questions."

"She won't talk to you," the old druggist said.

"Let me worry about that," Dub answered.

"She'll curse you and feed you to her little *maziks*," he said. Dub didn't know what a mazik was, but he didn't like the sound of it. "You go now, huh?"

"No," Dub said, trying to stay firm. "I came a long way. Help me. What happens to me when I walk out this door isn't your concern."

"Fat lot you know," the old man said, shaking his head. "*Every* man is *every* man's concern, huh?"

Dub started to say something glib but thought better of it. "Please," was all he could manage, and Spiel gave him directions. Two rights, three lefts, then right, then one more left; this street, that street, this street, etc. Dub's head nearly swam, trying to soak up the directions as they were given; he didn't want to ask a second time. Then he bought a Coca-Cola from Spiel, paid for it with a half-dollar, and was on his way.

Now the Cola was gone and he stood in the shadows of a towering, frowning old shithole of brick and ash-colored mortar that was probably older than the whole Lower East. The place looked so ancient and rotted it might well have been standing when the Dutch cheated the Red Men out of Manhattan. It sported the same rank plumage as its neighbors—seemingly forgotten laundry flapping on dry-lines stretched like the decrepit, soot-besotted webs of old, dead spiders in the alleyways, climbing all the way up the sides of the tower, with gaping forward windows barely retaining any glass and a general feeling of *wrongness* about the whole mess.

Beneath his shirt, against his skin, he felt his Legba *veve* pendant lifting from his chest, pressing gently against his shirt, drawn to the magical cesspool that stood before him.

Well. Guess this is the place.

Dub marched right up to the cancerous old brickworks and only stopped when a pack of dirt-faced little ruffians—the oldest no more than eight or ten years old—blocked his path. They appeared quickly, scurrying out of the forward cellar windows and the many trash-piles thereabouts like a bunch of two-legged rats. They fanned out and surrounded him before he even had the chance to say hello.

Maziks? he wondered.

He tried to smile and felt his grin failing him. "Fellas. How do this afternoon?"

No answer. The tallest one, whom he assumed to be the leader, glared at him, dark eyes big in his bony, grimy face.

Dub suggested the building they guarded. "This where the old lady live? The one they call Magda?"

Again, no answer. Dub offered his empty Coca Cola bottle. "You wanna take this back to the druggist, he'll probably give you the deposit. That should be a few pennies, I guess—"

The lead urchin snatched the cola bottle, and in one swift movement, bent and smashed it on the pavement. Now, holding its neck, he raised the jagged fragment, lunged, and took a swipe at Dub.

Dub slid backward and arched to keep his middle clear of the whizzing bottleneck. He felt a sear of pain in his left thigh, heard fabric rip, and knew the little bastard had drawn blood. Without stopping to check the wound, he hopped back three more steps, putting a good distance between he and the now-closing street urchins.

"Little man," he said, putting on his best stern schoolmaster's voice, "you're in for a heap'a trouble over—"

He saw one of them lunge in the corner of his vision; heard a barely-perceptible whizzing. He ducked instinctively, and he was lucky; a fat chuck of broken brick—probably with a jagged edge—sailed right past his crown and hit the pavement on the far side of him. If he hadn't ducked, it would've hit his temple square-on. Might have put him down, dazed and starry-eyed.

And he didn't want to find himself in that state, at the mercy of *these* little cretins. The demonic brats meant business.

Another one lurched at him from the left, swinging what looked like the broken shaft of a broom handle. Dub swirled the overcoat draped on his left arm round to blind the kid for a moment, danced back a few steps, and suddenly found himself sprawling: one of the little buggers had thrown himself down in Dub's path, tripping him. Down he went, whacked his head good and hard on the littered pavement, and amid the swirls of darkness and fireflies, saw the ghostly figures of the filthy little blood-mongers closing in around him.

"Son of a bitch," he muttered, scrambling, trying to get to his feet again. *Papa Ogou*, he thought, *remind me again why I didn't come downtown horsed?*

He floundered backward, hands scraped and cut on shattered cement, old brick, and bits of broken glass. The little demons closed. Dub was trying to blink away his starry-eyed daze and get back on his feet to make a run for it. With one hand, he searched for a piece of litter large enough and solid enough to defend himself with.

Then something strange happened. The urchins stopped their advance. All their beady, dark eyes rose, focused no longer on Dub, but on something new coming up behind him. His vision was just clearing. He needed to be on his feet and fleeing this place, now; *right now*. He'd come back in the night; come back horsed, armed, ready. *Then* let these little bastards—*maziks* or whatever they were—try to harass him.

But just as he was getting his feet under him and lurching upright, a pair of strong hands fell upon him, wadded up the slack of his suit coat, and yanked him upward. Dub found himself staring into the broad face of the biggest, baddest Son of Abraham he'd ever seen. Standing beside him was a smaller fellow, no less menacing for his lesser stature, so bright were his hate-filled, flashing eyes and the sneer on his narrow, pursed lips.

"Who the fuck dropped you off below Canal Street, Sambo?" the little one snapped.

"Must've got off at the wrong subway stop," Dub offered. The big Abe answered Dub's smartassery with bare knuckles. Dub saw stars and tasted a mouthful of pennies.

"Teapots ain't welcome down here," the little one said, and to prove his point pulled out a switchblade and popped it. The shining point hovered in Dub's view, splitting right through the new flock of seagulls and storm clouds that squealed in his ears and blackened his vision. "This is Spector's territory. *Fish* territory. *You*, blue gums, keep your chocolate-brown ass *uptown*, got me?"

"My mistake," Dub managed, though he was finding words hard to form at the moment. His tongue was in revolt, and his teeth felt decidedly loose in their roots. "You wanna unhand me, I'll just be on my way."

His big friend did just that, but not before laying another big kosher brisket-sized fist in Dub's breadbasket, then tossing him a good ten feet to come crashing down on the pavement and skidding to a halt amid the detritus. Dub stirred, eager to make sure all his limbs were still working. They seemed to be. He wanted to stand up, but he wasn't sure which way up was.

"You fuckin' jungle bunnies... think just 'cause some dumb white men put suits on you and taught you to speak you can have the run of the town. Well, we're here to say it just ain't so."

Dub was up, though he still couldn't quite stand straight. His head and knees kept wanting to hold close commerce with one another. He nodded, drawing breath deep and slow. "Lesson learned, sir. I'll just be on my way—"

Then the little kike screamed. Dub, more shocked than curious, stood bolt upright and blinked. The urchins were on Chicken Big and Chicken Little now, sniping with old brick-chunks while the smaller ones dove into the fray under the covering fire to pick the gangster's pockets. The little fellow swiped blindly and missed. The big one waded into the storm of little street rats, huge fists sweeping this way and that. But he never touched any of them. They were too small; too fast.

"Little bastards!" the diminutive Hebe gangster squealed.

Dub knew a good thing when he saw it. He left his good overcoat where it lay ten feet shy of him, dusted off his crumpled, dirtied fedora, and loped off on his merry way, eager to find the nearest taxi or train station.

Maybe he'd return in the night, with Ogou riding him, to pay Magda a visit.

Or maybe he'd just wash his hands of the Lower East side and figure out another answer to the mess at Aces & Eights...

XX

After finally making it home hours later than he intended, Dub showered, dressed in his dead man's duds, then mounted the secret spiral steps to his peristyle on the fourth floor. He chanted the *Afonga Alafia* as he lit the hounfor's battalion of slow-burn worship candles, and when that was done, he cranked up the Victrola. The familiar thump of the wango and the mambo croon filled the room. He gave offerings—dates for Erzulie, loose tobacco for Legba, rum for Ogou—and the doors between the worlds groaned as they opened wide.

"You were right," Dub said, pacing the perimeters of his patrons' *veves* on the earthen floor. "It's somebody else's magic. And now it's spreading."

So it ain't somebody else's problem anymore, Legba answered.

Dub held his tongue. This was typical: he was the protector; the avenger; but his patrons often would not approve his involvement until formal petitions by their worshippers had been made.

The Queen Bee called a mambo, Erzulie said softly, *and the mambo failed with what we gave her. That means we're still bound to try and wrest this thing.*

"*I'm* bound to wrest this thing," Dub corrected.

You do nothing without us, Ogou snarled around his cigar.

"Forgive me, Papa Ogou," Dub said, anger flaring, "but sometimes it seems I do nothing *with* you, either. Why did it take you this long to make this my problem?"

We got to wait 'til we're called, Legba said.

"*I* called you," Dub answered.

You ain't a petitioner, Ogou countered. *You're a soldier. Soldiers don't go to war 'til their generals order them to.*

"Order me," Dub said.

Impatient, Ogou said, chuckling a little, the sound like a whetstone drawn along the length of an eager blade.

The parties aggrieved get parlay before you bust in, guns blazing, Legba reminded him.

That's right, Erzulie said, *you act first as our mouth before you act as our sword.*

Dub was eager, the hunger for action pulsing through him like a junkie's urge. He moved to the Ghede altar and started donning his gear: skull-face powder and bootblack, gravedigger boots, waistcoat, long coat, dreadlock wig and top hat. "It's House, isn't it?" he said as he prepared. "He's the one that planted that thing. He's the only one who'd stand to gain." The coiled *Serpent d'Ogou* scarf went on last.

We can't say one way or the other, Legba answered. *You just pay him a visit. Let your eyes and ears tell you what they can.*

Dub snorted. *Typical.* But it was a start. He drew breath and opened himself.

"Do it, then," Dub said, checking his pistols and holstering them. "Horse me."

This is a parlay, Legba said worriedly. *That's all it is! Why you gonna go out packin' to a parlay?*

Dub kept himself from snapping. Legba might have the form of an old man with a cane, but dangerous powers lurked behind the veil of that form. Best not rouse them. He spoke slowly. "Well, I can't parlay with a killer like Solomon House in my suit and tie, Papa," he said through gritted teeth. "This ain't a job for Dr. Dub Corveaux—this is a job for a baron."

Lay off, Ogou growled at *Legba. I ride him... let me worry about it.*

"Come on, then," Dub said, loving the sure weight of his guns in their matching shoulder holsters.

Ogou mounted. The Dread Baron opened his black eyes.

11

Papa Solomon House owned a six story walk-up off 5th and 126th Street. Most of the fifth floor was an ad hoc casino, with games going on in the various apartments, the adjoining doors between them open wide to allow heel-toe access from one end of the floor to the other without ever stepping out into the central hallway. He had craps in one room, spades in another, hold 'em in a third. The rooms across the hall were linked the same way, and comprised a brothel. It was the short and sweet sort, full of curtained booths, not rooms, for blow jobs, dances, and quick pokes. House kept the sixth floor vacant, and there held court in a series of well-appointed suites. Behind those doors, he entertained guests, held sit-downs and negotiations, passed quiet hours with his favorite whores, or played cards with his lieutenants. The building was fitted with an elevator, but the operator only stopped on the fifth and sixth floors, for House or his special guests. The tenants on one through four used the stairs. They had no reason to complain, though. He gave them all a break on rent.

And if they *did* complain, he just fed them to Napoleon.

So here he was, walking the floor to assure himself that the croupiers and dealers were doing their jobs properly and not working any flimflams; that the patrons stayed jingle-brained and loose with their change; that the house was winning, the suckers were losing, and the whores weren't spending more than a fair tick on their dumb, drunk Johns. He got smiles and greetings and handshakes and well-wishes, but he knew that everyone who smiled at him wanted him dead. They were his best customers; slaves to his games; suckers for his tricks; gassed on his bathtub gin or syrupy on his rooftop-grown weed. He had them all by the balls, and they knew it. Given the chance, they'd all stick a knife in. If he was gonna prove he knew their game and wasn't afraid, he'd better show his face. So he walked the floor; smiled, nodded; offered free hooch or a snort or a toke on the house. He gave them just enough, and kept their swinging nuts in the palm of his hand.

Exploit vice; exploit fear. Papa prided himself on keeping Harlem well in hand. He just needed to push north. If he could get that high-toned yaller dame the Queen Bee out of her uptown digs, he'd have the whole knot in his pocket, and he could stroke it at will. She was just too entrenched, that was all.

You had to work such problems at their roots. Kill them. Shorten them. Then, when the tree balked, you tore it right up out of the ground and down it went. Simple as that.

He'd have her out soon enough. The hoodoo he'd worked on the supper club was first blood. If that worked out, he'd follow with some body blows, and finally, the knock-out.

He didn't come here from Trinidad and soil his soul and dare so much blood and violence and build the walls he'd built around his heart and mind to have some high yaller bitch in heels as his superior. *No sir*. He'd have her, and he'd fuck her good.

So Papa finished his walk, got quickie reports on the state of the union from his doormen and floor bosses, then took the stairs up to six to have a drink before he made the rounds to his other vice dens around lower Harlem. On his way upstairs, he turned and ordered Wash back down again. "Go get those two new twists from the cat rooms."

"Which ones, boss?"

"Fucked if I know their names, Wash. The Dominican and the Rican. And if the girls get mousy, tell 'em I just want to talk a bit. Get to know 'em."

Wash did as he was told and headed downstairs. Papa hadn't tasted them yet. He needed to taste all the merch before it spent too long on the floor and ruined his rep. Timmons carried on at Papa's elbow, and in two shakes they were up on six, marching down the carpeted hallway, ending in the big, broad chamber that Papa thought of as his home-away-from-home: the Roost.

It was a posh suite, furnished with red leather sofas and easy chairs, traced with stained cherry wood paneling and warmed by expensive wallpaper in a deep gold pattern that made House think of the pagan faces on ancient South American idols. There were palms and ferns in pots and all sorts of Old African hoodoo jigamawhats—masks and shields and crazy paintings by hop-headed Harlem artistes whose names he'd forgotten. It was just eclectic enough—by accident, not design—to be tasteful instead of tacky. But it was his, and he felt comfortable there. Six floors above the dirty streets, surrounded by *his* guns, locked behind *his* doors. He was the only one with access to a lately-installed elevator, and he kept a private stairwell at the back. There was even a cache of weapons stowed in a nearby closet. From the southeast windows, he had a great view of the rest of Harlem, stretching away from his lower enclave toward the north and east, and he stood there many a night, dreaming of the power and influence he'd one day wield.

Presently, three of House's hired guns bent over a small table in a corner, playing Hearts and drinking watered-down Canadian whiskey. His bookkeeper, Cornelius Luddard, busied himself in a far corner, at a large cherry wood desk, laying down the law for his new apprentice, a kid House himself had picked from a policy bank because he had a supernatural memory for numbers and could work figures faster than your average fourth-generation Yorkville Shylock. Ames was the kid's name, and from what Cornelius told House, he was working out just fine.

The card players all slammed down their hands and stood when their boss marched through the door. House gave them deferential waves and they nodded and went back to their games. He always acted like they didn't need to stand for him when he entered, but truth be told if he ever had one of them refuse to do so, or not *think* to do so, he'd probably make said insubordinate's life misery just as an object lesson. Fear kept them tight and frosty; fear must remain.

House nodded to Cornelius and the Ames kid, then strolled to the wet bar. He poured himself a Bacardi over ice, then added a twist of lime. He slammed it back fast, then poured himself another to sip slow. Satisfied, he drew a cigar from the case in his inner coat pocket, clipped the end with his teeth, and braced it between his lips. Timmons was there to light him and he drew a deep drag, savoring the tobacco.

"Everything copacetic this evening, sir?" Cornelius rumbled from his desk. His eyes never rose from the figures he was walking Ames through, line by line, explaining the coded annotations for graft payments and hand-outs.

"Cool as can be, Cornelius," House said, stripping off his coat and taking a seat in his favorite chair. "Working late, I see."

"The boy's a fast study," Cornelius said, suggesting young Ames as if he weren't there. "Figured why stop when he's still sharp?"

"I like that," House said, smiling at the boy and thinking that he should watch him carefully. Eager beavers and quick studies could be boons, but they could also get ambitious fast. Yessir, he'd have to watch him *real* close.

The door to the suite opened and Wash entered, followed by the two new girls from the cat rooms, one a long-legged Latina with wide hips and firm, pomegranate tits; the other a small but curvy Dominican the color of a Brazil nut shell.

"Ladies," House said, smiling. "Hope I wasn't interrupting anything?"

Both smiled a little, shook their heads, and lowered their eyes. Did they not speak English? "Parlay vous? Habla Englés?"

He got non-committal yeses from each. House rose and strode to them. He towered over both, making him feel a little like a dirty old man but not caring. The Dominica would do fine on her knees. The Rica's long legs were built to be shock-absorbers: she'd be on top.

Glory, glory. He smiled at the thought.

Then, just as he reached out to stroke the latina's long, dark hair, there was a rending crash and the room was invaded by a walloping wall of cold night air. The cards stormed off the table. Cornelius cursed as his books fluttered and an inkwell tipped, staining the ledgers.

As House turned toward the commotion, he saw objects flying out of the cold night air, arcing left and right.

Grenades! he thought, then one of the objects hit the floor by his boys playing cards, two more smacked Wash and Timmons, and a fourth shattered on his right, near Cornelius and the Ames kid. House heard a sound like shattering, hard-baked clay, and the room was filled with a storm of crazy blue and red lights.

His boys at the card table fell in heaps, all now wrapped in diaphanous blue flames. Their breath plumed in what seemed a shroud of almost visible cold air, and they screamed and cried and shuddered with the bone-deep chill. Ditto Cornelius and Ames behind the desk: the blue flames had them, and they cried out like children for their mammies, curling in on themselves, screaming about the cold—the penetrating, crushing *cold*.

He looked to Wash and Timmons. Their fate was separate, but equal. Red flames engulfed them but did not seem to burn them—at least not outwardly. Still, they flopped and writhed and screamed. Their eyes squeezed out tears and their hands gnarled arthritically and they screamed to wake the dead. It burned, they said. It burned, *Christ, how it burned!*

House heard something amid the howl of the wind, then: the flames didn't just burn or freeze—*they spoke*. They moaned and they wailed, as though they were full of unquiet spirits; shame and dread and raw, elemental fear.

What the fuck is this? House wondered.

The girls screamed behind him. House ignored them and turned toward the shattered windows again, looking for the intruder.

And he found him.

The cold night wind drove right into House's face and he had to blink against it for a moment, but when he saw clearly, he saw a shadowy figure standing near the now-shattered picture windows; saw the glint of something hard, black, and oiled in his gloved hands, leveled right at him, at House. Heaters. Colt .45's by the look. Their barrels yawned like twin tunnels in a mountainside.

It was the Hoodoo Man; the Witch Doctor; the one who'd taken out the gun car just a few nights previous. Top hat; skull face; natty tangle of dreads; long black coat; serpentine red scarf—the whole shebang, just as poor, dumb Wooley had described him.

The Cemetery Man smiled under his spook paint.

The wind died. House heard the girls behind him, still screaming, babbling prayers in their native tongues. "Shut your traps!" he barked, and they tried, but their fear was too great. They kept muttering their prayers, and he supposed that was the best they could do.

"Solomon House," said the Cemetery Man.

House answered. "You owe me a window."

"You owe Harlem a lot more than that," the Cemetery Man growled.

"You couldn't use the front door?" House asked.

"'Fraid you might've shrugged me off," the stranger said. His voice sounded like a file drawn slowly over rusty iron in some deep, dark prison cell.

"Well, here I am, Hoodoo Man," House said, still puffing on his cigar, determined to show this son of a bitch no fear. "What've you got to say?"

The stranger lowered his guns a little, his whole stance seeming to relax. "First question: you the one planted the curse engine at the Queen Bee's?"

House felt his face flush. *How the hell... ?*

"What if I was?" House said. "What business is it of yours? You on her dime?"

"Ain't on anybody's dime," the stranger said. "People hereabouts need somebody to look out for their interests. That's me."

"Queen Bee don't need another gun watching out for her interests," House said. He was closer now. The stranger smelled like stale cigars, burnt rum, and coalfires. He got an idea and reached for the inner pocket of his coat.

The Cemetery Man's right hand drifted up with lightning speed. There was a click as he thumbed back the hammer on his Colt and leveled the deep, dark barrel right between House's eyes.

"Care for a cigar, Baron?" House offered, opening his coat and showing the stranger the case. "Maybe a swig of rum?"

"Ain't here for offerings," the stranger said. "I'm here for a short, sweet parlay."

"Well, then, parlay. And get the fuck outta my roost."

The Cemetery Man smiled under his fright face. "Queen

Bee's trying to put a lot of people to work and put some money in colored pockets; *legit* money, more or less. Your little tiff with her does the people on her payroll no service—"

"They could just as easily be on *my* payroll and make out," House said.

"Well, that barely matters now, because whatever seed you sowed in the basement thereabouts is spreading. It'll blight the whole neighborhood soon."

House smiled, satisfied. "The people up that way flock to her, they're *her* hands and *my* enemies, see? So if my dealings with her trickle down... fuck 'em. They had a choice. They made the wrong one."

"That ain't the answer I'm after," the Cemetery Man said.

"Fuck what you're after," House snarled. "You gonna dig a canoe in my dome, Hoodoo Man, or are you gonna stand there in the draft stinkin' up my parlor all night?"

"One more time," the Cemetery Man said, looking as though he wanted to pull the trigger but couldn't. "You gonna call off that hex on the supper club? Leave the Queen Bee's operation be?"

"One more time," House said. "The Queen Bee and all her little drones get just what they deserve if they stand in my way. Now, blow, spook. And don't come back, else I'll see you planted *in* the cemetery 'stead of guarding it."

He saw fury under the white painted face; saw the gloved finger tensing on the trigger; saw the frustration in the vigilante's eyes.

Why can't he just shoot me? House wondered. *He wants to. Why don't he?*

"Next time you see me's the end," the stranger said, lowering his pistol. "This is all the warning I was required to give you."

With that, he turned, mounted the window sill, and launched himself into the night. House hurried forward to get a good look at the Cemetery Man's escape. Four stories below, the baron landed lightly on the peaked roof of a little two-floor tenement, then slid down the slope of the roof and leapt again, disappearing into a deep, dark alleyway.

House heard Timmons and Wash. They were on their feet

again, still shaking, looking beaten though there wasn't a mark on them. "Boss?" they both said, like sleep-eyed children.

"Quit gapin'," he snarled. "Clean this mess up." He turned and marched toward the door, stopping before he got there. "Timmons, what time is it?"

Timmons, gape-mouthed, pulled out his pocket watch. "Going on eleven-thirty, boss."

"Enough of this," House muttered, and drew a long, soothing drag on his cigar. He blew the smoke out slowly, and it wreathed round his head like a diaphanous crown. "Get Chuck and Willie on the phone. They should be over at the Eight Ball."

"Boss?"

"Do it," House roared, and Timmons did.

XX

Willie and Chuck *were* at the Eight Ball Billiard Bar, eyes on the back room card games. When House reached Willie, he gave orders: grab a dozen good trigger- and fuse-men, split the party in two, and hit the Queen Bee's smaller policy banks—the ones on 134th and 146th Streets. They were fronted by a laundry and a hardware store, respectively, and they would be easy targets. The Queen'd never expect hits that deep in her territory this late at night. The key was to move fast and hit hard; lead spray if there were bankers present; firebombs if the places looked dead. House wasn't after money now: he was out to hurt her. He didn't give a flying fuck if every dollar stored in those joints went up in smoke; he just wanted the flames to cook the Queen Bee's striped tail and make her think twice about crossing him.

And the Hoodoo Man—well, if he didn't work for her, he'd certainly assured that she'd bear the brunt of Solomon House's fury. See if he came to Madame Marie's rescue. That would flush him out and show what side he was on, right quick.

So Willie and Chuck swept up their gangs, improvised hasty Molotov Cocktails and dug up a couple of old potato-masher style grenades from the Great War, and off they went into the night.

Somewhere around one in the morning, sleepy Harlemites in the quiet tenements around the uptown bolito banks awoke to a storm of gunshots, the music of shattering glass, and the big crescendos of grenades popping and gasoline cocktails fueling hungry fires. The fire brigade was called out and the fires were doused come early morning, but already the word was out. Everyone knew what the laundry and the hardware store had fronted for. Everyone knew that the cash therein had probably gone to ash. But most importantly, everyone knew who owned the fronts and the policy they banked.

And now they knew she had an enemy that was not to be trifled with.

12

Dr. Dub Corveaux was already well into a full slate of patients when Miss Fralene Farnes appeared mid-morning and begged Cecile for just a few minutes of the doctor's time. Dub was happy to see her. He was sweet on her, he feared. But that sweetness went a little sour when he invited her into the examination room and she obliged, looking more dutiful than eager.

She started in on him almost immediately, not even offering a hello, or a how-are-you. "You've heard the news, I suppose?" Fralene asked.

He imagined he knew what she meant but he wanted to be certain. "That news being?"

"A laundry and a family hardware store firebombed in the night? Talk of an all-out gang war? No one was hurt this time, thank God, but that might have just been dumb luck!"

Dub tried to play it light. He grinned. "You in a gang you didn't tell me about, Miss Farnes?"

"This isn't funny, Dr. Corveaux," Fralene answered, clearly not amused. "This could escalate quickly. This is bad news, and you know it."

Dub nodded soberly. Clearly, she wasn't in the mood for levity. "Bad news for bolito bosses like the Queen Bee and Papa House."

"Bad news for everyone!" Fralene persisted. "If gangsters like that Merriwether woman and Solomon House start a war, then you know damn well innocent people will suffer! *They're* the ones who get caught in the crossfire! *They're* the ones whose children get recruited as soldiers! *They're* the ones whose businesses get firebombed and whose incomes get taxed for protection from these, these, these—"

She couldn't find the right word. Dub considered offering one, but he figured that would just make her more angry. She was in quite the twist this morning. He tried to calm her a little with cold, hard facts. "Somebody's business gets firebombed in the course of a gang war, ten to one, they fronted for a policy bank, and you know that."

"And *why* did they front?" Fralene said, holding her ground. "Probably because someone strong-armed them into giving up part of their precious store space and soiling their good reputation in order to have a squeaky-clean façade—"

Dub couldn't listen to any more. "That's naïve, Fralene, and you know it. I can't speak for Solomon House, but from all I've heard, Maybelle Meriwether doesn't strong-arm anyone into fronting her policy banks. She's usually *invited* in. Or she owns the business outright. The 'innocent people' whose stores get firebombed or who end up strong-armed for protection money are willing participants, not victims."

He wanted to drive that point home, so he said it again, perhaps a little too harshly. "Get that through your head, Miss Anne. There are *no* victims."

"I told you not to call me that," she said through gritted teeth.

He sighed. This was going nowhere. "What did you come here for, Fralene? I've got patients—"

"My uncle's hosting a dinner tonight for some community leaders. Councilmen; teachers and clergy; some of Harlem's most powerful businessmen—"

"If they're not in with the Queen Bee or Papa House, they're not too powerful," Dub muttered.

"I'd like you to be there," Fralene said.

Dub knew that was impossible. He was already eager for sundown; sure that tonight would be the reckoning. He'd begged the *lwa* for some sort of full-bore *juju* to put to use against the curse engine. No doubt he'd have little time to spare. Tonight was the Queen Bee's Grand Opening, and with all that psychic energy loose, the thing in the drain would be active, firing on all cylinders.

"Impossible," he said.

"Why is that?" she asked.

"I've got plans tonight," Dub answered, then suddenly realized that he hadn't constructed a solid alibi. What could he tell her? *I've got to play body-host to a lesser African deity and do battle with the infernal powers loosed by Papa House in the Queen Bee's new supper club. Could be a long night. Don't wait up for me.*

"What sort of plans?" she demanded.

"None of your business," Dub snapped, and regretted it almost immediately, because he could see it hurt her. He carried on, trying to rationalize his way out of it. "Look, Fralene, I admire your concern, I do... but someone like you isn't going to do a damn thing to change the fact that there are people like Maybelle Meriwether and Solomon House running the show in this world. So long as people want booze, games, and whores, *they'll be there.* So long as people want to throw nickels and dimes at a daily lottery in the hopes of winning a week's worth of groceries or enough scratch for a new car, *they'll be there.* And as long as white cops and white crooks and white politicians control bigger rackets with bigger money and bigger ambitions, then our folk are gonna be stuck looking to the Queen Bees and the Papa Houses of the world for their *own* sort of protection and fair-dealing. It ain't right, but it's the way of things. All your do-gooding isn't gonna chase their sort out of Harlem."

She stared at him, and he had the terrible feeling that he'd never see her again. Perhaps that would be for the best. Perhaps, with his own slate of nocturnal activities, he didn't need to be getting involved with anyone so... so... *pure.* So sure of herself and her place and purpose in the world. That wasn't him—all evidence to the contrary.

"I can't believe what I'm hearing."

He shrugged. "I'm sorry to disappoint you."

"All the words I've read penned by your hand, published under your name... everything you've just said flies in the face of those words."

He shrugged again. "I've written a lot, and no doubt I'll write more. I write when the muse is on me, and I write about whatever's troubling me at a given time. That doesn't mean I'm living my poem or my essay, Fralene. It just means I had a thought and wanted to share it."

"You're just like one of *them*," she said, and he knew by the venom in the statement that she meant *white*; *bourgeois*; self-absorbed and unconcerned. "You're just here to leech off this community, make your fortune, and retire to some neat little clapboard community out on the island, or into the lazy practice of some country doctor—"

"Last I checked," Dub said, feeling his ire rising, "healers aren't leeches, Miss Farnes."

She turned and opened the door. "Just because you do no harm doesn't mean you do any good. Afternoon, doctor."

Before he could say something, she'd slammed the door, and he could hear her heavy heels clicking on the floor of the hallway, shrinking, carrying her right to the front door.

Hell.

XX

The Queen Bee sat in her favorite seat, on the dais, facing the stage. The club was a hive of activity around her, but there was a muted, nervous silence that belied the activity; a sense of dread that turned what should have been eager mirth and light work into dirge and drudgery. She smoked a cigarette and stared at a stage crowded with band podiums and lit for a night's entertainment. The band would probably show up around noon to start warming up, but she guessed that the pall on the place would make their "Muskrat Ramble" sound like "A March to the Scaffold."

Gideon approached, mounted the dais, padded near like a caged panther. He took a seat adjacent to her, pulled out a cigarette of his own, lit up, and puffed placidly.

"Well? What's it gonna be?" he asked.

"What else can it be?" she countered.

"We could postpone."

"Like hell," she said. "We've got a full slate of local lights and downtown high-rollers. We're set. They're coming. We can't back out now. We postpone, those doors *never* open. It'll only get worse."

"The booze turned up."

She smirked. "Did Officer Heaney and company get their commission?"

"They did."

"One of these days," the Queen Bee said, "I'd like you to deliver his fat head to me. I think it'd make a fine foot stool."

Gideon smiled a little. "That it might."

"Hell," the Queen Bee said, and stabbed out her only half-smoked cigarette in a nearby ash tray.

"Maybe nothing'll go wrong," Gideon said.

The Queen Bee turned slowly and studied him. "It will," she said. "You know it will."

He nodded. "I know it will."

"We've just got to be ready," she said.

"For what?" he asked.

She shrugged now. "Anything."

"What do we do about the banks?"

"We've got more," she said, and lit another cigarette, as though she'd already forgotten her last.

"Those hits were a challenge," Gideon pressed. "We've gotta answer them."

"*This* is our answer," the Queen Bee said, suggesting the club around them. "Aces & Eights opens. Papa House can't stop us."

"Maybe he can," Gideon said after a long pause. "Either way, though, we can't just ignore those bank-hits. We lost too much money to just pretend—"

"If we buck up guards on the banks this evening, or send more to hit House, we'll be light hereabouts. We need all hands on deck this evening, in case things get hairy here."

"We could get help," Gideon countered. "Contract some hands outta St. John's? Some of those strivers from over Sugar Hill way?"

"Can't trust 'em," the Queen Bee said. "Besides, those Sugar Hill boys are nothin' but swells and queers. We need muscle tonight, not hustlers."

Gideon lost his patience, and she couldn't blame him. She was being childish and sulky—and she knew it. "We've gotta trust *somebody!*" Gideon snarled. "We've gotta start making friends and consolidating territory before House makes bigger and more brazen moves. You know it's comin'. If you do nothin' to get ready for it, you're failin' everybody! *These* people! *This* place! *The boys!* And *me!*"

That shook her out of her reverie. She turned and stared at Gideon. He leaned forward now, elbows on his knees, hands clasped as if in prayer, but his face was not one of supplication; it was one of challenge.

"Don't fade on me, Queen Bee. I need you, and all these people need you. It's gonna get worse before it gets better. *So what?* You ain't a quitter, you're a fighter. So fight, woman, and don't waste my time sulking like the little princess I know you are not."

She studied the room; the warm bodies drifting through it, laying table-cloths and place settings, placing fresh-clipped flowers in table vases and dusting the deep red runners round the stage and on the proscenium. She drew a long, deep drag on her cigarette.

"You think that's what it'll come to? Tying ourselves to those street punks in St. John's? Bank-rolling those pinstriped peacocks up by Sugar Hill?"

"If we don't, House will. Numbers count."

"Go get 'em then," the Queen Bee said. "And when you come back to me with more hands, bring a plan with you."

He smiled crookedly. "I've got a few already."

The Queen Bee smiled at her majordomo. "Why does that not surprise me?"

XX

Papa House studied the fat brown kid in the dim light of the warehouse, doing his best to melt the edges of his chocolate-colored skin with his eyes. "You straight on this, Calvin?"

The kid nodded emphatically, and Papa half-feared the instructions would come tumbling out through his gaping mouth. "Show up at the back door with the crate," Calvin blathered, "tell 'em it's an emergency delivery; put it wherever they tell me; hightail it out within five minutes or I'm toast."

"Fair enough," Papa said, nodding.

They were in the Foree Imports and Exports Warehouse; the one closest to the Queen Bee's turf, fronting the river; the one where House kept Napoleon the Alligator in his muddy crib.

Calvin seemed to be thinking something over. "Awful small bomb, sir."

Papa frowned. The kid's dim brain made ticking noises nearly as loud as that on the explosive timer. Where did he get off making such judgments? "You tellin' me my business, boy?"

"No sir," the kid said, shaking his head. "Just wanna do right by you, is all. My brother, Collie, he used to make bombs, sir. Planted 'em in Klan houses whenever we could find 'em. They was good bombs. Blew up big and bright."

"You your brother?"

The kid seemed to think about that for a moment. "No, sir."

"You make bombs as good as *he* did?"

Again, a long consideration. "No, sir." His answer came with a screwed-up face, as if the boy were insulted House would even suggest it.

"Then stop beatin' your gums," House growled. "You do as you're told, you hoof it. Savvy?"

"Yes, sir. Clear as a bell."

"You play this right, Calvin, you's and your mama's rent is set. Six months, square."

Calvin nodded again and House decided he'd done all he could. It was a simple errand and Calvin was a regular delivery driver for the Queen; he should be able to carry off his role in the night's proceedings and get out without trouble.

Still, he was dim. House looked to Wash and Timmons as the three of them marched away to thread a path back through the warehouse, followed by others—gunmen, hired and regulars, all gearing up for a turkey shoot.

"Best you could find?" House asked, meaning Calvin.

Wash shrugged. "He's a safe face around the club. Likewise, figured if we lose him in the blast, no great loss."

House nodded, puffing on his cigar. "Fair enough."

XX

Evening was nearly gone and night on the precipice, ready to fall. Dr. Dub Corveaux knelt in his fourth floor peristyle, surrounded by the *lwa*, receiving instructions. His guns were loaded, and he had belted up nine *govi* grenades

So his weapons were ready; all that remained was to be blessed by the *lwa*.

And to get horsed.

Ain't no easy thing, Legba was saying, *drawin' out bad* wanga *of this sort. You gotta work some serious* maji; *all alone; without us.*

Dub was impatient. "Just give me what I need," he insisted. "And tell me how to use it."

First, Erzulie purred, *whatever you're gonna draw's gotta be bound; like a tourniquet to keep venom in the bit limb and away from the heart. For that you make a circle with the* Petro Packet.

Dub saw the *packet* she referred to; a long-necked gourd bedecked with beads and a rainbow of colored threads, stopped with a cork. He lifted the *packet*, found it heavy and full, then slipped it into one of the deeper pouches within his coat.

"So I make a circle—"

Then set it aflame, Erzulie reminded.

"—then set it aflame. Protective proscriptions. Basic magic one-oh-one."

Make the circle big enough to contain the quarry, Erzulie said.

"Of course," Dub said.

And yourself, she added.

"I'll be *inside* the circle? The *flaming* circle? *With* the beast?"

Ain't no other way, Erzulie answered.

Dub sighed. "Fair enough. Then?"

You got it bound, Legba said, *you gotta flush it out. Make it manifest. That's what the mummified dog's for.*

Dub studied the cluttered altar, saw the shriveled, dead black pup that Legba suggested, and lifted it. The little corpse felt like a wad of crumpled paper in his hands, and just as hollow. He carefully stowed it in another side pocket of his long black coat.

You place the pup on the hex engine, Legba instructed, *then annoint it with some of your blood. That should wake the beast up and draw it out. hungry. Full-on.*

"Okay," Dub said, nodding.

Be ready, Erzulie interjected. *What springs forth when you bloody it won't be pretty.*

"I can handle it," Dub said, eager to be on his way. "Once the circle's lit and the thing's drawn out, then what?"

Then you kill it, Ogou said, and Dub could almost hear the bemused chuckle in the war *lwa's* voice.

"Understood," Dub said, trying not to let his frustration sound through. "Will standard lead-loads do, or do I need something else? Iron? Silver?"

Silence. He waited. None of them replied.

"Well?"

Still no answer.

"Give me *something*," he said testily.

It ain't our maji, Legba huffed, as if insulted.

"*I'm* your *maji*," Dub snarled. "*I'm* doin' *your* dirty work, and you ain't givin' me the tools to do it. You want your people protected, you gotta give me more than just a shield to hide behind and a horn to call my quarry with.

"You gotta give me a sword."

A long silence followed.

He's ready, Ogou finally muttered.

Put that in his hands, there'll be hell to pay, Erzulie purred. *Ain't there another way, Ogou?*

Thing ain't gonna flee for Florida water and incense, 'Zulie, Ogou countered.

He's got guns, Legba whined.

Lead's like flies to the Furies, Ogou argued. *He'll do little more than piss it off.*

"I've got work to do," Dub snarled.

And then, as if in answer, the air seemed to open before him. He smelled brimstone and coal-smoke, and something heavy and metallic thumped on the dirt floor before him. Dub, having closed his eyes to palaver with the *lwa*, opened them. Before him lay what looked like a long, broad knife in a beaten leather scabbard.

A machete.

He laid one hand on the grip, the other on the scabbard,

prepared to loose the blade. He heard Ogou in his ear, as if the god of war stood just over his shoulder.

That's my saber, the war *lwa* said. *The Machette d'Ogou. She's thirsty, doc. You loose her in the night, she's gonna want guilty blood before dawn.*

Guilty human *blood.*

"So you're tellin' me this'll do against the Furies," Dub said, "but I still gotta give it some *human* blood before the night's done?"

Just so, Legba said gravely.

"And if she doesn't get it?" Dub asked, still waiting to draw the machete.

If she don't get blood from the guilty, said Ogou, *she'll take it from the innocent. If you sheathe her before she's tasted it, she'll put the hunger in you, and you'll never be rid of it, long as you live.*

"Can I see her safe hereabouts?" Dub asked, sure he could hear the machete cooing at him, purring inside its scabbard like a woman awaiting his touch; eager to be undressed and caressed.

Just this once, said Ogou.

Dub drew the machete from the scabbard.

When it touched the air, the blade caught fire.

13

Sooner or later, for everyone, the time comes to jump or walk. That time came for Aces & Eights, and the joint jumped. By seven 'o clock, the dining room was filling, the first courses were served, and the band took the stage to start the night's entertainment. They opened with a piece called "Minor Swing," and it swung like a juke joint Jezebel with dislocated hips. Waiters careened among the tables and chairs, bearing their trays of seemingly-innocuous soft drinks (usually spiked with something from the secret bar in the larder), cigarette girls with long legs clad in complimentary fishnet hose and big bright smiles made rounds, and anyone standing lower stage right, staring out on the crowd, would note a curious fact about the ever-denser sea of faces filling the club.

They were all sorts: black, white, yellow, and everything in between. In one breathless, deft fell swoop, Harlem had integrated, and almost no one had noticed.

The Queen Bee had that view of the proceedings when she emerged from the stage right corridor into the dining room. It did her heart a small measure of good, and she allowed herself a smile and a moment of warmth.

But there were some patrons she wasn't so happy to see.

Harry Flood, for instance, had a table beside Teddy Michansky. High-rollers, sure, but they were predators with their eye on the place, and their beer baron bulldog, Dolph Storms, sat nearby looking just as greasy and unwashed as the day he'd tried to strong-arm Madame Marie into buying his suds.

There were none of the old greaser Dago families represented—they didn't go in for jungle bunny swing or jungle bunny company—but some of the young turks were on hand. The

Queen Bee recognized Carmine Dicicco, a young slick she'd heard word of, marked by an olive face, blue eyes, and red hair. Just to judge on the eyes and hair, he looked more Mick than wop, but the skin tone was right, and so was the air: Old World cool; a certain nonchalance and stillness. She could see instantly that the kid had quality and she made a mental note that she'd have to track him more carefully.

Butch Vena—who was Guinea by birth but hung with the Irish—and Ralph Mandolare, from the Bronx Italians, were also on hand. They were small-timers looking for angles to play— the sort of men who'd never rise above captain rank, though they probably sported hard-ons when they dreamed at night of bigger and better things. Little matter. Their presence here, like the presence of all the others, made one thing clear: there were parties interested in acquiring an interest in the club. They'd try to charm and finesse her if they thought it was a success; they'd try to strong-arm and terrify her if they thought it was a slam-dunk. She told herself to remember that: the harder they pushed to partner, the more attractive the club was to them. If they came at her hard in the weeks to come, she knew she was doing something right.

And she'd hold her own. No matter how hard they pushed, she wouldn't sell even the smallest interest. This place was gonna stay in her hands—black hands—and it was gonna put money in black pockets and feed black families. That was that.

So she put on her best cathouse moll's grin, shook hands, accepted kisses, laughed, welcomed and generally spread warmth and love and gaiety. All the while, the band blew hot, swaying the guests about in their seats, and the smells of hot victuals, spiked drinks, and new cigars filled the room. The Queen Bee rode a wave of frolic and good will, and for a little while, she almost forgot about the pall on the place; the furtive, benighted malignancy that seemed to drip from the rafters and seep from the walls and came oozing up out of the foundations like Texas Tea.

She *almost* forgot... until Dolph Storms slapped the waiter who delivered his tenderloin.

XX

At more or less the same moment that Dolph Storms slapped a waiter on the floor, Gideon Mann heard a terrible racket near the side stairwell just outside the cavernous kitchen and followed the commotion. Within moments, he'd come upon the deliveryman, Calvin, tangled up with a number of busboys and waiters amid a mess of fallen, shattered plates and glasses, dirty old dishwater and half-finished cocktails. The busboys were trying to clean the mess and get back on their feet. Calvin floundered wildly, trying to loose himself from the tangle, a wild look in his wide, dim eyes that suggested haste; hurry; *fear*.

Something was up. Gideon got a fistful of Calvin's collar and hauled him to his feet. The dummy blinked at him and shook his head.

"Ain't done nothin', sir!" he stammered. "Ain't done nothin'. I's just deliverin' the goods, like told. Full case! Good champagne! I did what I's s'posed to do, sir! If I could just go—"

"What're you on about, Calvin?" Gideon demanded. "Who sent champagne?"

"Son of a bitch," one of the busboys muttered, cleaning up the mess.

"Blind, deaf, and dumb," another one spat.

"Run right into us, Mr. Mann!" the third grated. "Boy, why don't you watch where you's goin'?"

"Ain't done nothin'!" Calvin kept saying. "Just deliverin' the goods, like I's told." He was yanking against Gideon's grip, eager to hit the door.

"Who signed him in?" Gideon asked the busboys.

"How the hell should we know?" one of them asked.

Gideon heard a new voice—Lyle, one of the line cooks.

"He just brought a crate in, Mr. Mann," Lyle said. "Bubbly. Had him put it back in the second larder—"

"Show me," Gideon said, and Calvin went crazy in his grip, wiggly as a feral cat.

"Aw, please, hell, sir!" he bawled. "I's just doin' as I's told! Just makin' a delivery!"

Gideon understood. He shoved Calvin into the waiting grip of the three busboys. "Hold him! Knock him out, if you got to!"

he said, and marched away. "Lyle!" he roared, "Show me the crate!"

Lyle led Gideon into the second larder, adjacent to the north stairs, pulled open the huge sliding door, and pointed at the case of champagne in question. Gideon lunged for the crate, tore off its loosely-nailed lid, and drew out four bottles at once, two in one fist, two in another.

Beneath, he saw the clunky mess of loose wiring that he hoped he wasn't going to see. He yanked out two more bottles; two more; two more—*the gizmo underneath took up the whole floor of the case!*

"Mr. Mann?" Lyle asked.

"Go help the busboys hold Calvin!" Gideon shouted, and finally tore the bomb loose from the floor of the crate. It was a jury-rigged raft of stick dynamite, electrician's tape, loose wiring, and the clacking guts of an old alarm clock. Gideon held it out before him like a hot plate, ripe for delivery on the floor, and made a bee line back through the kitchen toward the loading dock and the alleyway.

"*Out of the way!*" he roared as he raced. "*Everybody out of my way!*"

He saw terrified faces; confusion; consternation; puzzlement. He heard screams, sighs, mutters, the clack and clatter common to kitchens the world over. He moved faster, bearing the construction out before him and knowing it would do no good whatsoever. If it went here, in his hands, in the kitchen, he'd be blown to bits and Aces & Eights would lose its ass-end. He had to get it out; out into the alley way; out where it could do as little internal damage as possible.

He caromed past Calvin. The bumpkin still fought and flailed against the four pairs of hands now holding him. He screamed girlishly when Gideon came tottering forward, the bomb held out before him, as though the Queen Bee's main enforcer might make him eat the thing.

"*Aw Christ! Nosir, nosir, nosir!!!*" he sang.

Gideon cut left, toward the loading doors; toward the dock and the wide alley out back. Spare hands on their cigarette breaks at the doors saw him coming; saw the bomb; spat all sorts of curses and scattered every which way.

Gideon rushed into the open air and heaved the bomb into the alley. Just as it left his hands, he heard the old, rusty bells of the gutted alarm clock start clattering.

XX

But before all that came to pass, there remained the matter of Dolph Storms manhandling of one of the Queen Bee's servers. When she'd heard the commotion, she made for Storms's table. Storms leveled one pale, bratwursty finger at the waiter and growled in his sick, fucked up accent something about *jig, spit, steak, son of a bitch.* Madame Marie arrived and tried to keep her best hostess's smile on her face. The beer baron smelled, per usual, like a *brauhaus,* and his tuxedo hung ill on him like something untailored mounted on the wrong dress form.

"Is there a problem, Mr. Storms?" she asked. The waiter who'd gotten clipped stood at attention like a soldier, staring straight ahead. She could see he was wrestling with shame and fury. He wanted to hit Storms right back—but that wouldn't fly. Not tonight.

"This son of a bitch spit in my food," Storms said.

Madame Marie looked to the kid. "Wally?"

"No, ma'am," he responded. "I told the gentleman I did no such thing."

"You lyin' little jig fagot! I can see it on your face! I saw you as you came out the back hall—"

His voice rose, carrying over the hoot and holler of the band on stage. Madame Marie bent nearer. "Mr. Storms, would you like another plate?"

"I wanna see this little shit whipped like he oughta be! Make it part of the evening's entertainment! Liven this place up!" He smiled crookedly, saw a pale-faced downtowner staring sideways at him, and shot to his feet, lunging. "What're you lookin' at, fucko!?!"

Somewhere nearby, a lightbulb in a wall sconce exploded with a corkish *pop.*

Things would spiral out of control—she felt it coming—unless she could get them nailed down fast.

Harry Flood approached then—a broad little fireplug of a man, well-groomed and neatly put together. This was Storms's boss; the de facto head of the Irish racketeers out of Chelsea. Marie knew he'd be cordial—he was a good businessman—but he was also not to be crossed. He took a place beside Madame Marie and crossed his hands before him. "Is there a problem here, Madame?"

"Mr. Flood, good to see you."

"Wouldn't miss it," the Irishman said, not a trace of brogue in his measured voice. The Queen Bee knew the Flood Brothers came off a boat when they were kids. How long did Harry have to practice to lose his Belfast clip? "Nice place, madame. You know how to pick 'em."

"My thanks," she said.

"Christ a'mighty, Harry," Storms howled, rolling his watery eyes. "Where do you get off, talking sweet to a yellow dame like this?"

"Dolph," Flood said, maintaining his permanent cool. He had a cigarette clamped between his fingers, and he poked it toward his bulldog to punctuate his statements. "We're guests this evening. Try to show a little grace, eh?"

"Grace, *hell!*" Storms howled. "This black bastard spit in my—"

"You can have a new plate, or you can have a refund and be on your way," Madame Marie offered. "What'll it be, sir?"

Storms was on his feet now, towering over her, blowing his beer, brat, and sen-sen breath in her face. "And who the fuck are *you*, Granny Bluegums? Talkin' to me that way?"

Marie shivered. Had the temperature dropped? She took a quick look around; noted a number of the lady guests in their off-the-shoulder numbers drawing up their purely-for-show mink and fox fur stoles as they shivered.

They felt it too. The chill.

Despite her relief at having Harry Flood to help her wrangle a gorilla like Storms, Marie felt a new fear. Something *else* was happening. Something *wrong*. She saw the eyes of all the patrons on her; felt their fear; their nerves; their growing restlessness.

Then she heard Harry Flood, speaking beside her, still berating his cohort.

"She's the owner and operator of this establishment," Flood said coolly. "She's your host, Dolph, and you're my guest here this evening. You will show her the proper respect, or you can go enjoy an evening elsewhere."

Storms glared at his boss, teeth bared in something between a snarl and a grin—the Queen Bee couldn't tell which. "This is how it's goin' down, Harry? You're sidin' with a nigger against me?"

"This isn't siding, Dolph," Flood said. "This is being a good guest. You wanna roar, go do it in one of your own places—one of those Yorkville chophouses that serve your piss and let you walk all over them. Here, you're on *my* tab, and you're in *her* joint; you'll show some goddamn respect or you'll leave."

Storms snapped his fingers at the thick Bavarian moll who sat opposite him and she shot to her feet without a word. "Then I'm leavin'." He turned to Madame Marie, poking a finger in her face. "You're on the shit list, lady."

"Everyone's on your shit list, Dolph," Flood muttered. "Get out of here before you make any more of a fool of yourself."

Storms yanked his date away from the table and marched toward the entryway. Just before reaching the foyer, he lunged toward a potted palm nearly as tall as he was and toppled it, spilling its earth and fertilizer on the polished hardwood floor.

Just as the palm's big pot shattered, a pair of ellipsoidal lights above the band sparked and exploded with pops as loud as gunshots. The band's groove faltered. Some of the folks seated down front shrank and ducked, as though someone had opened fire.

Storms saw this, thought it a wonderful, well-timed coincidence, and laughed all the way out the door, pointing and grabbing his belly like a school-yard bully who'd just shoved a skinny kid into a puddle of mud. As his laughter faded, Marie noticed something more.

Another fight had broken out down front, this one between two white men in tuxedos. They were well-scrubbed and no doubt perfumed, but they'd come to fisticuffs nonetheless.

"Mr. Flood," the Queen Bee began, by way of excusing herself.

"Come around later," he said softly. "When things are under control."

She moved away from him, toward the rumpus. A fist flew and one of the white men reeled. The ladies at the table with them screamed.

Behind her, something shattered and someone else screamed: a man this time. She jerked toward the commotion and saw a fat old Negro in a fine suit singing Dixie, holding aloft a bleeding hand. His drink glass had, apparently, exploded in his grip.

The band lost its beat—or rather, found a new one. The jazzmen in their dinner jackets looked to the drummer on his dais. He hunched over his kit, face straining, as though under some alien influence. The veins in his temples and throat throbbed, his eyes narrowed, and his teeth gnashed. He pounded out a new beat: primitive, relentless, arrhythmic—blackest midnight in 5/4 time.

What the hell is happening? the Queen Bee wondered. But she already knew.

Then there was a sudden, shattering thunderclap from somewhere out back—so loud that it rocked the building. The drop lights swayed and the crystal sang.

Everyone shot to their feet and stampeded like a herd of maddened buffalo for the exit.

XX

The bomb blew mid-air, at the crest of its arc, after Gideon heaved it. Gideon was thrown backward a good ten feet by the blast.

It hurt. He couldn't breathe and his ears rang. But he was alive. Blessedly alive.

In moments, all sorts of kitchen folk surrounded him, alternately yanking him to his feet and encouraging him to sit down.

"Where is he?" he shouted. "Where is that little bastard?"

He tore through the crowd of onlookers and concerned faces, trying to locate the bomber. There he was: Calvin. Slack-faced, melon-headed Calvin. He fought the grip of those three busboys and Lyle the line cook, screaming, crying, a dark spot on the crotch of his coveralls where he'd pissed himself.

"I's just doin' as I's told!" he screamed. "Please, sir! Please, sir! Please, sir! Papa said he'd cut the rent! I had to pay the rent!"

Gideon burst through the cordon of onlookers. He tore Calvin from the busboys' collective grasp and punched him square. He felt Calvin's front teeth give under the weight of his fist, and his nose collapsed with a squelchy crunch. Calvin fell, but Gideon held him. Blinded by shock and by the gout of blood and snot from his broken nose, Calvin cried out of a mouthful of broken teeth.

Gideon dragged the fat feeb across the kitchen floor toward one of the prep stations—a chopping block where the raw beef and poultry was prepared.

Nobody seemed to understand what was happening. They just watched, curious and still in shock from the explosion.

Calvin kept screaming, trying to wipe the blood from his eyes, unable to break Gideon's grip.

Gideon heaved him against the chopping block. Calvin's head connected with a hollow thump, and down he went, moaning and reaching for his thumped noggin.

Gideon felt a strange satisfaction. He'd *heard* the hollow thump of Calvin's skull. His hearing was already returning. Good news.

But business was in the offing. He snatched up a big meat cleaver still tacky with beef gristle, lifted it high, and brought it whistling down.

When the blade cleaved Calvin's thick melon skull, he heard that too.

XX

The Queen Bee fled the rush and backed herself toward the windows at the front of the club. As the patrons clotted in the doorway to the single front exit, she turned and tore back the high, sheer curtains on the front windows to get a good look at the street below. A few trickled out at first, then more, and finally, like a dam giving way, something seemed to burst, and a glut of well-dressed bodies burst forth in a panic, flooding the street. Screaming, they scattered and collided. Some fell, trampled in the stampede.

For just a moment, the Queen Bee thought that someone had called the cops: there were a number of black sedans fanned out in a loose formation across Lenox Avenue, all attended by small detachments of men in coats and hats.

And masks. Simple, loose face masks, like those worn by desperados in a western flicker-show.

Then the Queen Bee realized that the men on the street were all carrying guns.

Someone gave an order and they opened fire on the fleeing customers.

The Queen Bee turned away from the window. She needed to sit down. Her head swam and her knees felt miles away. She'd sit, and she'd wait, and when Gideon found her, she'd ask for his piece and she'd shoot herself. Most of the time, she was a fighter; a scrapper; she took shit from no man and she turned lemons into lemonade. But this was her breaking point. She gave up. She wanted a bullet in the brain, and she wanted it with all expediency.

She barely made it three steps, though. Before she could take a seat and wait for someone to come and relieve her suffering with a bullet, she fainted dead away.

XX

Harry Flood knew that the imperative of the moment was to stay upright. His bodyguards Mikey and Doyle, made that a little easier but they were caught in the crush, too. Once on the street, Flood had been eager to break from the crowd. He pressed himself back against the front face of the building next door to the club and waited for the panicked patrons to disburse.

But then the shooting started.

Flood tugged Mikey and Doyle in front of him and crouched, back to the brownstone's brick façade, the two big Irishmen towering before him like bulwarks, guns drawn.

The crowd circled and seethed like a swarm of ants after someone had stepped in their pile. Machine gun chatter and the boom-chaka-boom of shotguns roared in the night. There were screams, but from Flood's hiding place, it seemed as though the people in their evening finery barely understood. When the guns sang, those that didn't fall to the hail changed direction and collided with more of their fleeing fellows. It was a mess; a turkey shoot.

It had to be House. Flood cursed the West Indian warlord and gave him due respect all in the same breath. That was a helluva play: set off a bomb out back; chase the clientele out front; wait with loaded weapons; open fire.

Ten to one, the bastard wasn't trying to slaughter the lot, or even pick out strategic targets. No, he was just doing his damndest to make the Queen Bee's business tank in night one. Nobody would patronize any supper club she opened now, thinking that House or some other player uptown might cause a ruckus of this sort and use the patrons for target practice.

The man had balls as big as meteors; Flood had to give him that.

And he made a mental note to see the bastard killed if he could: wet works of this sort—big, loud, messy, and non-particular—were bad for business. House had to be silenced, for good.

The guns kept snarling. A knot of scattering Anglos in furs and pricy coats hit the pavement not a stone's throw from where Flood hid, their blood steaming in the cool night. Flood heard someone in House's retinue laughing behind his outlaw mask, urging fire this way and that—*Down them slicks! Take out that bitch in the fox-fur! Bottle of rum if you can get one of the fellas to use one of the ladies as a human shield!*

Fucking savages!

A clatter of machine gun fire and Mikey withered, crumpling to the pavement. Flood immediately drew himself sideward, using big, broad Doyle as his main shield now.

"Boss, we gotta skin!" Doyle shouted, crouching lower, returning fire with his Smith & Wesson six shooter.

"Up the avenue!" Flood shouted above the racket. "Bust into that pharmacy about a block north! Tell me when the fire goes after a crowd running away from us!"

Doyle nodded. Flood waited, breathing deep, preparing himself.

Then he saw a shadow on a brownstone façade across the street detach itself, and come plummeting down, landing hard on the roof of one of the parked gun-cars. The windshield and windows shattered. The gunmen nearest the car shrank and cursed.

Flood blinked.

It looked like another Negro, but this one was dressed for Halloween: a long, black coat; a flowing, serpentine red scarf; a scowling skull-painted face under a mess of natty black braids and a top hat.

Not a second after landing, the skull-faced Negro's hands shot forth and tossed something into the midst of the gunmen. They were small and round, and Flood thought that they were grenades. But then they burst in the midst of separate, closely-spaced knots of gunmen, and Flood saw explosions of spectral blue and red flames, and heard the gunmen screaming and falling to the pavement, and wondered what grenades made those colors. Flood couldn't see the men engulfed in those flames, but he heard their screams. And their screams didn't stop.

Then the stranger had a heater in each hand—twin .45's, black finish, gleaming in the darkness. As House's gunmen turned their smoking barrels on the stranger, the stranger put those heaters to use.

The .45's spat fat tongues of flame, fanning a lightning-quick barrage into the nearest gunmen. Before that group had fallen, the Witch Doctor leapt off the car he stood upon, landed on the roof of another, and laid down another hail of fire. More of House's men fell, guns all clattering to the pavement.

"Boss," Doyle said. "What the—"

Flood barely realized that he was on his feet now, watching, eager to see what unfolded as—

Every gun in House's retinue swung toward the witch doctor and opened up. The Halloween spook emptied his pistols into the firing line, leapt off his car mount, hunkered down while the machine guns and shotguns tore into the Buick's opposite flank, and reloaded. It took him three seconds, maybe four. When the .45's were full and jacked, he stowed them in his coat, lifted a pair of Tommy guns fallen beside a pair of dead hoods nearby, and sprang up to meet his assailants again.

Flood couldn't believe his eyes. The crazy spade skated sideward in a long, broad arc, a Tommy gun cradled in each arm, and opened up on his assailants. House's men swarmed for cover or returned fire. Half of them fell in the blazing lead rain. Flood was sure the Witch Doctor took direct hits, but the Tommy guns kept chattering away in unison. Finally they both came up empty.

The Witch Doctor was still standing. He dropped one Thompson, gripped the other by its charring-hot barrel, and laid into the nearest gunmen using the machine gun like a Louisville Slugger.

Doyle's need to flee had evaporated, just like Flood's. The two watched, amazed.

House's gunmen thinned. No more than a dozen remained. As three more went down, blatted head-on by the Witch Doctor's arcing Thompson, the others fell back to reload.

But they were too slow. Just as the first raised the muzzle of his weapon, Flood saw that the skull-faced stranger now had a shotgun in hand. He jacked it, hipped it, and let it rip. The blast took two of House's hoods in their faces, and both dropped, heads half-sheared.

The rest of the gun-barrels rose: reloaded, hungry, ready.

The Witch Doctor pulled his .45's and finished the job he'd started. In moments, after the loud bang-clatter of his guns fell silent, there was no more gunfire on the street... just the sound of men bleeding and men dying, and the patrons who'd not succumbed entirely lying about on 5th Avenue, crying out for help, for lovers, for cops, for ambulances.

Flood watched from his safe distance. The Witch Doctor put bullets in a pair of still-moving hoods who crawled toward fallen weapons, then raised his .45's high and fired off a short burst into the air. It had the desired effect. The crowd put their heads down, screaming, terrified.

Then, as Flood stared in amazement, the crazy spook charged the façade of Aces & Eights, leapt off the pavement, cleared the jutting marquis, and crashed through a second floor window lickety-split.

A running jump, on pavement, arcing twenty feet up into a second-floor window. *After* taking out about two dozen hardened Harlem gunmen.

Now *there* was something you didn't see every day.

Flood was duly impressed.

14

Gideon left the line cooks to clean up Calvin's remains and rushed toward the main dining room when he heard the commotion of hundreds of feet pounding for the outer door.

He, Dorey, Croaker, and a few others climbed the stairs beyond the kitchen and stomped up to the second floor. The stairwell gave out onto a short corridor, and that corridor opened onto the dining room, down front, near the stage.

Intermingled with the thump-thud sounds of their own shoes pounding up the stairs, they heard the rattle of gunfire from the streets. The rattletrap thunder continued, punctuated here and there with shotgun blasts and small arms fire, as they made the second floor and rushed out into the dining room only to find the place empty.

Well, mostly empty. A few dancing girls, stage-hands, and bandies still fled the wings. And across the dining room, on the dais, Gideon saw the Queen Bee lying unconscious in a heap on the floor, surrounded by a slow-closing circle of strangers. Gideon shouted before he even saw who surrounded her.

"Queen!" His voice rocked the room like an explosion.

The patrons surrounding the unconscious Queen Bee turned to face him—and Gideon realized they weren't patrons at all. It was Papa Solomon House and his West Indies, circling her like a pack of jackals. Some had their guns drawn. House had his walking stick. They seemed to be studying her with an eye toward how to finish her.

Gideon still held the bloody cleaver he'd used to whack Calvin. Throwing it at this distance wasn't an option. So in one smooth motion, the cleaver moved from his right hand to his left, his now-free right hand dove into his coat, and his chrome-plated .45 jumped free. Gideon leveled it at House.

"Hands off, you son of a bitch!" he cried.

House gave command and one of his big bodyguards knelt to snatch up the Queen Bee. As Gideon squeezed the trigger, House's other bodyguard—the one called Wash—stepped in front of House, raising a sawed off shotgun to his shoulder and letting loose with both barrels.

Gideon knew his shot took Wash, but he didn't know where. He threw himself down; felt the sting of buckshot, spread wide at such a distance, but still drawing blood. Then the picture windows at the far end of the room shattered and House and his soldiers were all shouting, terrified by some new arrival.

Flat on the stage, Gideon craned his neck and tried to get a look at what, or who, had just arrived.

It was a man with a skull-face under a top hat and a nest of dreadlocks. He wore a long black coat; sported a slithering red scarf; bore coal-black .45's in each gloved hand.

Baron Samedi—the Cemetery Man.

The Dread Baron.

Gideon wondered who the Baron had come to collect. In the next instant, he got his answer.

The Baron opened fire on House's men, sweeping his twin pistols right to left in a broad arc, muzzles throwing tongues of flame, casings leaping this way and that like a swarm of brass flies. Gideon wondered what his men were doing behind him but didn't care. He had to get the Queen away from House and his goons. He had to move.

He checked behind him to see that his boys were backing his play, then gripped the meat cleaver in one hand, his pistol in the other, and charged.

He saw Papa House and Timmons dragging the limp Queen Bee between them toward the entryway. Wash scooted sideward before them, ready to lay down cover fire and act as a screen. Gideon raised his automatic but knew he couldn't fire without risking the Queen.

He tried to circle wide, to put the Queen out of the line of fire and give himself a better bead on Wash.

Wash saw this, threw down his empty two-barrel scattergun, and drew a pair of Webley pistols from his long, camel hair coat.

As Gideon bore on, another of House's goons retreated out of the line of the Dread Baron's barrage of hot lead. The goon turned just in time to see Gideon bearing down on him; raised his .45 to take out Gideon and give House and his bodyguards a clean getaway.

Gideon planted the meat cleaver edge-on into the goon's face, splitting it down the middle. The soldier convulsed under the strike and his hands spread. His gun fell free.

Gideon snatched it into his now-empty left hand.

All this unfolded in a breath; two at most. Gideon raised his pistols, two-fisted, ready to blast Wash a storm of new assholes.

Wash's Webleys cocked and bore down on Gideon, barrels wide, black and staring, like the eyes of some sea beast.

Behind him, Gideon heard the Dread Baron beating a thunderous death-march with his twin .45s. Gideon joined the march and opened up on Wash.

Wash opened up on Gideon.

Dozens of slugs passed in mid-air, whizzing murderously toward their quarries. Gideon felt two tear into his leg and down he went. Wash took two—one in each shoulder—and toppled, still pulling the triggers on his empty wheel guns.

Down they went, each granted a reprieve.

Gideon blinked, vision astir with darkness, ears ringing, nostrils singed with the scent of cordite and freshly-spilt blood. A moment later the world came back into focus. His boys stood before him, guns trained on something above and behind him, cursing, telling whoever it was to drop his heaters, *now*.

Gideon rolled over and saw that the Dread Baron was the only man left standing. He'd taken out all of House's men alone: close to a dozen of them, lying in a heaped, scattered semicircle on the dais amid overturned dinner tables and the shattered glass of the front windows.

As Gideon watched, he noted that the Baron's pistols were both jacked open, mags and chambers empty.

Clack, clack. The slides snapped forward again. The ejection ports clinked shut.

Empty? Or just freshly-reloaded?

There was a long silence as the Baron stared, guns high. Gideon's men waited.

"Your move," the Baron said, and the sound of his voice made Gideon's spine crawl.

"Stand down!" Gideon managed, barely finding the breath to speak.

"Boss?" Dorey asked.

"Took two in the leg, but I'm breathin'," Gideon answered. "Put your guns down before the Baron here adds you assholes to the body count."

The Baron dared a glance down at Gideon, where he lay heaped on the floor. "Smart," he said.

"You wanted us dead, we'd already be there," Gideon said, and coughed, breath suddenly short.

"Your boss needs a doctor," the Baron said, addressing the men.

Gideon still held Samedi's gaze. "They got the Queen," he said, then pushed himself upright, sitting now. He got a nasty head rush and a wave of nausea for his trouble.

"See to your boss," the Baron said, giving orders without compunction. "She'll be at Papa's warehouse by the river." The Baron never lowered his guns or took his eyes off Gideon's men. Gideon was glad the men listened. He wouldn't have been able to stand without Dorey and Croaker speeding forward to help him up. As he rose on shaking legs, leaning on his captains, he looked to the Cemetery Man.

The Baron was circling them, guns still drawn, on-guard.

"Where you goin'?" Gideon asked.

"My business is hereabouts," the Baron said. "You got something nasty on the premises. Needs extraction."

Gideon didn't quite understand, but he accepted that answer. He turned to see what had become of Wash.

House's first officer was gone, nothing but some blood and his fallen sawed-off remaining where he'd collapsed only moments before. When Gideon craned his neck round to look back over his shoulder and question the voodoo man, he found him gone as well.

Son of a bitch. Busts in through the front windows—second floor windows!—and takes off without a word.

"Boss?" Croaker asked, sounding like a scared little kid.

Gideon couldn't blame him. He felt the same. All the rage and fight had gone out of him. It was replaced now by nothing more than weariness, pain, and fear.

Fear for the Queen.

Fear of the Cemetery Man.

"Let's get the fuck outta here," he said, and the men did as they were told.

XX

Dr. Dub Corveaux was not himself. He was horsed by Ogou, the warring; the contentious; the iron-willed; the bloody-handed; the all-powerful *lwa* for whom war, fire, bloodshed and death were house pets; the stuff of daydreams as well as nightmares. Dozens of evil men had fallen to the thunder in his blood, the rage in his heart, the hunger for justice in his gut. By all accounts, being horsed, victorious, and *unstoppable*, he should have felt no fear.

But fear still lived inside him. It coiled in his hot guts like a cold, clammy serpent. Killing men—criminals and hoods— that was one thing. The Furies awaiting in the cellar of Aces & Eights... that was another entirely.

You ain't a man, Ogou snarled in his ear, riding his back like a junkie's monkey. *You're my fire and sword; you're the nail-studded staff in my right hand, the machete in my left.*

Dr. Dub Corveaux, in the guise of a man of the grave, marched forth toward the side corridor that Gideon Mann and his soldiers had emerged from; the corridor that led to the side stairway; the side stairway that led to the ground floor; then the ground floor corridor that led to the basement stairs.

The basement. The entryway to the underworld that he would have to brave and return from—like Orpheus or Dante—if he hoped to survive the night. He marched with purpose, guns ready, back straight, knowing that the Queen Bee's men might glance back and see him here. And if they did so, they should see him upright; staunch; unafraid.

But he *was* afraid. Beneath his terrifying skull-face and the rough armor of his great-coat and the *Serpent d'Ogou* round his throat, he *was* afraid, as any man might be.

You ain't a man! Ogou growled. *You're my soldier!*

I am a man, Papa Ogou, Dub answered inwardly, *and I do feel fear.*

Anything hurts you before the sun rises, I take that hurt when I depart, Ogou assured him. *Sunrise comes, you're good as new.*

And what if it ain't done with me by sunrise? Dr. Dub Corveaux asked.

Ogou didn't have an answer for that. A long silence followed Dub's wondering. Finally:

Don't think about it, Ogou said. *Just do what you came to do.*

Ogou, speechless. That gave Dub little comfort.

XX

The droplights in the lower corridors swayed to and fro like the earth itself shook beneath them. Deformed, elongated shadows danced on the floor and the walls. The Baron pressed on through the narrow corridor, toward the swinging door at the far end the opened onto the foyer. He had nearly made that door when he heard something behind him.

It came from the kitchen; the slough-drag of heavy feet; something large and awkward moving slowly, deliberately, toward him. The Baron froze in the corridor, the whole world around him tilting crazily in the drunken, swaying light and tarantella of the shadows.

Slough-drag. Slough-drag. Slough-drag.

"What in the hell... ?" he croaked, Ogou's rusty-iron voice sounding from his lips.

At the far end of the long corridor, the kitchen lay beyond another swinging door with a small, round, porthole-like window in it. Beyond that tiny window, the Baron saw a slow-moving silhouette appear. It filled the porthole, and then the silhouette set its weight against the door and pushed.

The Baron decided the time was ripe for a reload. In the two or three breaths it took for the heavy, slow-moving form to push the swinging door wide, the Baron popped his mostly-empty magazines, pocketed them, drew out his spares—two of the last four remaining—and slammed them home in the stained walnut grips of his pistols. The slides were jacked and fresh rounds rammed home in the still-warm barrels. He held his guns aloft just as the form from the kitchen came stumbling, herky-jerky like a drunken marionette, through the swinging door.

It was a thick young man, dead as Noah, his melon cleaved wide open like a crack in some old boulder on a mountaintop. Even in the swaying, feverish light of the corridor and the backlight from the kitchens, the Baron saw the glint of bloody gray matter in the open-air skull; saw that the young man's whole, bulky, lifeless body hung loose and raggedy, a puppet whose half-stitched limbs were all tearing loose.

Someone had taken an ax or a meat cleaver to the kid. But here he was, slumping jauntily toward Dub with dead, white eyes and a gaping mouth.

No need to waste bullets. The Baron could easily outrun the dead thing. He pushed through the swinging door at his back into the front foyer, knowing that the stairs down to the basement waited fifteen feet dead ahead of him.

Fifteen feet—choked with more of the upright, animated dead. Some were well-dressed townies, probably casualties from the turkey shoot outside; others were House's dead men from upstairs, tilting and toppling as they thumped down the stairs from above with stiff-legged, mindless determination. All their wounds gaped black and crimson; their eyes were clouded like the long-uncleaned windows of houses marked for demolition; their strange gaits made it clear that they were no longer living men and women, nor conscious. Someone—some*thing*—was animating their corpses; directing them; closing in, moment by moment, on the Dread Baron.

The curse engine knew he was here to end it. It was fighting back with the best weapons at hands: the dead who'd fallen under its watchful, eldritch gaze; whose blood-sin and evil fed it even as their souls fled to their final rewards.

Save your bullets, Ogou said. *They won't do any good.*

The Baron holstered his guns.

Then he drew the *Machette d'Ogou*. The flames of the machete burned bright in the dark and crowded foyer and the Baron felt its heat on his skull-painted face.

The cleavered kid burst through the swinging door at his back just as the crowd of street-dead and House's minions filled the last empty spaces between the Dread Baron and the basement stairs.

Behind the mask of the Dread Baron, Dr. Dub Corveaux's human fear melted in the infernal fires of the *Machette d'Ogou*, and he laid into the dead without mercy.

The machete screamed as it sliced the air, cutting wide arcs back and forth across the corridor. Heads were severed and rolled like stones in a landslide; grasping hands and arms were hacked and strewn about like jungle vine on a pathless march through the Congo; torsos were cloven wide to spill out their steaming contents; legs were cut out from under tottering, deathless husks in motion.

They kept crowding him, reaching for him, their mouths yawning as though they were hungry and they wanted his flesh to feed their deathless appetites. He hacked; he slashed; he yanked and shoved and clove and strove, keeping his eyes on the stairway, so close and yet so far away, through this tangled, grasping forest of the undead.

In moments, the Dread Baron laid waste to the zombie horde, his white skull-face stained with the gore of slaughter. The bodies twitched and flopped about him, still struggling in vain to reach their quarry and failing. The pulsing flames of the *Machette d'Ogou* stank of brimstone and smoke-filled charnel houses.

Move, Ogou said, *before it comes up with something else.*

The Dread Baron did as bade, sheathing the *Machette d'Ogou* and racing toward the dark stairwell that would take him into the cavernous cellar.

XX

The air grew cold and damp as he descended, so swiftly and surely that he knew it could be no natural change in climate. The Dread Baron thumped down the long flight of wooden stairs, through a door, and found himself in the northwest corner of the basement, at the head of a small cellar antechamber that opened onto a larger one. Beyond, in the next large cell, sentinel rows of towering industrial shelving stacked with canned goods, boxes, crates, and nameless, purposeless bric-a-brac awaited. He marched forward into the larger storage chamber, made it five steps without incident, then heard a groaning in the rafters above.

The shelves, anchored to the roof beams, tore at their bonds and broke free. One by one, the shelves surrounding him began to sway, like prisoners bound in chairs rocking back and forth in an attempt to topple themselves. The Dread Baron couldn't wait. He sped down the center aisle as the shelves heaved sideward, spilling their heavy contents with a clamorous, apocalyptic roar. If the animated dead could not stop him, perhaps an avalanche of forgotten junk could.

The demons denned below Aces & Eights would bury him, one way or another. They would bind him; break him; end him.

The Dread Baron ran faster as the roar of the falling shelving rose around him and the air filled with choking, ageless dust. Midway through the long, narrow cell, he crossed the broad central aisle of the basement and made a hasty, careening left turn. The old, plugged sewer line where the curse engine waited was fifty yards, dead ahead.

The avalanche raced alongside him, the shelves along the large center aisle now tearing loose from their anchorage in a thundering rain of champagne, fine china, and spare silverware. The Dread Baron called on Ogou's strength and launched skyward on his boot heels, sailing up and over the dusty, creaking miasma of rent iron and splintered lumber. He sailed twenty yards in a low arc until gravity took him, then down he went. He landed hard on a newly-made mound of debris, tripped on jutting ironworks and splintered slabs of lumber, then dove into a roll to stop himself.

He came to rest amid a central conglomeration of shelving that was double-bolted to the rafters. Like their fellows, they creaked and strained against their bindings, but they could not free themselves.

This was the place where he'd discovered the curse engine just a two nights before. They'd double-anchored the shelves here because they'd already fallen once.

Trying to crush him.

No time for caution now. The double-bolting would buy him some time.

The Dread Baron marched forward and tore the hundred-pound manhole cover off its maw. The stoppered pit beneath vomited a cloud of rotted air and gravesmoke.

There at the bottom of that pit lay the sculpture of skulls, bones, and animal detritus that was causing all the trouble.

Magda's curse engine.

Waiting.

Ready.

Dub tore the stoppered gourd containing the *Petro Packet* powder from his coat's deepest inner pocket and set to work, pouring out the powder in a broad, circular cordon nearly 20 feet across that encompassed himself and the forgotten well.

This would lock it in—and he with it.

Circle of protection in place, Dub next fished the mummified dog from its pocket and laid the paper-light corpse down in the well, atop the curse engine. Now all that remained was to invoke the powers of the Furies, to draw them like hungry beasts into the baited trap of the mummified little pup with an offering of blood. And once the Furies were trapped therein, he could destroy the mummified pup and let the whole thing be consumed in flame.

Dub drew a soldier's bayonet from its sheathe and held his hand out above the well, the pup, and the curse engine.

You're forgetting something, Ogou said.

Dub ignored him. He had forgotten nothing. He knew that the *Machette d'Ogou* would be the weapon of choice when destroying the beast upon manifestation. He wasn't a fool.

He said the words of offering, invoking the Furies by name as though they had been *lwa.* "Vouchsafe this offering as the purest I can obtain," he said, resting the sharpened edge of the bayonet against his outstretched, uncovered palm. "Nemesis, Alecto, Megaera, and Tisiphone—I bid you fill the empty vessel I've provided, and show yourselves to me as a humble petitioner."

He drew the bayonet over his hand. His blood welled, steaming in the cold of the haunted cellar, and he made a fist to bring it forth faster.

The blood splashed down, wetting the mummified pup and the curse engine beneath it. As Dub watched, the little, wrinkled animal stirred, moving with some semblance of life.

Fire, Ogou said urgently.

The Dread Baron drew the *Machette d'Ogou*, and its fire filled the darkness. He readied himself to yank the pup out of the well at the first sign of manifestation—the first indication of supernatural life.

Not that *fire*, Ogou said.

The mummified pup stirred, warped little paper-twist legs suddenly kicking. It shot upright, emitted a strange, throaty yelp, and then the Furies made their presence known. As the Dread Baron watched, suddenly sure that this would not play out as he'd hoped, the mummified pup sprouted and grew like some cancerous tumor.

The pup turned itself inside-out. Tendrils of old, dried muscle and sinew burst through the papery skin, engulfed its tiny form, then spread out, grasping, toward the edges of the well. As the Baron stared, the tendrils thickened and grew more maleable—ropy and alive. These tendrils sprouted shoots; the shoots sprouted flesh-flowers; the flesh-flowers sprouted more tendrils and more shoots.

It happened in the span of two or three breaths. First it was a mummified pup; then it was a creeper vine of flesh and cartilage and sinew and gristle; then the whole mess roiled in on itself, burst outward, filled the well, and rose toward Dub where he stood at the well's rim.

He threw himself backward. The roiling mass burst up and out of the well, blooming toward the ceiling and the edges of the protective circle. Suddenly, the Dread Baron understood what Ogou had been trying to tell him.

Fire. He needed to light the *Petro* powder and seal the protective circle.

He brought the flaming *Machette d'Ogou* whistling down onto the protective circle. With a sound like a great, in-drawn breath, the whole circle suddenly threw up a wall of heaving flames, twenty feet across. The tendrils hit the firewall and shrank, seeming to emit a high, quailing scream. The thing swelled and knotted then in protest, pressing outward on all sides. As the Baron crouched on guard, fire at his back, blasphemous, grasping malignancy before him, a quartet of the heaving, whipping tentacles rose above the center of the mass. They were long, thick, and ready to burst, like giant bean pods, or bloated, pus-filled sacks of flesh nursing deep infection.

The pods burst. Their tacky contents unfurled: a quartet of leathery, translucent wings, criss-crossed with spiderwebs of black veins and the ghost of a taut-but-elastic musculature.

A new knot of pods on its flesh-vines swelled and burst, revealing bloodshot, glaring eyes that leaked crimson tears and sought the Dread Baron's crouched form with malevolent assurance. More pods burst and revealed flexing, ragged, crab-like appendages that Dub supposed were fingers. A pair of pods at the center of the writhing mass tore open with sounds like ripping farts and revealed the assimilated skulls of the curse engine beneath, now clothed with thin veneers of alien skin, the jaws hanging askew from their roots and the gaping mouths quailing like the maws of hungry baby chicks.

Fear. Revulsion. Horror. Wonder. All these assailed the Dread Baron in the same instant. Then, a moment later, he felt the weight and heft of the flaming *Machette d'Ogou* in his grasp, felt the towering walls of heat that surrounded he and the beast, and he knew that the fire would not stay contained for long. It would spread and consume the whole cellar, then all of Aces & Eights above.

And here he crouched, at its epicenter, trapped with a fiend from beyond hell.

"Well, shit," he muttered. Dr. Dub Corveaux let the man in him shrink to a pinprick. He was the Dread Baron now; a horse of Ogou and Samedi and the Ghede; saber of the *lwa*. If this thing was Fury made flesh, he was fiery, fearless justice. A lopsided grin split his skull-painted face. He launched himself toward his quarry.

The tendrils lashed out. The wings swooped toward him like razor-edged folding fans. The strange, grasping fingers sought his softest exposures and extremities.

Then one of its insectile finger-blooms contracted into a fist. It rocketed toward him, faster than he could raise his blade or skate sideward. He took the blow in the sternum. The Dread Baron's breath left his lungs; his feet left the floor. He landed in the cordon of fire and lickety-split, his top hat, dreadlocks, and the mantle of his coat were hosting hungry flames.

So much for self-confidence.

The Baron rolled forward and thrashed, eager to put himself out. From the corner of his quaking vision, he saw a pair of the beast's tendrils and another of its razor wings dive toward him. The Machette d'Ogou flashed amid the inferno surrounding him and hot, thick juices from the pair of hacked tendrils sprayed his face.

But the wing still dove. He got his feet under him just as the barbed edge of the flesh-fan dug deep into his left shoulder, tearing through his coat and drawing blood from his bare flesh beneath. His flesh burned from the inside out as though the thing's barbs left some infernal acid in their wake.

Pain. Blood. These were new to the Dread Baron. He took bullets all the time; occasionally knife-wounds or mortal blows. But Ogou absorbed these; Ogou took their pain, and their force, and so long as Dub Corveaux made it home before sunrise, the wounds were healed and left no marks.

But the damned thing towering before him, shrinking from the fire surrounding it (and him), striking at him with all lethal intent—that *thing* had dealt him a bleeding, painful wound while horsed.

"Ogou?" the Baron snarled through gnashed teeth.

You're gettin' everything I can give you, Ogou answered.

The beast struck again. The Baron danced backward from the lurching blows and almost tripped into the flaming cordon again. Even the *Serpent d'Ogou* scarf around his throat cringed from the flames at his back.

And that seemed to save him. The *Serpent's* dangling ends rose in protest as they swung near the flames. Again the beast before him lurched forward and brought a knot of its whipping tendrils whistling down toward him. The *Serpent d'Ogou* rose, its ends like two striking snakes, and caught the thickest, longest tendrils, holding them. The three shorter tendrils between them stretched, trying to reach him, nearly whipping some foul venom from their oozing ends into his eyes.

The Baron struck. The lesser tendrils collapsed and the thicker strands broke from the *Serpent's* grip, retreating, and the beast squealed.

You don't retreat anymore! Ogou barked in the center of Dub's fevered consciousness. *The air's hot and thick, you got flames at your back and a fiend in your path—attack! No retreat, and no surrender!*

Dub felt a surge of strength and fury flow through him and knew he couldn't resist it, fear and good sense notwithstanding. He submitted to that red wave and charged, leaping right up onto the towering malignancy's foul bulk.

The *Machette d'Ogou* swept left and right in broad, smooth arcs. Its flaming iron hacked horror-flesh. Its flames boiled black blood and ichor. When its wings dipped to encircle him, he thrust with the machete and tore them like old drapes and their juices painted him. When the grasping, crab-like fingers curled to ensnare him, he kicked and quelled them with the heels of his gravedigger's boots; with his flaming machete from beyond; with his bare, brawling fists. When its gaping, toothy mouths and mewling orifices sought his flesh to feed their hunger, he drove the machete and its flames in deep. He tore at its joints and crevices with the flaming blade and reveled in the demon's shrieks and gibbers of agony.

Twice more the beast struck and wounded him. He went down on his knees when the thorny tip of one of its tendrils drove point-on into the meat of his right thigh. Down in a half-crouch, another knot of tendrils sought his throat, coiling with startling speed and trying to strangle the life from him. But the *Serpent d'Ogou* came to his aid, wrestling the constrictor vines loose with its own considerable strength and freeing him for a final, desperate onslaught.

He couldn't even see anymore. The flames made him squint. The smoke stung his narrowed eyes and filled them with tears.

He felt the heat of the flames and breathed the poisonous smoke of the cellar, but he didn't care. His mortal mind knew a fiery death or a choking one lay just around the corner if he didn't soon finish his business, but all he saw was the wounds that he opened in the flesh of his enemy, and the murky red haze that ebbed and flowed across his vision in answer to the bloodlust inside him.

Soon enough, though, he was crusted in gore—its foul, alien, all-blackening gore. Without faltering, he fought and hacked and slashed and thrust. He tore and he pummeled and his own heartbeat thundered in his ears and nearly drowned the hungry, gathering roar of the flames as they spread through the cellar in all directions, devouring everything in their path.

At last, the thing had no more tentacles to grasp with; no more talons to tear with; no more wings to flap or flounder. Its mouths and orifices worked, but they were like the gills and mouths of a fish out of water. Beneath him, though he could still feel some foul life pulsing through it, the Dread Baron knew that the whole beastly mess was somehow shrinking; diminishing; collapsing inward on its own vascular bladders and withering knots of cord and limb. He threw himself off of it, landing hard just beside the encircling wall of flame, and watched as the Furies were drawn from the shriveling flesh like poison from a wound; drawn right out of their plane of existence back into their own; and then, staring, he knew that he'd won. All that remained was an empty remnant of lifeless, ruined tissue.

And the fire; all around him, a fierce, roaring blaze that leapt and devoured every scrap of fuel in its path. Now the fire was the beast, and it would not be satisfied until the cellar, and the club above, had sated its voracious, charcoal appetite.

Breathing was torture. His eyes were two pools of boiling water. His leg throbbed. His shoulder burned.

"Time?" he asked Ogou.

Time, the war *lwa* answered. *High-tail it, soldier. You're needed elsewhere.*

The Baron sheathed the machete and stood best as he could. "Elsewhere?"

Papa House still got off with the Queen Bee... 'less you wanna leave her to him.

The Dread Baron drew the deepest rattling breath he could in the smoke-choked cellar. It was hot and thick as an iron foundry.

"What gives?" the Baron asked. "I ain't feelin' tip-top here, Papa Ogou."

We've just spent a heap 'a maji. *I'm givin' you all I got, horse, but even I get tired.*

The smoke was thick now, the fire roaring. "Reckon you can give me a little more?" the Baron urged. "Take me through to dawn?"

Why you still talkin'? Ogou countered.

The Dread Baron smiled in spite of his weariness... in spite of his pain. What was one more miracle? He launched himself through the roaring wall of flames, seeking the shortest path to smokeless autumn air.

15

Gideon and company arrived at the Foree Imports Warehouse right after House and his goons did. Gideon saw the Queen Bee, now conscious but with her hands bound and mouth gagged, being dragged into the warehouse, a cavernous brick-and-steel structure on east 132nd Street, just south of the Park Avenue Bridge, fronting the lazy, slate-gray Harlem River. House took her inside, flanked by Wash and Timmons. The rest of the West Indies made a cordon of their cars across the face of the warehouse, entrenched, and opened fire. Gideon and his boys were pinned down from the first, and though they gave as good as they got—making mince of House's auto fleet, downing a couple of his men, and generally making a hell of a racket—the stalemate persisted and would not break.

Gideon cared little for the ache in his leg from the bullets he'd taken at the club. All he cared about was doing right by his employer; the mother of the streets who'd found him, raised him, and made him a better man than he had been when found. For all he knew, the firefight had gone on too long; she could already be dead within, and House miles away, fleeing in a boat up or down river, or crossing to disappear into one of his safe-houses in the Bronx.

But what of it? Gideon couldn't give up; not now; not when the Queen needed him.

So he hollered orders to his men, saw ammo spread among them, and kept the hot lead flying.

And it was in the midst of that stalemate, when their ammo was dwindling and Gideon thought he heard the faraway whine of police sirens, that a bounding shadow swaddled in a billowing black coat and serpentine red scarf came leaping into the fray from a nearby tenement roof. The Cemetery Man cut a fast track across the peaked roof of a nearby warehouse adjacent to Foree Imports; slid down the sloped forward eaves; steadied himself; then launched himself into the fray on the far side of the West Indies' automobile cordon.

"Down!" Gideon screamed, making it clear he wanted his men out of the line of fire. As they all stopped firing and hit the deck, they heard House's soldiers cursing and shouting from their entrenchment; then, the savage *snap, crackle*, and *pop* of gunfire, now directed inward, criss-crossing the warehouse forecourt. Little by little, the gunfire dwindled, and men died under a new hail of thunderous gun-music made by a pair of smoking, fire-tongued, cold, black .45's.

And just as quickly, there was silence. Gideon raised his head in time to see the Cemetery Man—that darksome, carnival figure with a skull face and a jauntily-angled top hat—walk through the quiet warehouse forecourt toward the front entrance. The cocky bastard was almost strutting. Or was he limping? Either way, the door didn't even stop him. The Cemetery Man just lowered his shoulder and barreled right through it with a bellow. There were some choice words and a quick volley of gunfire from within, then silence.

The Dread Baron was inside, and the cordon was down. Gideon told his men to spread out. "Snap up any ammo on these sons of bitches and meet me at the door."

"We're goin' in *there?*" one of the boys whined. "With the Cemetery Man?"

"Goin' in?" Gideon snarled. "Shit, Cleve, we're gonna back him up—come on!"

XX

House heard the noise from out front, but he didn't care. He was seconds away from his vengeance, and he'd have it. He would've preferred to see the Queen Bee ruined in the public eye first: bankruptcy, scandal, the loss of power and turf by increments until she was left with nothing, begging to be put out of her misery.

But as he had her here, now, in his grasp, he supposed feeding her to Napoleon would have to do.

House and his goons were gathered on the high wooden catwalk that encircled Napoleon's muddy pen below, a sunken pit that gave out onto a stretch of the cold, quiet Harlem river. The gator looked a might pernicious; annoyed by the change of seasons or just plain hungry, House couldn't tell which. He gave orders, though, and his men set to stringing the Queen Bee up by her wrists on a hook and winch. The plan was to swing her out over Napoleon's pen and lower her little by little. House knew the big bastard could jump if the right food was dangled above him. He wanted the gator to start with the Queen Bee's feet and work his way up.

The Queen Bee bucked and floundered in her bindings, cursing through her gag. As the men had her prepped, House stepped forward and tore the gag off her. He wanted to hear her beg for mercy when the gator took her pretty little yellow feet off; wanted to hear every curse and cry as she was dipped lower and lower, disappearing in large, ragged chunks down the gator's throat.

"Hell on earth is comin' your way," the Queen Bee snarled. "Hell on earth such as you never dreamed of! You hear me, House?"

"Well, come it may," he said, "but I'm guessin' it won't arrive before Napoleon's had his fill of your long, pretty legs, Queen Bee."

The Queen Bee turned and saw the gator then. The beast saw her as well. House let himself believe the toothy beast grinned, then bellowed as though in search of a mate. It slid forward through the cold mud.

"Swing her out," House said.

The goons nearest her lifted her legs. Another worked the long, steel arm of the little crane that she was roped to. He swung the arm sideward and the Queen Bee's body tipped over the wooden railing and she went dangling out over the empty air above Napoleon's pen. Her legs kicked and wheeled in the empty air, and her high heels fell free, bouncing harmlessly off Napoleon's long, blunt, upturned snout.

"Forward!" House ordered. "Get her farther out there!"

Two more of his boys laid their backs against the crane and the whole mess slid along its track. The arm from which the Queen Bee dangled moved forward, outward. Now she was farther from the railing, still dangling a good 12 or 15 feet above the gator and his cold, muddy pen.

Eager, Napoleon sounded another throaty bellow, rocked back on his thick tail, and launched himself skyward, jaws gaping wide.

The Queen Bee drew up her legs, screaming. She missed losing one of her dainty little feet by an inch or two. Napoleon's jaws snapped shut with a thunderous finality and he fell back to the mud, snarling from somewhere deep in his gullet.

House and his men all laughed. "You got good reflexes, Queen Bee!" House offered. "I do believe we'll just have to settle in for a long, slow show, eh?"

"You can go to hell, House!" the Queen Bee spat.

"After you, mam'selle," he said coldly, and lowered his eyes.

Napoleon was preparing for another spring.

Suddenly, the laughter of House's men was swallowed in the roar of gunfire. The three stationed by the crane sagged against the machinery, then slid to the floor, all having sprung crimson leaks.

House and his fellows spun on their heels, searching the vast, cluttered gloom of the warehouse for the source of the gunfire. House heard voices in the distance: a volley nearer the warehouse's entrance. The Queen Bee's men had broken through!

But they still seemed far away... just pouring in through the front doors...

House turned as Napoleon sprang again. The Queen Bee drew her whole body upward, snapping her legs nearer as she did. Napoleon missed her by a hair-breadth and fell back into the mud. She got a quick, terrifying glimpse of her left shoe tumbling down the gator's gullet.

"Somebody get on the crane," House ordered. "Lower the boom. She's goin' all in."

Two of his men moved to answer his orders. They were shot down, too, and House saw the muzzle flashes this time, bright, white-hot flames cast out of the rafters down toward their place on the catwalk.

"Up there!" he said, pointing toward the source of the sniper fire.

His boys all raised their weapons—Tommy Guns, shotguns, pistols—and prepared to fire.

Then a thick swatch of shadow loosed itself from the darkness and plunged toward them, letting loose with a pair of roaring .45's in its night-black hands.

House threw himself sideward. His boys opened fire, but the shadow had the drop on them, every shot a winner. Blood sprayed the catwalk, stained House's camel-hair coat. His men withered, snapping off shots in their death throes as they collapsed.

Then the gunman hit the deck on all fours, like a cat. It was the Cemetery Man—the same bastard who'd busted into House's headquarters the night before. He staggered but quickly steadied himself, the landing from the twenty-foot fall seeming to trouble him a little.

Maybe he was mortal after all. House would find out.

There was more gunfire from below, moving nearer by the moment. The Queen Bee's men were inside. His own men were thinning, skinning out. Only half a dozen remained around him who hadn't fallen in the first volley from the Baron.

House threw himself at his nearest henchmen, snatched a Tommy Gun from one goon's hands, then wheeled round behind them to use the little crowd of henchmen for cover. "Take him out!" he shouted.

As they moved to do his bidding, he snapped back the bolt on the Tommy and swung the muzzle toward the dangling Queen Bee.

Then the world was a storm of fire and smoke, and House barely knew what was happening.

XX

The Dread Baron saw the Queen Bee dangling over the leaping gator; saw the half-dozen henchmen now lowering their weapons to ventilate him; saw Papa House beyond them, using their bodies as cover, taking aim at the helpless Maybelle Meriwether.

"Speed, Ogou!" he snarled, and didn't wait to see if Ogou would listen.

He leapt, climbing up onto the crane and scrambling toward the fulcrum where the arm was anchored. Reaching out sent sharp pain through his shoulder. The weight on his leg made his thigh throb. He'd pushed himself too hard—his power was waning.

House's gunmen opened fire, following him right up the length of the steel arch, and the warehouse was awash in the ringing clatter of hot lead bouncing off cold steel.

House couched the butt of his Tommy Gun, ready to throw a burst at the Queen Bee.

The Baron, with a better angle on the bastard from high up, bounded out onto the narrow length of the crane arm, blasting away at House below. He caught two of House's henchmen in their faces and down they went; splintered the railing of the catwalk; planted a hot barrage square into the Tommy Gun's flank and through House's left wrist.

House screamed. He let loose, finger squeezing the trigger, but without his left arm to brace it, the Tommy swung with the recoil and all the shots went low and wide, stitching a line through the muck in the gator pen below.

The gator leapt again toward the kicking, flailing Queen Bee. With a scream, she snapped up her legs and narrowly escaped losing a limb.

As the gator fell back to the muck, the Baron whipped off the *Serpent d'Ogou*—the 20 foot long coil of red silk that was curiously alive in his grip, awaiting command. And though it seemed feather-light to the touch, it had heft when he whipped it downward and wrapped a length of it, taut as a bullwhip, round the thickness of the arm of the crane.

He launched himself into space, fell, felt the *Serpent* go taut in his grasp—God*damn*, he felt that!—then he was whipped backward, swinging like Tarzan on a vine beneath the Queen Bee, dipping down toward the mud of the gator pit.

The gator saw him, opened its maw, and sprang.

The Baron drew one of his pistols from its holster and emptied the clip down the gator's throat.

The gator rattled under the weight of the gunshots and fell out of the air, mid-spring, dead as Judas.

The Baron's swing carried him upward. Momentum yanked the arm of the crane sideward and the whole structure swung toward the catwalk; toward Papa House; toward his last standing goons.

The Baron opened fire on the goons and downed the lot—though his head shots favored one eye or the other, and his center-mass clusters hammered more lungs and livers than the hearts they were aimed at. His swing brought him up toward the catwalk. The crane arm followed him, pivoting under the force of his swing. He kicked and shattered himself a path right through the bullet-riddled railing, then loosed his grip on the *Serpent d'Ogou* and sailed right toward House. He slammed into him with terrific force, and down they went.

The Queen Bee screamed as the crane arm swung and settled her dangling form down, pretty-as-you-please, on the wooden catwalk. With a place to plant her feet, she could pull herself loose of the hook easily, and then set to wriggling out of her bonds.

The Dread Baron crouched atop House's massive, fallen form. He struggled to catch his breath as he popped the empty clip from his .45 and went rooting for another.

You're tryin' me, boy, Ogou said.

"We'll finish this soon enough," the Baron said aloud.

House seemed to take those words—intended for Ogou—as a personal challenge. The Baron thought he was out cold, but the crime boss suddenly bucked, roaring like his pet gator, and threw the Dread Baron off of him as though he were light as a child.

Strong, that one. And desperate.

The Baron was done playing. He threw down his pistol and drew the *Machette d'Ogou*. It's black iron blade bled heat and flame.

House dove for a nearby revolver.

The Baron sprang, raising the machete high.

Then a new form slammed into him broadside—one of House's goons, not quite dead, still showing a little fight despite a couple of seeping wounds. The big Negro drove the Baron hard into the outer railing of the catwalk and the Baron felt the whole mess splinter and give a little beneath him.

House raised the revolver.

The Dread Baron planted one elbow in the goon's flat face, and as the moose stumbled backward, the Baron brought the flaming machete round in a bright, flaming arc.

The goon's head whirled into the gator pit; his body collapsed on the catwalk.

House pulled the trigger. The Baron felt a hammer-blow in his left shoulder.

Ogou! he shouted inwardly. *That came through loud and clear!*

Gettin' tired, the lwa said. *Sun's comin' up soon.*

Then there were shouting voices, heavy footfalls, and new arrivals. The Queen Bee's soldiers had made it to the aft end of the warehouse. They fanned out on the catwalk, lowering all their weapons toward Papa House and telling him to drop his gun.

But House didn't listen. He shot one sidelong glance at the Dread Baron—his new mortal enemy—and smiled crookedly.

The Baron raised his pistols and asked, "What?"

"You're bleeding," House said and nodded toward the Baron's shoulder.

The Baron glanced, just for a second. There was no blood. House squeezed off three more shots—every one taking the Baron square in the chest—then dove off the catwalk into the mud and muck of the gator pen below. The Baron, still upright and breathing, reeled from the kill shots.

Ogou... he whispered inwardly.

I got you, boy, the lwa said.

The Baron recovered as the Queen Bee's soldiers, led by the unstoppable Gideon Mann, all crowded at the railing and lowered their weapons. Before they could open fire, House dove right into the river.

Every weapon barked thunder, spat flame. The Baron lit up both barrels. The Queen Bee's troops slung lead right beside him Their bullets tore the surface of the cold, gray Harlem River... but the Dread Baron knew they'd missed him. Papa House was a survivor. He'd turn up again.

But that wasn't the Baron's problem anymore. Now, he just had to get the hell out of here and get the lead out of his chest and shoulder before the sun came up. Once the slugs were extracted, Erzulie could mend him.

He moved to the crane, and with a flick of his wrist, urged his lively scarf to disengage. With another upward toss, the *Serpent d'Ogou* coiled itself mid-air and settled round his throat, a serpent at rest on its master's shoulders.

Gideon was at the Queen Bee's side. Both turned to study the Baron. There was a long, strange silence, no one sure what precisely came next.

The Baron launched himself nimbly upward, perching on the fulcrum of the crane.

"Wait a minute!" Gideon said. "Where're you off to, Cemetery Man?"

The Dread Baron smiled. The answer, though hardly honest, came easily enough. "Back to the cemetery."

"What's your name, then?" the Queen Bee asked. "You gotta have a name?"

No one had ever asked him. And he'd never thought about it. Once more, the skull-face smiled. "Just call me Doc."

After that, there was no more to say. He sprinted the length of the crane arm, leapt up to the rafters twenty feet above the catwalks, threaded a nimble, feline path through the beamworks, and finally launched himself upward into the night through an open sky-light.

The night air on the roof of the warehouse was cold and hard, just like a gun left long-unused. He marched forward to the warehouse edge and saw that there were new arrivals below: the cops, en masse. He watched them for a time, and thought for a moment that some of the milling boys in blue below might see him, wondering at the crazy figure he cut against the dark night sky: a figure in flowing black, with a skull face and a fiery red serpent round his throat and a top hat perched jauntily on his crow's nest of natty dreads.

Let them talk, he thought. *And let them fear...*

With that final determination, the Dread Baron melted into the darkness of the Harlem night, and left the aftermath of all that evening's travails to more earthly authorities.

16

Dr. Dub Corveaux let Sunday slide by in blissful isolation. He ventured out for breakfast and for a stroll in the park, but he spoke to no one and was happy to do so. The day was sunny but cold, and everyone seemed to be talking about the upset at Aces & Eights the night before; of gunmen and crooked cops and nearly two dozen dead and scores more injured, both grievously and otherwise. The nightclub was a charred ruin. It was a minor miracle that it hadn't taken the whole block with it. Strangely, when folks talked of these things in the good doctor's hearing, they did so not with sorrow or shame or fear, but with a sort of bottled-up excitement: Imagine! All that unfolding, right here in Harlem! Things were really heating up! The Queen Bee was lucky to still be upright and breathing!

And then there was the talk of the Cemetery Man. The folks were already amalgamating his many names—the Dread Baron, the Cemetery Man, Samedi, the Witch Doctor—and Dub heard at least two men separated by many blocks and many hours refer to him by the same name.

Doc Voodoo—Harlem's own dread baron.

The good doctor supposed that would have to do.

He did not look for Fralene, and on that Sunday, she did not seek him out. Legba, Ogou, and Erzulie made no demands of him come sundown, and Dr. Dub Corveaux ended the day as he began it: alone; rested; ready to meet the coming week and its challenges as they came. He slept hard and had no dreams.

By Monday, lunchtime, Fralene had found him again, and she apologized for leaving him in such a huff on Friday. She acknowledged his right not to get involved in Harlem's social troubles, but she made it clear she hoped to change his mind in time. For her part, she would not tire. She'd keep holding meetings; keep beating down the mayor's door and making demands of their councilmen; keep fighting to make Harlem the Negro Mecca that she knew it could be.

Dr. Dub Corveaux assured her that he would have expected no less—then asked her if he could take her to dinner once more before the week was done.

She made him wait awhile for her answer, but her silent smile said yes before her voice did.

XX

It was late and the streets deserted when the Dread Baron piggy-backed a downtown train and disembarked on the Lower East Side. The very same tenements that he'd marched beneath a day or two before in broad daylight—still looming, still shadowy, still wafting blight and decay like yawning mouthfuls of carious teeth—were now not half so intimidating. After dark it may be, but he was armed, and he was horsed. There was nothing for him to fear in his present state of readiness.

At least, he hoped so.

He heard voices speaking a dozen languages on the night air, heard the squawl of tomcats on the prowl and smelled fires and stewpots and boiled cabbage; he even heard the sound of raucous singing in crowded basement taverns and winesinks; but no one was on the streets. Clearly, even those who dwelt on the Lower East Side knew better than to wander its paved boulevards and cobbled avenues alone after midnight.

Thus, he found his way back to Magda's building without encountering a single soul.

That was good. He was on a mission. He would have hated to cause trouble in someone else's neighborhood when all he intended was an exorcism, followed by a little much-needed demolition.

The old witch's tenement squatted on its foundations, twice as ugly and malevolent and malignant in the muddy early morning darkness as it had been in the light of day. Nonetheless, something was different. He sensed it immediately when he stood before the empty doors and broken windows of the place. When he drew out his Legba *veve* and let the pendant sway free in his outstretched fist, he knew his senses didn't lie.

Old Magda was gone. She'd taken her deadly little *maziks* and all the terrible, festering black magic resident in the tenement with her. The place still radiated a blunted and diffuse malign intent—the remnant of old entities, embittered desires and vicious impulses—but it was a dead husk now. A shell. A scar on the world attesting to evil's presence, devoid of all vitality.

He felt a twinge of regret. If he'd come here horsed from the start, he might have exorcised the evils that the old witch cultivated in that place—maybe even punched her ticket as well. But clearly, she'd sensed his presence, even though he'd been unhorsed, and she'd moved on, seeking a new place to plant her poisoned garden in.

Well, he wasn't going anywhere. He may be uptown, and she downtown, but he wagered that sooner or later, he'd get his shot at her again. And next time, he wouldn't hesitate.

Alone on that street, swaddled in its inky darkness and penetrated by the loneliness and despair that it bred in any human soul unlucky enough to traverse it, the Dread Baron knew there was only one thing left to do. He drew out the half-smoked stub of a cigar, lit a match with his thumbnail, and puffed away, cultivating the fire in the close-packed tobacco with deep, thoughtful draughts. When he knew he had the fire good and hot, he drew out a souvenir claimed from one of Papa Solomon House's abandoned weapons caches, a souvenir ferried all the way down here to the Lower East Side, with Magda's name inscribed on its round and slender length.

It was a small stick of dynamite with a twenty-second fuse.

Ambling into the deeper darkness of the tenement's ground floor, he sought out a doorway to the basement. Locating it, he lit the fuse off the end of his cigar and tossed the explosive right down the open gullet of the empty building the old witch had, until recently, occupied. Then he strolled back out into the dark and breezy night.

The explosion tore the rotted old tenement's ground supports out from under it and pulverized its rotted foundations. With a roar and an enormous belch of smoke and ancient dust, the superstructure imploded and the whole, haunted mess came crashing down. The Dread Baron didn't even look back. He was already marching up the street, eager to steal a windy ride on an uptown train.

Down a sidestreet, he heard a woman scream. Her words were in some guttural Eastern European language that he didn't know, but the gist was plain enough. When he heard male voices booming predatory laughter in answer, and the woman's words devolved once more to wordless screams, the situation became clear.

The Dread Baron stood still in the street for a moment, considering. It wasn't his neighborhood. It wasn't his problem.

But he was here, now. A cry for help was the same in any language.

He made sure that his pistols were loaded. There were govi grenades in his coat pockets.

Then he marched off in answer to the call.

XX

The Queen Bee was surprised to find Harry Flood in her parlor on a Monday morning. Still, she played the good host, offered the bullish little Irishman a drink and some of the late breakfast that had been prepared for her, and he accepted. He carried a briefcase and he was accompanied by two bodyguards. New faces. The Queen Bee figured his former draft animals had been lost in the mess on Saturday night.

They drank, they ate, they chatted. Finally, Flood produced some papers and photographs and let the Queen Bee study them. He let her study them for a good, long while before he even spoke his offer aloud.

"The Kit Kat Club," he said, suggesting the paperwork and the photos. "New place I've been prepping, up on 7th Avenue. I'd like to make you a partner and have you run the place."

"A partner?" the Queen Bee asked.

"Forty-nine percent," Flood said, "with an option to buy me

out once I've recouped my initial investments, plus profits. Say, a year at the soonest; three years at the most."

The Queen Bee studied the photographs. It was a nice place. And Seventh Avenue didn't have a spate of supper clubs yet like Lenox did. But why? Why would the Irishman want to do business with her?

He seemed to read her mind. "You're wondering what my angle is?" he asked.

The Queen Bee smiled and nodded. "Doesn't everybody have one?"

Flood smiled. "Of course. The angle is money, Miss Merriwether. There's money to be made in Harlem on supper clubs. I don't know what precisely went wrong with your previous venture—it seems you were the unhappy recipient of some rather negative attention, possibly by competitors hereabouts. But the best way for you to bounce back from that mess is to go into business with me. We'll both make out. And people will see that you're not afraid to get thrown off the horse without getting back on again."

He had a point at that. Still, the Queen knew that Flood's angle, however seemingly generous to her, had to benefit him in the long run to a greater extent. She was selling part of her own stake in Harlem and surrendering her name and her reputation, being hitched henceforth to Flood's wagon; to the wagon of the Chelsea rackets.

But in the state she was in—ruined on Aces & Eights, arguing with the insurance companies about the cause of the fire and the damages, trying to shrug off responsibility for those shootings in the street—could she really afford to turn Flood down?

What would Gideon say? she wondered. *He's young and he's proud, and he's all about making no man—especially a white man—his master. He'd say that Flood was taking advantage of your bad fortune and trying to use you to burrow in deeper here in Harlem. He'd say that if you seriously considered this business and went in for it, you'd be selling yourself, and selling Harlem.*

And he'd be right.

She sipped her mimosa.

But Gideon's not here. And I'm the Queen.

"You mind if I have my lawyers look over this offer, Mr. Flood?"

Flood smiled warmly. Part of the Queen actually felt safe with the Irishman. Another part felt a piece of her soul shrivel under his gaze and grin.

"Take your time. Consider carefully. I'll be eagerly awaiting your call."

The Queen smiled back and offered her hand.

God damn Harry Flood: he already knew he had her.

XX

Clayton Carr craned his neck back and forth again, made sure that no one was watching, then strode quickly across the pavement to the waiting Cadillac and slipped in. Franco Nasario was waiting inside, along with a fat Irish cop that Carr vaguely remembered having met at some point, though the cop was dressed in plainclothes and his name escaped Carr at present.

The car hitched forward, took the three of them for a ride. Carr slumped, eager to make sure that no one made him in the vehicle with a known mafioso.

"This won't do," he said. "That's the message I've been instructed to give you by the men I serve. This. Will. Not. Do."

"For once, Mr. Carr, you and I are in complete agreement." That was the fat Irishman.

"You know Officer Heaney?" Nasario asked Carr.

Carr only nodded and offered his hand. "Officer."

"Harlem's his beat," Nasario continued. "He's seen some of this strangeness first hand, and he's our contact in the department up that way."

Carr thought it strange that an Irish cop would align himself with Italian gangsters, but then he reminded himself that a fellow like Heaney was probably a contact for lots of downtown mobs on his uptown beat. He was probably on three different payrolls and would only declare absolute allegiance if caught in hock or backed up to a wall.

"They invaded a whole quarter of prime real estate," Carr said, trying to boil down the base elements of the arguments of his masters. "They made a little paradise for themselves above 110th street, and we didn't complain. But if they think they'll do as they please up there and not render unto Caesar, like everyone else, they're sadly mistaken. And this lawlessness... good, white citizens, gunned down in the street by colored hoods armed for war. I repeat, gentlemen: this will not do."

"Suffice to say," Nasario answered thickly, "we're on the same page. We just want assurances that if we take steps to bring some law and order to Harlem, we won't end up arousing the ire of City Hall."

Carr swallowed. "I have been authorized to assure you that so long as we are kept apprised of the broad sweep of your activities uptown, only the coloreds will feel the weight of justice. Yourself and your associates will be protected."

Nasario looked to Officer Heaney. He wore a shark's grin and Carr didn't like it one bit. "Hear that, Officer Heaney? That sounds like an invitation to the dance to me."

"My ears hear the same, sir. I suppose all that remains is a friendly swig on it, eh?" He drew out a flask, unscrewed the cap, and drank. He then offered it to Nasario. Nasario drank and offered it to Boss Clayton Carr.

Feeling a little sick at his stomach, Clayton Carr took a long, deep swig.

Downtown had just declared war uptown; City Hall had just sold its soul to the rackets.

And Harlem was about to be set on fire.

XXX

ACKNOWLEDGMENTS

"Writing, at its best," wrote Ernest Hemingway, "is a lonely life." This is true. But I'm here to attest that said loneliness is sometimes ameliorated by the warm support and keen criticism of friends and colleagues kind enough to read a work in progress. Mark Owens, Melissa Campos, and Keith Gouveia all read this one, and the final product benefited from their attentions and insights.

In addition, I'd like to offer my gracious thanks to my publisher, Matt Peters, for unleashing the Dread Baron on an unsuspecting world. Even when risks are calculated, they're still risks. He's done me a great honor by taking this one.

And I thank my wife, Gisely, whose love, faith, and incredibly low threshold for B.S. continues to motivate and inspire me.

Now, with the candles lit, the offerings laid, and the chants all sung—let's get horsed . . .

ABOUT THE AUTHOR

Dale Lucas is a novelist, screenwriter, civil servant, and armchair historian. His short stories have appeared in *Samsara: The Magazine of Suffering* and *Horror Garage*, and his film reviews in *The Orlando Sentinel.*

He lives in Los Angeles, California.

Find him online at *www.facebook.com/AuthorDaleLucas.*

CPSIA information can be obtained at www.ICGtesting.com
Printed in the USA
LVOW101828111112

306760LV00003B/1/P